Never Let H

Never Let Her Slip Away

Kay Christopher

CHAPLIN BOOKS
www.chaplinbooks.co.uk

First published in 2015 by Chaplin Books

ISBN 978-1-909183-97-1

A CIP catalogue record for this book is available from The British Library

Design by Michael Walsh at The Better Book Company
Printed by Imprint Digital

Chaplin Books
1 Eliza Place
Gosport PO12 4UN
Tel: 023 9252 9020
www.chaplinbooks.co.uk

'I have heard the mermaids singing, each to each
I do not think that they will sing to me'

The Lovesong of J Alfred Prufrock, T S Eliot

Contents

He stepped out from the hedge in the darkness and swung the spade wildly in a kind of arc as soon as the car-door opened. The spade was heavier than he expected, its metal handle and shaft cold against his hands and slippery from where his palms had been sweating. He wished he had thought to wear gloves. He had mis-timed the strike, the sharp edge of the blade glancing off the rim of the door and smashing into the side window which cracked with a loud report. The jolt of the impact ran from his hands right up to his shoulders.

Moving back slightly, he raised the spade again, crouching in order to find a better angle. The man in the car, still sitting in the driver's seat, reached out to try and pull the door closed but was too slow. This time the aim was better and the spade came down neatly on the man's arm, halfway between elbow and wrist. The man let out a gutteral howl and fell out of the car sideways onto the gravel driveway.

Holding the spade horizontally across his body, he looked down at the figure illuminated by the light from the car. A 'courtesy light', they called it, and the incongruity of it made him give a bark of laughter. The man looked up at the sound, cradling his broken arm as if it was a precious new-born baby or some valuable antique artefact. 'Please please please,' saying it over and over again. He raised the spade once more, this time two-handed, and brought the flat of it with a satisfying swoosh down onto the back of the man's head. As he began to raise it again, the man let go of his injured arm and grabbed the other end of the metal shaft with a surprisingly strong grip. They wrestled for a moment, both tugging at the spade for possession, until the man suddenly shoved the spade towards him, the handle catching him a direct blow on the nose. He staggered back, astonished at the pain and at the amount of blood pouring from his face.

The man was kneeling now, throwing the spade away from him like a javelin into the rose-beds and then lunging at him, grabbing his ankle so that he toppled over backwards, his head hitting the tiled border that marked the edge of the lawn. The arm of his coat had caught on one of the shrubs and he tugged at it to free it, unable to see properly in the darkness and bemused by the pain in his head, but somehow taken with the thought that he shouldn't tear the fabric.

When he looked up again, the clouds had moved away and the moon was visible, just a slender slice of moon almost resting on the roof tiles of the house. The engine of the car started, the gears made a graunching sound and the gravel spurted up as the car reversed, the driver's door still wide open, its edge just grazing his chest as it went by. The car swerved crazily in the drive, turning and glancing off the brick gatepost before reaching the road. He rolled over and watched as the door swung to, half-fastened, and the car roared away in first gear.

Spring

Barbara Blaize was not a liberated woman. She had never strode bra-less through the streets of Southampton, proclaiming on a banner the rights of women. She had never read *The Female Eunuch* or *Sexual Liberation*, nor had she ever been a member of a feminist movement that met for earnest discussions about sexist power structures or the female orgasm. When she married Andrew, back in the so-called swinging sixties, she was an old-fashioned girl. She had not walked down the aisle in a mini-skirt to the strains of 'Hey Jude', with flowers in her long red hair, but had worn a classic gown and veil and promised with all her heart to 'obey' her bridegroom. In fact she had obeyed people all her life. Marrying Andrew was all part of the obeying; a nice clean-cut boy, her mother had said, with a promising future – Andrew was studying to be an architect – and good taste. Her mother didn't dwell on the affluence of Andrew's parents (which would have been in bad taste) but clearly marrying someone who would still be a student for the next four years would simply not be practical unless the prospective parents-in-law could support them. The alternative, Barbara shuddered at the thought, would have been for her and Andrew to share her childhood bedroom at home, having to creep about the house for fear of raising the wrath of her father, with her mother continually hinting about when they were going to start a family. Barbara had been barely twenty-two when she married Andrew and moved into a 'starter home' in Chandlers Ford – but, in her mother's eyes, marriage could not come soon enough, anxious as she was about the possibility of a 'shotgun wedding' in that make-love-not-war era.

Now, twelve years on and childless, Barbara felt that life was slipping away far too quickly. And what was her life exactly, she wondered, other than looking after the house, ministering to Andrew, arranging the flowers at church and going to boring coffee mornings with old busybodies she really didn't want to talk to? It was a comfortable life but a life in which she felt she was an adjunct – a wife, a daughter, a sister – rather than a person in her own right. A year ago, she had made a small move towards independence. She had developed an interest in antiques, and had been buying at auctions and selling at antiques fairs, where she hired a stall for a day, usually a Sunday. The rest of the week she stayed at home. Every summer she and Andrew went to the Oxford music festival for their annual holiday. Every Christmas they shared out between her parents and Andrew's mother, his father having died of cancer five years ago.

So when Barbara decided to announce to Andrew that she would this year be taking a separate holiday, it was not without a certain trepidation. There was also a hint of defiance, since she knew Andrew would not readily agree.

She decided breakfast would be a good time. Toast and marmalade stage, so that Andrew would have very little time to argue before having to dash off to work.

"By the way, there's an antiques convention I'd like to go to – it's in a village near Andover." Barbara paused as Andrew lowered his copy of the *Daily Telegraph*.

"Oh? Well, why not?" he said, smiling. "What is it – a one-day session?"

"It's a residential course actually – for a week."

Andrew resumed his reading but said from behind his paper: "It's not going to be possible, I'm afraid. The music festival this year is first class. Rostropovich is coming and there's a premier of a new work by that Finnish chap whose name I can't recall at the moment. So we can't miss that, and I can't take any more leave."

"It won't affect your leave – I knew it wouldn't interest you, so I just booked one place, for me. I can still go to the festival with you because the antiques convention is the third week in April and the festival is not until June." She hoped that would wrap it up.

He looked up. "You mean you're going alone?"

"Well, yes. It's only six days actually and I'm very lucky to get a place."

“I must say, Barbara, you’ve been a bit underhand, booking without telling me.” Andrew had rearranged his usually complacent expression into one of petulant injury.

“I’m sorry darling – I really didn’t think you’d mind.”

“Well I don’t know what my mother will say.”

“What on earth can it possibly have to do with your mother?”

“If I tell her you’re going away on your own, she’ll think our marriage is on the rocks. She’s a bit old-fashioned about things like that.”

“Surely I don’t have to ask your mother’s permission? I’m thirty-five years old, for heaven’s sake. Just don’t tell her I’m going away if it bothers you so much.”

Andrew pushed away his plate and drank the last of his coffee. He got up.

“I really can’t imagine what’s come over you.”

“Nothing has come over me.” Barbara felt a growing irritation. “I just thought this year I would do something of my own choice. And it’s a study group, not an orgy.”

Andrew Blaize was not really a male chauvinist pig – he had never gone along with his father’s idea that a woman’s place was at the sink or in the bed. But on the other hand he had never experienced even the slightest doubt that as soon as he qualified as an architect, Barbara would automatically give up her shorthand-typing job to become a housewife. The idea of marrying a ‘career woman’ – which was how he thought of Fiona, Barbara’s older sister – would never have occurred to him, just as it had never occurred to him that Barbara would want to take a holiday alone. He had never asked whether she enjoyed the music festivals, but had taken it for granted that she would want to come with him. That’s what wives did.

Barbara could see that the conversation had been something of a shock to Andrew. He was wrestling to achieve some kind of compromise, she thought. Trying hard to be fair. Packing his morning paper into his briefcase, he said: “I suppose I could give up a couple of days of the festival and come with you." He smiled with the satisfaction of a problem solved, a noble sacrifice made. Barbara could hardly believe it. Since she had been selling antiques at her weekly local fairs, Andrew had been entirely uninterested. He didn't know the first thing about anything made before 1940. His only role had been to drive her there and back.

"But darling. you can't come. I booked ages ago – they only had a few places left."

"Ages ago? I see. Well, it doesn't matter. Are you sure you want to go on your own?" Andrew spoke as it was the Middle East that Barbara was going to instead of twenty miles away.

He was offended – Barbara could see that. But she was determined not to give way this time.

That evening he was still sulking.

"I'm worried about you going on your own," he said, out of the blue, as they were watching a television programme on the jungles of central America.

"For heaven's sake, Andrew – it's only in Andover." Actually Barbara was more concerned with how Andrew would manage without her. She supposed he was capable of taking a meal out of the freezer and popping it into the oven. And Snob would be quite happy as long as Andrew remembered to leave out his fish and milk each day. She fondled the cat's black silky ear as he dug his claws in and out of her new skirt.

As the weeks passed, Andrew Blaize accepted the idea of Barbara's week away without actually condoning it. He had explained to his mother very carefully that it was a study course necessary to Barbara's antique dealing.

*

Barbara vividly recalled the previous year's music festival. She had hated it all – not that she had let Andrew know, of course: he was under the illusion that she had enjoyed it as much as he had.

The preparation had started at least a month before they went. Andrew had bought the sheet music to half a dozen of the most important pieces that were due to be performed and spent hours – thankfully with his headphones on – listening on his B&O hi-fi, the sheet music open on his lap, his arms waving in imitation of conducting. For Barbara, preparation was more about what to pack, who would look after the cat, and what she was going to wear. Not that there were many other wives there. Because the festival was organised by a hi-fi magazine, it attracted a mostly male clientele with what Barbara thought of as a 'trainspotter' mindset. She recalled the drinks party after the Schubert concert last year. An earnest chap, who had one of those strange beards that had no moustache, and who was wearing a corduroy jacket with elbow patches, had cornered her and gone on about the seating arrangements and how, being at the far end of a row in the concert hall, the balance of sound was completely distorted with the violins overpowering everything else. Barbara had nodded sympathetically, while scanning the room to plot her escape. She'd eventually located Andrew, but he was locked in a discussion about sub-woofers so it was hardly an improvement. He had seemed oblivious of Barbara for the entire festival, so she could not imagine why he was hurt that she could not accompany him this year. He'd had a tendency to introduce her as 'my wife' as if her presence didn't even warrant a name.

The only respite had come when an orchestra from Moldovia had performed some selections from Italian opera. Barbara and Andrew had had a seat almost at the front of the stalls and Barbara had enjoyed the proximity as much as the music. She was fascinated to see that, although the musicians were all in regulation black, that their dress suits were faded and fraying at the cuffs – they were clearly penniless. After the concert, they had joined the audience at the reception, huddled in a corner, nursing their drinks, ignored by the very people who had applauded so warmly just half an hour before.

Andrew hadn't been impressed, however: he regarded opera as low-brow, the sort of thing that errand-boys would whistle in the street. Barbara had had a job not to laugh – the only errand boy in Ampfield was Bert, 75 if he was a day, but much more likely to be whistling something from the Top Twenty than an aria. Barbara had wandered over to the Moldavians and praised their performance. They were eager to talk, even if communication had to be mostly at the level of single words or gestures. After a few minutes, however, a tall, heavily built man with a shaved head – clearly their 'minder' – had come over and Barbara had taken the hint and retreated.

*

Gilbert Smart had been in verbal combat with Myra ever since he had finally plucked up enough courage to tell her about the antiques course.

"I've told you before – it's not a proper holiday," he explained, "it's an educational thing."

"You didn't ask me if I wanted to go."

Gilbert refrained from saying that the whole idea of his taking this holiday was that he needed to get away from Myra for a week. Instead he said: "I really didn't think you would want to go."

Myra banged the vacuum cleaner into the hall and pressed the switch, her adrenalin flowing freely in anger. Conversation lapsed. Later over coffee she said: "what if I get one of my turns when you're away? Have you thought of that?"

Gilbert had thought of it and dismissed it, since Myra's 'turns' in the past had stopped him from doing so many things he had wanted to do. Like the time he would have joined a chess club, or gone to the office Christmas party. Eventually Gilbert had given up the idea of doing anything.

"You haven't had a 'turn', as you call it, for a very long time."

Myra didn't answer. She looked out of the window at the neat rectangle of garden, mutiny on her face.

"Myra, it's only six days."

Silence.

"You could ask your sister to stay."

Silence.

"Well?"

"I don't want to talk about it."

Gilbert sighed. That evening he wrote out a cheque for the full course fee. The following morning he filled in the form and posted it, using the office stamps.

Sitting at the dressing table that night creaming her face Myra said: "In 16 years we've never been apart."

Gilbert could have added that they'd been 'apart', as it were, for years – far more apart than any geographic distance could put them.

"I just can't understand you," she went on. "Margaret thinks it very odd."

"Margaret thinks everything is odd," Gilbert shouted. "Did you ask her to come and stay?"

"No, I did not."

"Look, Myra, if you really want me to cancel this 'holiday', as you call it, I will." There – he had made the final gesture. He had played his ace and he knew by her silence he had won.

Nothing more was said until a few days before the course started. Gilbert had called in at Marks & Spencer's in his lunch break and bought himself some blue striped pyjamas. He had the parcel under his arm when he arrived home.

"What's that?" Myra's sharp eyes fixed on his plastic bag.

He explained about how his old pyjamas were faded and sad-looking.

"They were good enough for me," she said acidly.

He took them upstairs and put the parcel on the shelf in his wardrobe. He noticed the freshly laundered shirts hanging there, and his grey suit and tie. There was a little bundle of rolled-up socks and a box with clean handkerchiefs. Under this were his old pyjamas, carefully ironed and folded, and some fresh underpants. His plastic toilet bag was packed with his pills, a strip of elastoplast, two safety pins, a tube of new toothpaste and a small tin of talc. Myra had put ready everything that he wasn't using. All he needed to do was to bring down the small suitcase from the loft. When he got downstairs Myra was making a cup of tea.

"I see you've been getting some of my things together." He smiled, feeling almost warm towards her.

"I don't know why you wanted to waste money on new pyjamas," she said, her back to him. "What is she – blonde or brunette?"

Gilbert permitted himself a tight smile. "I should be so lucky," he answered, then – daringly – "pyjamas would be the one thing I wouldn't be taking."

Myra crashed the dishes in the sink and remained silent.

On Saturday, Gilbert had packed his suitcase with the items that Myra had selected. He was tempted to include his casual trousers but felt that Myra would put too much of a frivolous interpretation on that. When he left her, Myra turned her face away at his goodbye kiss and gazed stonily out of the kitchen window.

As he drove out of Forest Close and left Southampton, Gilbert experienced a sense of freedom he had never felt before. It was a freedom overlaid with apprehension. Since his marriage, life had taken on a very predictable pattern. Gilbert always arrived at the office at 8.50 promptly. He dealt with all the claims, had a break of 35 minutes for lunch, during which he had cheese and beetroot sandwiches and a rock cake baked by Myra, and at precisely 5 o'clock he locked his desk drawers and made his way home. Myra was a good housekeeper and an excellent though predictable cook. They had a pattern for eating: Monday was cold meat and salad, Tuesday steak and kidney pie, Wednesday a beef casserole, Thursday liver and onions, Friday plaice and chips, and Saturday beef burgers. Sunday was a full roast at precisely one-thirty. It never varied. Myra had no stomach for wine and Gilbert had no head for any alcoholic drink. They were both heartily against smoking.

They used to go to the cinema once a month until the films became too disgusting and they used to 'make love' every Saturday night. This, because they didn't have to get up early on Sundays. Each Saturday morning Myra would present Gilbert with his list of 'duties' for the day. If he didn't manage to get them all done, the items left would be added to the following week's list. Gilbert now had an extremely long list ranging from cleaning the drains to redecorating the outside of the house.

All in all, it was a marriage of no surprises. Even the conversations between them were predictable. Armchair battles, word strategy, blueprints for defence. Yet without the fights, Gilbert thought, life would be indescribably boring. Unfortunately there was never the joy of making up. Never anything to make up. Not even tears to dry since neither of them felt in the least upset by the barbs. Just the awful depression.

Gilbert swung the car off the by-pass and made his way towards Abbots Ann. He did not feel depression now. But it could come. Out of the blue. When it did, he would feel the enormous black shroud engulf him, and drag him down, down through an endlessly dark tunnel. The tablets were quite good but left him drained and zombie-like.

When he reached the drive leading to Wendells Court, he felt sick with fear.

*

Barbara had Andrew drive her to Winchester to catch the Andover coach. He seemed by that time to have become quite reconciled to his week alone. Barbara had left everything he needed for his comfort. Meals in the freezer, a couple of books from the library on topiary as he had mentioned that he was toying with the idea of digging up part of the front lawn to create a knot garden, and a whole series of notes marked Sunday to Friday reminding him of all the things he needed to know and was sure to forget – such as putting the bins out for the dustmen. She left her telephone number in case of emergencies and an envelope with Mrs H's money in it. She would need paying on Thursday.

"Are you sure you'll be all right?" he said, embracing her as the coach arrived.

"Of course I will. I'm looking forward to it."

"Phone me tonight, won't you?"

"I'll call at teatime – about 5 o'clock."

She handed her suitcase to the coach driver and joined the straggle of other passengers waiting to board. She turned to wave just as she reached the doorway, but Andrew had already got back in the car and driven away.

*

Wendells Court Conference Centre was used all year round for a variety of conventions from business seminars to religious congregations and from the brochure, which she read while waiting at Andover for a taxi, Barbara found out that the 'Working with Antiques' course had been taking place annually for nine years.

As her taxi pulled into the curving gravelled drive, flanked by parklike gardens, the setting was that of a stately home. Inside the Georgian house, however, the rooms had been over-modernised. Instead of faded elegance and deep comfortable armchairs, the owners had decorated the walls with overbright large-scale patterned wallpapers in strong opposing colours. Barbara flinched at the decor of the reception hall which looked as though the decorator had been using up remnants from a wallpaper sale.

During the war Wendells had been requisitioned for use by the Admiralty. They had torn out historic fireplaces and six-panel doors and had divided up the main rooms into small cells, which they had painted in cream gloss, the colour of margarine. Rows of toilets were installed with short doors, gaps at top and bottom, a bit like being at school, thought Barbara. Now, the small cell-like rooms had been turned into bedrooms. At the back of the house a new extension provided a bar and a large dining room.

Barbara checked in and was given the number of her room on the first floor.

"It's near the washrooms, so you're lucky," said the receptionist.

Room 105 was just around the corner of the corridor leading from the main staircase. Inside the single room was a bed – sagging slightly – a dining chair with a rexine seat, a dressing chest in shiny oak with a shaped mirror, and a single wardrobe full of wire hangers which fell off with a clatter as Barbara closed the door. A small window overlooked the gardens and in the distance Barbara could see the impressive outline of the stone lions on top of the entrance gate pillars.

She unpacked, selected a cream dress to change into, and decided to investigate the washrooms. There was a common entrance formed by a wide corridor, then a few yards away the corridor divided into two narrow ones. Barbara entered the 'ladies only' area – no door, but as the corridor widened into a square it was lined with washbasins. There was no privacy. There were two bathrooms in the narrow section, both doors locked and with engaged signals showing. Barbara decided to wait for a bathroom to wash, and made her way back to the bedroom.

Along the corridor she passed a pale flat-faced man wearing gold-rimmed spectacles. Their eyes met briefly – a tentative smile touched Barbara's lips and she was left with an impression of a dark grey suit and sandy-coloured hair. He nodded but did not return her smile.

*

Gilbert already wished he had never come. His suit was wrong for a start – far too formal. His long-sleeved pullover beneath it made it uncomfortably tight. So far, the men he had seen were all in casual slacks and sporty pullovers. Some were even in jeans and open-necked shirts. His room was depressing too. It overlooked the car-park – a constant reminder to him of his 'fish out of water' state, his maroon Austin 1300 pinched in between the Volvo estate cars of immense proportions. After unpacking he knew he would have to face the ultimate ordeal of mixing with the others in the main reception room.

On the way down he followed the attractive lady with red hair that he'd passed on his way to the washrooms. She turned out of room 105 and walked a few yards ahead of him along the carpeted corridor to the rather grand staircase. When they reached the reception rooms she hesitated, then pushed open the swing doors. Gilbert followed. Almost at once, two men standing chatting close to the doors smiled at her and introduced themselves. Gilbert took a deep breath of confidence and walked purposefully into the main part of the room, his eyes scanning left to right as if looking for a friend. When he reached the middle of the now-crowded room, he stood on the edge of a noisy laughing group.

Gilbert found it extremely difficult to project himself. He supposed it was because of the quiet life he led with Myra. He glanced at his watch. He must not forget to phone her. Perhaps just before dinner would be a good time. Conversation about a sale someone had been to intruded on his private thoughts. The big man with his back to Gilbert was relating how he had run somebody up at auction on a bookcase. The 'somebody' was always following him and was always one bid ahead; using his experience, the man had decided to teach him a lesson. Unfortunately the big man had miscalculated and been left high and dry – paying more than the piece had been worth. Gilbert would have been appalled if it had happened to him, but the big man was relaxed and laughing. He stepped back in his merriment right onto Gilbert's left foot.

"Oh sorry, old man – didn't see you there."

Gilbert also apologised for being there. He moved to the edge of the room. At that moment, Barbara Blaize was extracting herself charmingly from the two boring men who had fastened on her so readily.

"Do please excuse me," she smiled. "There's an old friend of mine looking for me."

She slipped into the crowd thankfully and was just in time to see Gilbert, alone, make his way to the side of the room. She recognised him as the pale-faced man from the first-floor corridor. Another bore? Or shy? He looked tense and unhappy. She took in the formal grey suit, the high pale forehead – or was it a receding hairline? She walked up to him with a confident air. He was not tall, perhaps 5'8", the same as her.

"Hello. Do you mind awfully if I stand here and talk to you?" She smiled. He didn't return the smile but said "not at all."

"I've been caught up with the most awful bores," she explained. "I had a terrible job getting away from them."

Gilbert was relieved and flattered. "I'm glad to have someone to talk to – it's my first time here. Are you on your own?" He noticed her wedding ring.

"Yes, my husband isn't interested in antiques," Barbara said. "Music is his thing."

Gilbert wondered if she had a shop. Listening to people here he felt he might be the only one who was not in the antiques trade. He was just about to ask her when she said: "I really don't think people should take up places here if they are not genuinely interested. It's hard enough to get in as it is."

Gilbert felt a flush of guilt warm his face.

"So it's your first time and mine."

"Probably my last too," said Gilbert. "I'm not very good in crowds. I lead a very quiet life."

Myra would be preparing her beefburgers now; they always ate their tea at 5.30pm, as soon as Gilbert got in from work. "I must not forget to phone my wife," he said.

"Shall we go and find the telephones?" Barbara said, seeing the two bores approaching.

Gilbert felt rather than saw the envious glances as he left the room with the creamy-skinned redhead.

Barbara asked: "By the way, what's your name?"

"Smart – Gilbert Smart."

"Are you usually known as Gil or as Bert?"

"I prefer Gil."

The abbreviation made him feel much better. He didn't mention that no-one had ever shortened his name before.

"And you?"

She turned big hazel eyes on him.

"I'm Barbara Blaize."

They reached the payphones in a corner of the reception hall. Barbara took the left booth. "I'll phone Andrew," she said.

Gilbert dialled his home. The phone rang out about sixteen times. Four paces from Myra's chair to the hall, three paces from the cooker, and if she had to turn the gas down, another few seconds. She was deliberately delaying to worry him. Then the ringing stopped and Myra said "hello?". There was always a touch of suspicion in her voice whenever she answered the phone.

"You really should say the number." Gilbert had said this so many times.

"Why? You know my voice."

"It may not have been me, Myra."

She sighed.

"Anyway, I just phoned to say I'd arrived safely."

"Oh yes."

"And to see if everything is all right."

"It's as all right as it usually is. Nothing alters just because you choose to go on holiday. Just think of me sitting here on my own sometime, won't you, while you're raving it up?"

"I've told you, Myra. It's not exactly a holiday. It's a serious study group."

"Are there any women?"

"A few. Why?"

"I can hear a woman laughing," she said.

"It's someone passing through the hall. I'm in reception."

"The kettle's boiling," said Myra.

"Well, I'll let you go now," said Gilbert with relief. "Don't want to steam the kitchen up. I'll phone tomorrow."

Click.

Barbara Blaize was still in the next booth, her slim straight back towards him. What an apt name, he thought: Barbara Blaize. Gilbert suddenly felt she was the most fascinating person he had ever met.

*

In the booth Barbara laughed as she told Andrew about Wendell Court.

"If you saw my awful little bedroom you'd never believe it," she said.

"What about the people? Have you met anyone yet?"

"A couple of bores and a funny little man in a tight grey suit who looks as though he's just stepped out of the 1950s. How about you? Are you coping?"

"Of course. Actually I've been invited out to supper with Desmond and Leonie. They phoned as soon as they heard you were away. I thought it was very nice of them."

"Yes," said Barbara with irritation. "Very nice. If it was me alone they wouldn't dream of asking me. There's something about a man being on his own that brings out a woman's maternal instinct."

"Rubbish." Andrew laughed.

"What did they say about me going away on my own?"

"They were very discreet. Never asked very much at all."

"I hope you told them I was at a study group."

"No, I didn't expand on it," he said.

Andrew had somehow managed to make her feel very

guilty about being away. It wasn't exactly what he said but the implication behind it.

"Well darling." Andrew interrupted her thoughts. "I must go now – they're expecting me in half an hour and I want to take a shower first."

"Yes – well, we go into dinner shortly so I'll phone tomorrow about the same time."

Andrew said not to bother to phone tomorrow because he would probably go to the cinema more or less straight from work.

"Perhaps Monday," he added. "And by the way, Fiona called. She's desperate to talk to you. Sounded like she was in tears."

"She usually is." Barbara sighed. "I suppose I couldn't leave it until I get back?"

"Certainly not. She'll just keep phoning me and I've really not got the patience to deal with her so-called problems any more. Just sort her out, would you?"

*

Barbara joined Gil outside the booth.

"Well, that's that," she said, smiling. "Did you get through to your wife?"

"Yes," Gilbert answered heavily. "A short conversation. I'm not exactly popular at the moment." His eyes crinkled in amusement. Barbara looked at him with interest. He was, she supposed, just the right side of forty. His eyes a cool blue, rather hard, like stones. Except when he smiled, then the pallid skin seemed to come to life and the eyes twinkled and became softer behind the gold-rimmed glasses. His hairline was receding, she noted, with the hair on top straight and thin. She wondered what his background was.

"She didn't like you coming here alone?"

"That's right. The trouble is, I feel so damn guilty about it. She makes me feel as though I should pack up and go home."

“Oh surely not. I’m sure by tomorrow evening everything will be all right. I had similar trouble but I’m not going to let it get me down.”

“Did you?” Gilbert looked at Barbara and thought ‘I’m not surprised. If I had someone as beautiful I wouldn’t let her out of my sight.’ He sighed. She probably needed some moral support, he decided. Being so beautiful she could be very vulnerable.

“I think I’ll trot along to the lounge and have a cup of tea,” Barbara said. Gilbert looked uncomfortable.

“Yes, well I think I’ll take a turn around the grounds.” He moved away. “See you later.”

Gilbert’s personal black cloud hovered over him, blotting out the feeling of well-being he had experienced when he left home. Suddenly as he stepped out into the sunlight he felt the familiar melancholy, a sensation of dread.

Barbara watched as he went through the swing doors. She would have to take him under her wing, she thought. He was so very unsure of himself.

*

At the tea-queue, when she was waiting to be served, someone touched her shoulder. She swung around.

“Hello – it’s Mrs Blaize, isn’t it? Of course. I knew I couldn’t mistake that hair.”

A tall slim man in cream trousers and a green check shirt was smiling at her. Barbara hated this situation. She looked at him blankly.

“Don’t you remember me?”

Barbara said she knew his face. She was desperately trying to connect it with a name.

“Well, what a let-down. I couldn’t have made much of an impression.”

Barbara said: “I’m sorry – it’s a bad fault of mine.”

“Shall I jog your memory? Chichester – last July.”

"Of course – Ian Avery. We both shared the same disastrous day."

It all presented itself. Total recall. She had a stall at the annual Chichester antiques fair. Ian Avery had the stall next to her. She sold one small item and he sold nothing at all.

"You've grown a moustache – that's what fooled me," she laughed.

"I felt I needed a new image," he said lightly. "Look – you sit down and I'll get the drinks. We must catch up on news."

Barbara sat at the nearest free table. The moustache certainly gave him a rather trendy air. He must be in his late thirties but didn't look it, except around the eyes which had attractive little laughter lines.

He brought the tea and some brown bread, bramble jelly and fruit cake.

"It's your first time here, I believe?" he said, as he emptied the tray.

"Yes, is it yours?"

"No – my sixth. I'm on the committee actually. It's hell being new. I know most of the regulars so I'll introduce you around."

Spreading her bramble jelly, Barbara asked if he was still doing the fairs.

"Oh yes, but not the local ones, which is why I haven't seen you I expect. I'll never forget that awful day at Chichester. Poorly advertised – and the sunshine didn't help. Everyone had gone to the beach. Are you specialising in any particular branch of antiques these days?"

Barbara said no, just whatever she could get, although she had a fondness for porcelain figurines.

"There's a good course here on German porcelain. I expect you've signed up for it already, haven't you?"

Barbara nodded.

"Apart from the lectures, we also have a fairly good social side here too, Babs, and it is possible to make some good trade contacts."

Babs! No-one had called her 'Babs' before – not even her mother. And Andrew had always called her 'Barbara'.

"That's not the only kind of contact people make here either, if you know what I mean." He nudged her playfully with his elbow. "See that couple over there?" He gestured with his butter knife to a portly, dark-haired man who was standing with his arm around a blonde woman in heavy make-up. "They are both happily married to other people but every year when they come to Wendell Court, they resume their affair."

Barbara couldn't imagine how that would work or why anyone would want it to, especially with such an unattractive specimen as the man concerned. She stared at the couple over Ian's shoulder as he talked about the fairs he had been doing mainly on the Surrey circuit. When he mentioned Winchester was closer to home, she discovered that they lived within 15 miles of each other.

"Why don't we meet up in the bar after the new members welcome meeting? I'll introduce you around before dinner. We don't have a lecture tonight – it's a free evening."

*

Gilbert's heaviness gradually lifted as he went over in his mind what Myra would say if he returned home the next day. By the time he had walked around the grounds and down the main drive to the road beyond, he felt much better. He read the programme of events that he had folded into his jacket pocket. He decided he would find out which lectures Mrs Blaize was taking and tag along there. He supposed he could call her Barbara – after all, she had asked him his name. They were both new here. He was lucky. They would stay together.

By the time he reached the house his depression had lifted. He strolled towards the tea room casually. She was not immediately to be seen. He glanced around him feeling a slight panic. People were watching him looking for her. He looked behind him – no, they were all chatting, unaware of him.

Then he saw her, smiling and bright-eyed, pouring out tea and chatting freely to a lean man with a droopy moustache. The man seemed particularly friendly with her and as Gilbert watched, the man patted Barbara on the knee. Gilbert trembled inwardly and walked away, through the reception hall and upstairs to his room.

*

The welcome meeting was held in a small room off the main lounge. Barbara was surprised to see how few new guests there were – only about ten. Gilbert Smart was not there. Barbara looked to the door several times, ready to encourage him with a smile. The committee member in charge of the new guests droned on. Dinner would be at seven and lectures would start at 9.30 the next morning immediately after breakfast. Tuesday was a free day with coaches arranged for those guests wanting to go on antiques tours or visit stately homes.

*

Gilbert had the most atrocious headache. He'd completely forgotten the new members' meeting and would never have thought of it again had he not seen them all coming through the lounge as he sat in an armchair near the window. Barbara was talking to a rather stout lady in a floral dress. They passed by Gilbert without seeing him. Then the floral lady went off somewhere and the man with the droopy moustache reached Barbara just as Gilbert was about to get up from his chair. He took an instant dislike to the man. Barbara herself then left and Gilbert followed. Unfortunately he was delayed by some old codger who was asking where he could find a committee member.

"I'm afraid I've no idea," said Gilbert, sidestepping him. But Barbara had gone upstairs.

Just before dinner, Gilbert once more looked for Barbara, spotting her by the bar. She had changed into a dress the colour of pale jade and had coiled her hair around her oval face. She was standing in a small group next to the man with the moustache. Gilbert stood outside the bar area, half-hidden by a brick column. He could hear them talking.

"Mike – meet Babs Blaize. Mike has a little shop in Northam Road in Southampton. John here runs an open-air antiques market, and this is Beryl – she's a stall-holder from Guildford."

Gilbert heard Barbara's voice: "Will you excuse me for a minute?" He moved away quickly and pretended to be looking at a painting on the wall.

"Hello – what happened to you at the meeting? I didn't see you."

"I had a headache and decided it would be better to rest."

"Oh, you poor thing. Look – come and join us for a drink."

Gilbert shrank inwardly. "No, if you don't mind. I'm afraid I don't drink." He knew it was considered socially unacceptable if you didn't drink.

Barbara said: "Of course, but have a tonic water or fruit juice or something."

Gilbert allowed himself to be led towards the bar. Then Barbara was introducing him all round. The annoying man with the moustache was called Ian, apparently. He asked Gilbert if he had a shop and Gilbert was tempted to tell him to mind his own business.

"Er, no," he said instead.

"A stall?" Ian persisted.

"I collect," Gilbert answered desperately, trying to think what he could say he collected that would not get him into deep water.

"Let me guess – I'm good at this. Stamps? Pot lids?"

They went on like this for quite a while until Gilbert said, at random, that he collected furniture. It sounded vague enough.

"Furniture?" Mike, a fat man with a rather camp manner, raised his eyebrows. "What a large house you must have."

John, who spoke in a loud booming voice, then talked about some fantastic house clearance he had where he had come across a seven-piece drawing-room suite – spoon back chairs, cab legs, the lot. The only trouble was it was riddled with worm and rot and when he tried to move it the whole suite had collapsed. They all forgot Gilbert at this tragic piece of news.

At dinner Gilbert was remote and said little. Later he pleaded his continuing headache and left them to retire early.

*

It rained heavily that night. The hot spring weather of the past few days ended as usual in thunderstorms. Gilbert's room was next to the garages at the back of the car park and the constant hammering of the rain on the corrugated iron roofing kept him awake for hours. In the morning the air was fresh and sweet. The gravel below looked newly washed and golden, and the sun shone out of a clear cloud-swept sky.

Gilbert felt so much better. He met up with Barbara in the garden and shared her table for breakfast. As they walked in she indicated a table for four. He would like to have suggested a table for two, but felt he should be grateful for her company.

"You look quite relaxed today," she said. He thought she looked absolutely stunning in a buttercup-yellow sleeveless cotton dress with a white cardigan draped around her shoulders.

"I am feeling better," he said.

"I don't know how you can keep cool in that suit, though."

"I don't feel the heat," he lied. All around him the men

were in sports shirts. Gilbert would like to have taken his jacket off, but then that would have revealed his braces.

"The courses start at 9.30." Barbara took her programme out of her pocket and consulted it. "Let's see – I'm in the Blue Room." She looked at her watch. "I shall just have time to get my notebook and pen. Which one are you doing?"

"What do you recommend?"

Barbara consulted her programme. "Well, there's oriental china, or Art Deco bronzes. I'm doing German porcelain."

"How interesting – I didn't notice that on the programme. That's for me."

And that, Gilbert thought, was that.

He went straight to the Blue Room which already was filling up. He found two chairs together, sat on one and put his programme and book on the other. When Barbara finally came, he waved her to the seat.

Gilbert could not concentrate on the lecture. All he could think of was the lovely Barbara Blaize sitting next to him. Her every movement distracted him. One thing was certain. While he was around he would protect her from both bores and gigolos. The words of the lecturer were lost to him in a blur of terms like Meissen, Volksted and Sitzenberg, which had been listed on the programme notes as being included in the course, but which meant nothing to Gilbert.

*

Myra gazed at the raw chicken, pallid, soggy-looking and unappetising, on the fridge shelf and decided not to do her usual Sunday roast. There didn't seem much point in going to all that trouble if Gilbert wasn't there. She shut the fridge door, noting that the hinge was still squeaking and resolving to remind Gilbert to fix it, and walked to the newsagents on the main road. There was a strong breeze and litter was blowing along the gutters. When was it that people now felt it was acceptable to eat as they walked along? She remembered going out with her mother when she was about 20: they had bought a peach from a roadside stand and ate it as they walked, the fleshy, juicy flavour given a piquancy by the guilt they felt at 'making an exhibition of themselves'.

Once in the shop, she bought the newspapers that Gilbert did not approve of, *The News of the World* and *The People*, feeling a slight frisson as she did so. When the Pakistani man gave her her change, he pressed the coins into her hand with a lingering touch and she wondered whether he was flirting with her. She didn't dare look up at his face, but bundled her purse back into her handbag and hurried out of the shop. As she closed the door behind her, she heard him say something in his own language to the man stacking the shelves and thought the remark was probably about her.

Relieved to be home again, she made a cup of coffee, put her feet up on the settee and settled down to read the scandal and to plan the rest of her day. It felt very quiet in the house, so she got up again and turned the radio on for some company, but it was a religious service with a priest droning on about sin, so she turned it off again. The *News of the World* revealed that a woman called Cynthia Payne was in court for running a brothel where barristers, peers of the realm and even a few vicars paid for prostitutes using Luncheon Vouchers. She put the paper down and prowled around the house, restless. It was good not having Gilbert here, but somehow frustrating too: there was no-one to argue with. At this time on a Sunday morning, he'd always be out the front of the house, washing the car and drying it carefully with a chamois leather. What was he doing now? Learning about antiques. It was completely baffling: he'd never shown the slightest interest in antiques before and, although she had teased him about it really being about meeting a woman, she knew that couldn't possibly be the case. What kind of people went to antiques conventions? She'd seen them on *Antiques Roadshow,* of course, listening to Arthur Negus pontificate about some obscure bit of china that had looked more like an ashtray to her. The people weren't really interested in when it had been made or what the maker's mark on the underneath signified: you could see in their faces that they just wanted him to get to the bit where he told them what it would fetch at auction. She tried to imagine Gilbert holding forth as an antiques expert. Maybe he'd make a wonderful discovery of a valuable piece in a junk shop and make them all rich. She made a scoffing noise and swung her feet down off the sofa.

She had decided what she'd do about lunch: something she had never done in her life. She would go to the Chinese and have a take-away. Gilbert didn't approve of take-aways, so that was two acts of rebellion she would have achieved in a single day. She checked the amount of money in her purse, put a plate to warm in the oven and set off for the Mr Woo Chinese on Southampton Road. The shop was quite crowded and the window was steamed up. She spent some time outside, reading the menu, which seemed to have several hundred items on it. She strained her memory, trying to recall what it was that Sandra always had when she 'went Chinkee'. Sweet and sour balls of something or other. Inside, the other customers moved up so she could get to the counter. The kitchen door swung open and a young Chinese man carried through a great stack of foil containers, doling them out to the families who were waiting. As he went back through the door, Myra caught a glimpse of the kitchens, with two Chinamen clattering giant woks and shouting to each other over the noise. Perhaps one of these was Mr Woo himself.

"Yes please?" said the man behind the counter.

"Er, I'd like one portion of sweet and sour ..." Myra had forgotten what they were called again.

"Number 54?"

She looked blankly at him.

"Here on menu – number 54." He pointed to the laminated menu stuck to the counter-top. "Sweet and sour pork balls."

"Yes, that's the one," said Myra.

"Rice?"

"Does it come with rice?"

"No – is extra."

"Very well. Rice as well please."

He leant through the swing door and yelled something to the kitchen. After she had paid, Myra sat down on the rexine bench to wait. A TV was fixed to the wall, the picture on but the sound low. Below it was a large and gaudy red-and-green dragon made of plastic and on a low table was a pile of much-thumbed magazines. The food arrived suspiciously quickly, complete with a paper bag of complimentary prawn crackers, which looked a bit like polystyrene. She hurried home, anxious to eat her lunch before it got cold.

*

It had only been 24 hours, but Barbara was already beginning to find Gilbert Smart more than a little irritating. She had only to rise from her chair for him to be at her side. When she moved from one room to another he would shadow her like a faithful old dog. When her cup was empty he would spring to his feet to relieve her of it and would follow her relentlessly, once almost into the ladies' loo. He would hover near the lecture room or the dining hall waiting for her. If she talked to someone else he either stood there tapping his foot and ostentatiously looking at his watch, or he would interrupt the conversation and find some excuse to drag her away. If she evaded him, he would become moody. Yet, despite this, she could not be rude to him.

At the first social event of the week – an informal disco – Barbara arrived early and sat at Ian's table with Mike, John, Beryl and a young American dealer called Phil who said he was from Baltimore and specialised in marine antiques. Everyone else had made a bit of an effort for the disco, but Phil arrived in the same jeans and sloppy pullover he'd been wearing all day.

"Do you know that this place is a hotbed of intrigue and general naughty behaviour?" he said to Barbara, leaning close and speaking into her ear so the others at the table couldn't hear.

"I had heard that, yes," said Barbara cautiously.

"Beryl, for example – she and John have been having an affair for years. It's an open secret."

Barbara glanced up at John and Beryl. It seemed as unlikely as the couple that Ian had pointed out to her the day before. Perhaps Phil was just joking. The DJ – one of the committee members – dimmed the lights and put on 'Do That To Me One More Time' by the Captain and Tennille. Phil asked Barbara to dance. On the floor he draped himself around her, holding her so close around the waist that her face was buried in his chest.

Barbara arched her back trying to breathe. She said: "You're just in the UK for the course, then?", an obvious statement but anything to stop herself suffocating.

"Yep. Plus a bit of buying, and shipping a lot of stuff back home. Usually try to fit this place in."

Barbara didn't approve of England's heritage leaving the country.

"You move well," he said. "Get plenty of practice?"

Barbara laughed. "I haven't danced for two years at least."

She caught sight of Gilbert in the doorway, hovering, looking murderous. Phil leant back to look into Barbara's face. He smelt of beer – already. Barbara said: "Oh, there's Gil."

Phil followed her gaze. "Your husband?"

"Yes," said Barbara.

"He doesn't look too happy."

"No, he gets very jealous."

Phil slackened his hold. The music stopped.

"Thank you," Barbara said and moved away quickly towards Gil. She felt guilty about using him as an excuse.

"Hello," she said brightly.

Gilbert said: "I don't think much of your dancing partner."

Surprised, Barbara asked: "What do you mean? Do you know him?"

"I just didn't like the way he danced," Gilbert said.

"Oh, that. Well he's American – they always dance like that."

"Maybe next time he asks you to dance," Gilbert said, "you should refuse."

Barbara must have shown the astonishment she felt at his words.

Gilbert said: "I'm sorry – it's nothing to do with me, of course."

"Come and join us," Barbara said brightly in an attempt to change the subject. Gilbert joined them physically, but mentally he was clearly completely switched off. Ian whispered to Barbara: "what's the matter with your friend?" She smiled and shrugged her shoulders.

Phil said loudly: "Guess your husband's a bit sore at me dancing with you, Babs."

He leaned over to Gilbert.

"Can I get you a drink, sir?"

"No – I think I'll turn in. I don't feel very well." Gilbert, pale-faced as usual but tense and obviously unhappy, got up and left.

When Barbara passed through reception on the way back to her room, the well-groomed young man behind the desk called out to her, saying that he had a message for her. He passed over a slip of paper. Barbara noticed his manicured nails. As she walked up the stairs, she unfolded the slip and looked down at the four words it contained. 'Please call Fiona. Urgent.' Sighing, she crumpled up the message in her hand and flung it in the waste-paper bin on the landing.

*

"I have a confession to make," Gilbert said at breakfast. Barbara waited, spreading marmalade carefully on her toast.

"I'm here under false pretences." His hand was trembling against his coffee cup. "The thing is – I don't collect furniture. In fact, I don't know the first thing about antiques."

"But we're here to learn – you just have to be interested, that's all."

"I'm not even interested. I came to get away – from home – just for a while. I thought it would be better. A closed community. Everything laid on. But in a way it frightens me."

Barbara thought it better not to interrupt. He went on, all the time folding his paper table napkin over and over again.

"I've never been away before – well, years ago Myra, that's my wife, and I went to Cornwall. It rained every day. Just lately I've had some bad depression. A few months ago I wanted to die. I really did. I get this feeling I'm on a conveyor belt. Life is passing by. I can observe it. It rarely touches me."

Barbara wondered what on earth to say without resorting to platitudes.

"I know," she said. "I know what it feels like." She was annoyed with herself because that was surely the worst platitude to utter.

"Then sometimes," Gilbert went on, "the belt speeds up and I get the feeling I shall fall off the end of it. It's the inevitability that frightens me."

"Is that why you wanted to die?" Barbara asked gently.

Gilbert blinked. "What? Oh, no. It was when the belt stopped. It got stuck in a bad patch. Luckily I saw the advertisement for this course."

"Well you've stepped off your conveyor this week," Barbara said. "Life isn't passing you by now. You're part of it."

The first lecture bell rang. "Heavens." Barbara finished her coffee. "We'd better get moving."

"You're a very understanding person," he said. "I mustn't bore you any more with my problems."

Amen to that, thought Barbara. In the lecture room, she took lots of notes, on the difference between restoration and conservation.

"It must be tedious for you listening to all this," she wrote in the margin and pointed it out to Gilbert. Gilbert smiled and shook his head.

*

When Barbara phoned home that evening she was pleased to hear that Andrew was spending an evening in.

"Hello, it's me," she said.

"Oh, hello you. How's it going?"

Barbara said it was not going badly. She was learning quite a lot. They were a friendly crowd and the weather was perfect after the rain. The funny little man she mentioned before was rather sweet but a bit of an irritation. "I think he's made himself my bodyguard," she added.

"You seem to have that affect on people, despite your liberated views," Andrew said.

"Liberated views? Me?"

It was clear that after fifteen years Andrew had not the faintest idea of what made her tick.

"What I mean is," Andrew explained, "that you have the facility of looking lost and uncertain, but you know exactly what you are doing."

"Is that supposed to flatter me?"

"No – it just explains your funny little man's sense of chivalry. He probably beats his own wife."

Barbara laughed. "The pips will be going any minute and I'm out of change. I'll phone tomorrow – it may be late because it's the outing to Petworth House."

"Fiona has called three times for you. I don't think she believes you've actually gone away. I'm afraid she went on and on until I gave her the Wendell Court number. She sounded quite desperate."

"She always sounds desperate," said Barbara, as the pips sounded.

She made her way to her room to freshen up before the evening's quiz.

*

Gilbert knew he should phone Myra. It had worried him that he could not get through the night before. The engineer had said it was because of the rain – cables were waterlogged and work was going on to repair them.

Barbara, he noticed, had been phoning home. He wondered about her home. Was it modern or old, town or country? Would it be full of antiques? He could get no picture at all. In fact he had no picture in his mind of her husband either. He knew there were no children – she'd said so. Strange that he had spent so many hours with her and knew absolutely nothing about her. Somehow here it didn't seem to matter. She was just Barbara Blaize. But no – there was something – a cat. He recalled her saying something about a cat. Slob, no – Snob, that was it. Stupid name. Stupid creatures too with their superior attitudes. Gilbert hated cats. Myra would not have had any pet – messy, dirty creatures. Gilbert would have liked a dog years ago but Myra was too houseproud. It had caused a lot of trouble when they first married. If Gilbert got up from his chair briefly to fetch something, Myra would leap up and shake the cushions plump again. And on wet days his felt slippers would be in the porch so that he could take off his damp shoes before stepping onto the Wilton carpet. She wasn't quite as bad these days but a dog would still be out of the question.

They knew at the office that Myra was a bit of a tartar. He once heard them talking as he approached the open office door.

'I reckon old smartass is hen-pecked at home, don't you?' That was the office junior, Miss Green. 'All bumptious people are hen-pecked – it's the only way they have of asserting themselves.'

Miss Rendell's voice, stern yet sympathetic, said: 'I feel very sorry for Mr Smart. He's a lonely man, and very self-conscious. I can't imagine why he ever married that woman.'

Gilbert had retreated on tip-toe from the door of the office back to the cloakroom. He was hurt and embarrassed. It had taken him almost fifteen minutes to get up courage to go back, this time noisily.

Why had he married Myra? He tried to think back. He couldn't remember ever having been in love with her. She'd been pretty in a hard way. Her dark wavy hair had framed a neat little face with pointed chin. It softened the sharp expression in her eyes. She had been slim – giving no indication of the stockiness that would be her figure a dozen years later.

Gilbert fancied she'd married him on the rebound. She'd been the victim of a broken engagement and Gilbert had been taken by surprise by her sudden and intense interest. He'd allowed himself to be swept along by the waves of her enthusiasm. He remembered at the time thinking he could do worse. It had not taken him long to change his mind about that. But they had stayed together. Why? Perhaps because it was easier. Or had he not really thought about it – accepting his unhappy state as he accepted day and night – as inevitable? He wasn't always unhappy. He merely never questioned his feelings. That is, until now. Now, he felt that finally he was appraising his life. That he was finding Barbara Blaize on his mind more and more disturbed him. He had never met a more perfect person. He was under no illusions about her thoughts on him, however. After all, she was everything that he was not. Elegant, assured, kind, amusing, eye-catching, intelligent and warm. Gilbert sensed her warmth. He felt it his pleasure as well as his duty to look after her. To shepherd her to and fro to meals, select her place to sit, carry her folders, shadow her carefully so as to protect her from undesirable and brash characters. She would have been easy prey for the wolves.

Last night he had dreamed about her. She was missing and he had frantically rushed from room to room, fleeing into the garden when he thought he saw her by the fountain. But when he got there she had gone. then he had leaned over the stone parapet and seen Myra's face reflected in the water below. The shock had woken him. He was hot and his heart was racing. Since then he would never let Barbara out of his sight. From dining room to lecture hall, from coffee bar to reception. In the afternoon, there had been a valuation session where some members had brought along antiques for expert opinion. Barbara had brought an Elbogen Fairing of three little kittens having tea. It never occurred to Gilbert that the week would soon be over and he would be back home with Myra.

*

Barbara was feeling suffocated by Gilbert. She was glad to spend ten minutes alone in her room. Ian had said that people made useful trade contacts. She'd had little chance to mix. Because of Gilbert, she had made none.

He was waiting for her at the foot of the stairs.

"Just going up?" she said, rushing past him. "Can't stop – see you later."

She knew he was hurt by her rebuff. But if she were to get any sort of freedom at all she would have to be rude. She'd been here three days and hardly knew anyone. She didn't turn back, just walked on through the hall towards the common-room. A number of people had congregated there with cups of tea. She weaved her way through them and saw two people she had been introduced to on that first day. They smiled a welcome as Barbara joined them. She could not remember their names.

"How are you getting on, Mrs Blaize? Your husband not with you today?"

Barbara looked puzzled. "Husband?"

"Sorry – I don't know his name. I saw him earlier – he was looking for you."

"Andrew, here? Well I didn't know..." Barbara's voice trailed off because the man interrupted. He was looking beyond her now smiling.

"Talk of the devil – he's just walked in."

Barbara swung around scanning the room for Andrew. Gilbert stood just inside the door rather awkwardly, she thought. He was looking across the room but not at her.

"He hasn't seen you," her companion said. Barbara looked at him and saw that he was looking at Gilbert. She felt her cheeks grow hot suddenly.

"That's not Andrew," she said. "I mean, that's not my husband. That's Gilbert Smart – just a friend."

It was her companions' turn to look embarrassed now and, mixed with the embarrassment, the man gave a sly look at his wife.

"We thought ..." his wife began. "Well, we didn't catch his name earlier and since you were always together ..."

Barbara felt a flush of guilt. Why, she didn't know. A perfect stranger had made a very understandable mistake. Mixed with the guilt was a kind of anger. How dare he put her in this position, she fumed quietly. She would see that he never did it again. She smiled at the couple she stood with.

"I'm afraid he's becoming a bit of a nuisance," she explained. "I can't move anywhere without him. I don't like to be rude and tell him to clear off."

"Oh dear," said the wife. "I think he's looking for you now."

"Look," Barbara said. "Could you waylay him while I escape? I think if he came over here now I would be rude to him and I don't want to be rude."

Gilbert had almost reached Barbara when a tall woman tripped, grabbed him for support and began to apologise to him at length. When he turned away from her intense gaze, Barbara had gone.

"I don't think I know you, do I?" she said. Gilbert was forced to listen to her ramblings. Her husband then joined her and Gilbert was stuck.

Dodging Gilbert became an almost full-time job. Barbara skipped the after-dinner coffee so that she could get to the quiz early. She chose an easy chair between two elderly ladies who had staked their pitch before her, having forsaken their dessert. As the room filled up and the teams took their places, she watched the door for Gilbert's arrival with dread. When he came in, she lifted a magazine in front of her face – glad of the marble pillar that partly shielded her. When she looked again he had sat down on the hard chairs lined up near the door. The chair next to him was empty apart from the programme he had placed on it to reserve the seat. From the back he looked as though he could be tall. His body was long and he sat straight up. His fair hair, so receded at the front, was thick at the back. There was no sign of baldness. From the back he looked much younger.

As the quiz progressed, Barbara was amused to see Gilbert getting more and more agitated. Then at half-time for scoring she saw him get up from his chair and leave.

*

It was quiet in the outer corridor. Gilbert felt miserable and afraid. He searched all the public rooms but Barbara wasn't there. He went to his bedroom and to the washrooms. As he passed Barbara's bedroom he paused, listening, his heartbeat pounding in his head. A man came out of the room opposite and walked towards the washrooms. He glanced at Gilbert with curiosity and distrust. Gilbert knocked lightly on Barbara's door. After a moment or two, he went downstairs and found a small empty room with half a dozen writing tables and chairs. He pulled a chair into one of the window alcoves and sat there in the twilight looking out at the gardens.

*

Barbara enjoyed the quiz immensely. The questions were all on antiques and she gained quite a lot of knowledge. She was pleased to have guessed right a number of the answers and afterwards had had an interesting conversation about early lamps with a collector. Without Gilbert trailing her, she felt free to mix. It wasn't that he stopped her mixing exactly. It was that he monopolised her so completely. She assumed he had gone to his room. She wandered around the old house, looking at its architecture with interest and trying to decide where it had been altered over the years. At the far end of the lounge was a door. Barbara tried the handle. It was locked. So she went out into the corridor to see where the door would lead to. A few yards away to the right was a similar door, six-panelled and in deep polished mahogany, with 'reading room' across it in gold letters. One door, she thought, that had escaped the builder who 'modernised' the house. Inside it was semi-dark, giving the room an air of mystery. Vague shapes of tables and chairs. A pile of magazines and programmes on a side table. Two immense windows projecting into the garden forming twin alcoves. Barbara walked across the empty room to one window and gazed out to the moonlit lawn and fountain. It all looked very romantic. Very far away from home. She wondered what Andrew was doing now – at this very moment. It was nearly a quarter to ten. Most likely he would be listening to Vivaldi – with Snob on his lap like a sleek black miniature panther. Andrew seemed shadow-like at the moment. Barbara was surprised to find she could hardly remember his face in detail – that is if she was asked to identify it line by line. His eyes were brown, or were they hazel? His hair was goldish tending to brown. It had been thick and wavy when he was young but now it had lost some of its curl and was floppy. He had a few freckles when the sun caught him, and he was tall and slim in build. But somehow she couldn't picture him – his chin, and his nose and forehead were out of focus. If he looked like anyone it was Paul Newman. When they were young, she had gazed so long and lovingly at him that his face should have been etched forever on her mind.

Barbara wondered how she would feel if she never went home again. Would she miss him? Yes, she supposed she would. Or was it that she would just be missing somebody – anyone? What if it were Gilbert Smart sitting in Andrew's chair when she got home? She tried to imagine Gilbert sitting in the relaxer chair listening to Vivaldi. The vision wouldn't gel. Gilbert could never relax like Andrew.

Barbara was not a nervous person but a frisson of fear went through her as she heard a small sound just a few feet away from her. She stepped back quickly from the alcove into the room, putting a yard or two of distance from the sound. From the other window alcove she saw a shadowy figure emerge and realised that someone had been sitting there all this time. With a shock she saw it was Gilbert.

He stepped forward.

"Barbara." He was genuinely surprised. "I didn't realise it was you. I heard someone open the door. I thought whoever it was would put on the light. I'd have felt rather stupid sitting in the dark. But you didn't. I thought whoever it was would go away almost immediately – then it was too late. I thought I'd just sit quietly and wait. I'm so sorry. I should have spoken."

They stood facing each other.

"I think it's a perfectly odd thing to do to sit there in the dark," she said. "Like a spider."

Gilbert stepped closer. "You didn't come to the quiz. I saved you a seat."

"What's that got to do with sitting in the dark?"

He reached out a hand towards her. "Look, I'm sorry. I was just sitting here thinking."

Gilbert then did a surprising thing. Without warning, he caught her hand firmly and pulled her quickly to him. "You've been driving me mad. Do you know that?" he whispered, his face close.

Barbara leaned back a little. "Please," she said quietly, "let go of my hand."

Suddenly his mouth was on her face searching for her lips. She struggled and he let go and turned to the window. Barbara felt herself shaking with rage. They stood silently.

"I'm sorry," said Gilbert eventually. "That was a really stupid thing to do." Barbara could hear the tears in his voice. "I'll pack and go home tomorrow. I won't bother you any more." His shoulders sagged. Barbara could see the moonlight on his fair hair.

"It's all right," she heard herself saying. "It really doesn't matter."

"Yes it does. I'm so ashamed." He turned and passed her, making for the door. She caught him up.

"You don't have to leave, Gil."

Rather terribly he put his hands over his face, shutting her out. "I've never done anything like that before. I don't know what came over me."

"It's all right. You shouldn't have done it, but I am actually rather flattered that you wanted to kiss me."

He became very still as though he was listening for something. Then he moved away, recovered. He cleared his throat. "I'll just go and freshen up a bit outside." She let him go.

On reflection Barbara found the whole episode ridiculous. So, he'd made a pass at her? Ill-judged yes, but hardly something that should cause him such trauma. Or was he upset by the lack of control he had displayed? It was a necessary kindness to try to minimise it by being understanding: it was only a kiss after all – a blind, struggling, blundering kiss.

*

Gilbert could not sleep. He tossed backwards and forwards. He thumped his pillow and sat up at two o'clock to take a sleeping pill. It was after three before he began to relax. He'd made a bloody fool of himself. Whatever had possessed him to make a lunge at Barbara like that? How could he face her at breakfast? Tomorrow was the Petworth House trip. The alternative was browsing the antique shops in Arundel, with coaches supplied for both trips. Gilbert still felt more like going home. But what of Myra? What would Myra say if he came home early? Barbara's words kept going round and round in his mind: 'I am rather flattered that you wanted to kiss me.'

It was morning at last. Gilbert awoke with a throbbing head. His room was on the shady side of the house. the morning looked clean and chilly. Gilbert raised himself on one elbow, fumbled on the table for his glasses and looped them on crookedly to see the time. It was 8.40am. He groaned and subsided onto his pillow. Breakfast – the thought of which nauseated him, ended in ten minutes' time. Gilbert turned on his side and promptly fell asleep.

*

Myra unfolded the stepladder beneath the loft hatch and climbed cautiously up the first couple of steps. She never liked lifting the loft cover in case a spider was waiting to drop down onto her hair, but this time there was nothing. She clicked on the light switch. She could see the big cardboard box but it was just out of reach, even with her stretching her arm as far as it would go, so she climbed up another step, keeping one hand firmly on the top of the stepladder. Removing the lid of the box, she reached in and drew out a large photograph album and carried it triumphantly down to the living room. The day was chilly so she lit one bar of the gas fire and sat in the armchair alongside it.

The first few pages of the album were full of very small black-and-white photographs: Myra's parents strolling down the prom at Margate, caught by one of the seaside photographers that must have made a decent living from selling snaps to holiday-makers. They looked young, carefree and happy. Her father was wearing a belted mac and her mother a smart coat, a handbag held in the crook of her arm. The surface of the photograph was deeply creased from where Myra used to carry it around with her when she was a small girl. There was another one, uncreased, of Myra's mother standing next to a lifesize stuffed lion; she had one hand resting on its head and the other attempting to hold down her hair in the stiff breeze. The lion looked somewhat moth-eaten. On the following page, her parents were pictured with Myra at what she assumed was her Christening. Her little face could hardly be seen among all the lace-trimmings on the dress and her dark hair was enclosed in a bonnet. Later pictures showed her being pushed along in a huge pram, such a sturdy and deep-bellied structure that it looks as though it would have made a serviceable boat; at school, thin-faced and frowning, standing next to her friend Rose; and on Girl Guide camp in the New Forest, standing on her own, watching somebody else put up a tent.

The next section of the album blossomed into colour, that strange over-saturated colour that seemed to emphasise reds and oranges. The pictures, each slightly blurry, showed a very different Myra, as a teenager with long hair, knee-length boots, a suede skirt and a flowery blouse with full sleeves. Each of the pictures, originally square with broad borders, had been cropped in half. In one, a man's hand was just visible at the edge of the frame; in another, Myra was looking over to someone who had been cropped out of the photograph. She was laughing and pointing. She hadn't thought of Howard for years. He'd been a good-looking lad, tall and slim with glossy brown hair. Originally, she'd only agreed to go out with him because he had a car, a Morris Minor, but he'd become a habit. 'Myra-and-Howard', people used to say, as if they were indivisible. After six months and an engagement party, he'd chucked her one evening after they'd been out to the pictures.

She turned the page.

*

Barbara sat on the Petworth coach wondering if Gilbert would join her, unsure as to whether to be elated or miserable when he didn't show up for breakfast. She particularly wanted him to see that last night didn't matter in the least; that she had dismissed it from her mind. The thought that he might pack and leave halfway through his holiday because of her very much plagued her. She didn't know what his wife was like, but she imagined it would take a bit of explaining. From what Gilbert had said, his wife had not wanted him to come in the first place.

It wasn't the first time that someone had made a pass at Barbara since her marriage. There had been plenty of opportunities for infidelity. But she had managed to treat all overtures lightly and to sidetrack them neatly. With Gilbert it was different. He was clearly not a womaniser. His approach had not been calculated or expert which was why, she thought, she felt the need to reassure him that it was all right.

The coach began to fill up. She watched a number of elderly ladies helping each other up the steps. With these ladies you never knew whether they were highly successful dealers or just old dears wanting to fill up an empty week. Barbara chose to sit on the front seat. Ian stood outside talking to the driver. Then just before they were due to leave, Ian boarded and sat next to her.

"What a stroke of luck you being here," he said grinning. "I thought I'd be landed with one of the old biddies. I'm afraid it's my umpteenth visit to Petworth, but being on the committee I have to do it."

Barbara smiled: "I haven't seen much of you lately."

"Committee business," Ian said. "Although I could see you were not lonely. You were with your shadow – what's his name, Melville, is it?"

"Gilbert you mean."

"Oh yes, Gilbert. Funny sort of chap isn't he?" Ian stretched his long legs out in front of him.

"He's not a good mixer, not used to socialising," Barbara said. "A bit of a loner really. He seems to have rather taken to me."

"Can't say I blame him."

"Are you married, Ian?"

He laughed. "Very much so – Cass is pregnant."

"Oh." Barbara smiled. "How lovely. When is the baby due?"

"Not until Christmas – in fact, we've only just found out the good news."

When they reached Petworth, Ian left her and she teamed up with a lady doll-collector.

"I come to Wendells every year," she said. "People are so friendly."

The party gathered in the courtyard and went into the house en bloc. Barbara should have been enjoying herself – instead she found she was worrying about Gilbert. She had wanted to get away from his suffocating presence yet now she was free to mix, she could not get him out of her mind.

'Damn Gilbert', she said to herself. 'Why should I worry? He's nothing to me. In three days' time I'll wave goodbye to him and never see him again. Neurotic little man.' Nevertheless Barbara could not get him out of her mind and he might just as well have been there on the trip with her.

After the tour of the house, they were free to shop in Petworth village. Barbara found a little antiques shop and bought a miniature silver violin for Andrew and a china cat for stock. Then on a stall near the entrance she found a tiny pair of gold-rimmed spectacles in the form of a tie-pin. Impulsively she bought it for Gilbert.

*

Wednesdays were always a flat day for those few people who chose to remain at Wendells. There was little to do but make the most of relaxing in the comfortable chairs, usually occupied by others. Or enjoy tea without having to queue. Or wander through the now quiet grounds. Some would read the antiques magazines and thumb through the publicity leaflets announcing future fairs. Business cards, artfully placed on tables, would be studied, and the conference centre's own headed notepaper would be used to write frivolous notes to friends back home. Some would walk around the grounds, empty now of crowds, and imagine they were in their own spacious garden. Or a group would congregate in the lecture hall arguing about trends and the effects of the recession.

Gilbert did none of these things. He stayed in his room until noon when his headache lifted. then took a long leisurely bath, enjoying the experience of no-one trying the door handle. Skipping lunch, he grabbed a coffee and took it back to his room to compose a letter to Barbara.

'Dear Mrs Blaize,' he began. He scrubbed out 'Mrs Blaize'. It was only a rough – he could rewrite it once he had it sounding just right.

'Dear Barbara. I must apologise to you for my behaviour last night. I value your friendship and would not want to jeopardise it in any way. You have been so kind to me that I'm afraid I presumed too much. This morning I looked at myself in the mirror and thought 'how could someone as lovely as her possibly be interested in someone as ordinary as me.' Please forgive me. I know you were only being kind when you said you were flattered that I kissed you. Yours, Gilbert'.

Gilbert read it through, crossed out the 'yours' and read it though again. Then he scrunched it up and threw it in the bin.

He took another sheet and started: 'My Dear Barbara', and sat looking at it for a long time. Nothing else came into his mind so he tore it up. Then he retrieved the first letter from the bin, tore it into tiny pieces so that no-one could read it, put all the pieces into a blank envelope and stuffed it in the inside pocket of his suit jacket.

Just before the coaches were due back, Gilbert dispensed with the jacket and put a pullover on to cover his braces. He felt a little less formal.

He would await the coaches in what Barbara referred to as the 'sun room' on the first floor, directly looking over the broad sweep of the drive. Since he had time to spare, he decided to phone Myra.

She answered with a sharp 'hello'. He had forgotten the sharpness. "It's me," he said. "Sorry I didn't phone before. I did try but the lines were out of order."

"Where are you phoning from?"

"Usual place – the hall here."

"Oh." Myra sounded suspicious. "It has a different sound – the background, I mean."

"That's because most of them are out."

Myra said: "You didn't go?"

"No – I wasn't well. Just a bit of a headache."

"You had another depression I suppose. At least it shows that I'm not the cause of them."

"I never for a moment suggested you were," Gilbert lied, having been sure for years that she was the direct cause.

"It doesn't occur to you to ask how I am," Myra said. "I could have been dead this last two days."

Gilbert sighed. "Don't be dramatic, Myra. I rang to say I'd be home at around three o'clock on Saturday."

"I suppose you'll want some lunch?"

"No, we have lunch before we leave."

They seemed to have nothing else to say.

"All right."

"Well, bye."

"Bye." Myra put the phone down first.

Gilbert wandered back up the stairs to the half-landing and in through the door at the top, where a cardboard notice had been pinned. 'Committee Room' was printed on it and underneath in tiny handwriting, 'this room may be used by guests on Wednesday between the hours of 10.30 and 5pm and evenings after 9pm.' Gilbert had been told by Barbara that this was the sun room. He pushed the door open tentatively. There were three people in the room. Two looked up and smiled as Gilbert walked in. The other one was asleep. Gilbert walked across to the wide curved window which spanned floor to ceiling. Beyond the arc of the drive were trees and grass and beyond that the gentle curves of Hampshire's countryside. The first coach, the one from Arundel, arrived within a few minutes. It disgorged its passengers then moved around the arc of gravel. Five minutes later the Petworth coach pulled in. Gilbert watched with pounding heart as Ian Avery stepped out, closely followed by Barbara, who was smiling at him. Gilbert felt a tightness in his throat. She was wearing white jeans and a fitted black shirt, her red hair tied back with a black bow.

Gilbert decided to time his exit from the sun-room to coincide with Barbara reaching the first-floor landing. He wanted to judge her reaction when she saw him. As he reached the door, the man in the nearest chair said: "How are you enjoying the porcelain course?"

Gilbert looked back and the man fixed him eye to eye.

"Er, very good," Gilbert said, hand on the door handle.

"Not so good as last year," the man continued. "They've narrowed the field somewhat."

"Oh?" Gilbert was inwardly fretting. Barbara would surely have passed by now.

"The whole convention was much more comprehensive last year. They included all sorts of fringe items like militaria and musical antiques."

Gilbert said it was a pity, but he'd better be getting along – a small meeting and a bit late already. Then he was out of the door. The corridor was empty. Gilbert bounded up the short flight of stairs leading to the bedrooms and saw Barbara just before she turned the angle of the building. She was fumbling for her room key.

"Hello, Gil." He thought she sounded very natural. "What happened to you today?"

"I didn't sleep." His heart was pounding. "Woke up with a fat head."

Barbara had unlocked her door. "What a shame. It was a lovely day. Oh, I've got a little present for you. Come in and I'll sort it out."

Gilbert hesitated, then followed her in, standing awkwardly by the still-open door. Barbara dropped her bag on the bed and opened a carrier bag.

"Here we are." She took out a small tissue-wrapped packet.

"It's only a little thing – a memento," she said, smiling.

Gilbert hovered, unsure whether he should open the present at once.

"I don't know what to say. It's very good of you."

"Say nothing," Barbara laughed. "Just open it."

While he fumbled with the sticky tape, Barbara said how worried she had been that he had not been on the coach.

"I did wonder if you'd done what you said and gone home."

He looked down at his shoes. "I couldn't really do that. I would have taken too much explaining."

"I'd never have forgiven myself if you'd gone."

Gilbert's heartbeat quickened. Suddenly everything seemed all right.

The miniature spectacles amused him and he let Barbara fasten them onto his tie.

After he'd gone, Barbara berated herself for telling him that she had worried about him.

*

By Friday evening they, that is she and Gilbert, had attended four more lectures. Gilbert had been in 'faithful dog' mood, shadowing her everywhere. Barbara noticed he wore the tiny gold tiepin all the time. Several people had stopped him to ask about it. He had been pleased to show it off, she could see.

The last evening was to be a social event and most of the guests were in high spirits. The committee had booked a trio to play at the dance. In the lecture hall where the dance would be held, they had put up decorations and set out tables for four all around the room. The buffet table draped in white sheets was set at the end of the room. Barbara was glad she had brought a long dress with her, since she noticed that most of the ladies were formally attired. There were more men than women, which was unusual, Barbara thought, at any event other than the hi-fi magazine's music festival. Barbara had noticed that at all the evening classes she had attended over the years, men were in the minority – although they seemed to stick out the course better than the ladies.

Gilbert had said he would wait for her in the hall so they could go in together. Barbara had said no and to carry on because she might be a little late. She was, in fact, considerably early – another 'dodge Gilbert' move which amused her.

When she got to the room, Ian was talking to the band, telling them what time he'd need to announce the supper. The band would get one hour's break while people were eating. Then there would be another break at about 10.30pm for the farewell speeches. The band would finish off the evening until 11.30.

Some of the tables were taken already. Barbara waved her hand as Ian caught her eye. He beckoned her.

"Come and join us," he called. He led her to a table near the platform and introduced her to his companions.

"I did arrange to see Gilbert so perhaps I'd better ..." she began.

Ian pulled up another chair. "Nonsense. We'll pull another chair up – or why don't we push two tables together." Barbara agreed, glad at the prospect of some amusing company. She put her bag on the seat next-but-one to hers for Gilbert. Phil, the American, sat next to her. Ian was opposite. Phil was with a lady called Liz, so hopefully Barbara wouldn't have to be grappled on the dance-floor by him again. The trio, two guitars and a keyboard player, started in on their intro number. Somebody shouted 'lights!' and the room was dimmed leaving a few coloured wall lights. They had to draw the heavy curtains to shut out the still light evening. More people came in but Gilbert was not among them.

*

Gilbert was down to his last clean shirt – the pale blue. He chose a plain navy tie and pinned the gold tiepin to it. When she gave him the gift he had felt quite overcome. But what pleased him more than anything was that she'd missed him. He was glad now that he hadn't joined her on the coach trip. He felt that after all he had been better appreciated by his absence. The last two days, she had allowed him to be with her at all the meals and lectures. He had enjoyed fetching her tea, carrying her folder, saving her a chair in the lecture room. She had been very charming to him, but once or twice become confused about where they had agreed to meet and he'd lost her. Tonight he would have preferred to wait until she was ready and go down with her, but she had said she could be late. He had taken as long as possible getting ready so that there would be a good chance of catching up with her. Gilbert slipped into his jacket, took a last look in the mirror, fingered the tiepin and went out into the corridor.

*

The dance was warming up a little. The band was playing a lively Motown number and Phil was dancing with Liz.

"Come on," said Ian to Barbara, reaching for her hand. "Let's get them started. Some of these fuddy-duddies wait until the last fifteen minutes before they get up, then they want more."

Ian moved well on the dance-floor, twirling Barbara around a couple of times. At the end of the number, they returned to their seats and Ian asked her if she had many antiques fairs booked up for the coming months. Barbara said no, she hadn't because July and August were bad trade-wise – everyone was on holiday.

"I like to start again in September," she added, "But I buy my new stock in August if I can. What about you?"

Ian said he'd been thinking for some time about organising fairs instead of renting stalls.

“I’ve had such a bad run of luck lately,” he said, “that I’ve come to the conclusion that the only person sure to make money is the organiser.”

“That’s probably true.” Barbara had thought this before and had wanted to start up some fairs herself.

“I would have done it ages ago if I’d had some help. But on my own, it wouldn’t be feasible.”

Barbara was about to reply when the trio started up again and Phil whisked her onto the dance floor. As she and Phil swung around towards the door, Gilbert came in looking tentatively around him in the dim light.

“Oh, there’s Gilbert,” Barbara said to Phil. They were close to him now. “We’re at the table near the stage,” she shouted. “We’ve saved you a seat.” They danced on.

When the music stopped they went back to their table. Ian was taking orders for drinks. Gilbert had sat down in Phil’s chair, so Phil moved around, leaving Barbara to sit next to Ian. Barbara introduced Gilbert to everyone he hadn’t met. Gilbert was rather quiet. When Ian came back with the drinks everyone was chatting to their neighbour. Phil was telling Gilbert about some house-clearance he’d done and what a find among all the usual rubbish – a superb Georgian sextant and an engraved brass ship’s bell from the Royal Yacht of Queen Victoria. Gilbert gazed at Barbara, who was immediately deep in conversation with Ian. He wondered whether he could get up enough courage to interrupt Barbara and ask her to dance. He didn’t like Ian Avery one little bit. Phil droned on. Gilbert rather rudely said: “If you’ll excuse me,” and got up. Barbara looked up as he moved around the table to her chair.

“Could I butt in?” Gilbert asked with a smile that didn’t quite reach his eyes.

Barbara looked at Ian, who immediately said: “Sorry, I mustn’t monopolise you all evening.”

The dance was a slow one. Gilbert held Barbara carefully as he guided her around the floor. He was doing a chassis step at a different time to her. Gilbert said “I’m not very good, am I?”

"Don't worry about it. No-one's looking at us."

"Barbara." Gilbert thought the name sounded strange on his lips. He didn't remember calling her by her name before. He'd said it enough to himself, but never out loud. "Do you realise that after tonight we may never meet again?"

Barbara sighed. "I know – strange, isn't it? We're all here in this closed little community for a week and barely see the outside world."

"I've almost forgotten my home," Gilbert said thoughtfully. "I think I could forget about it all together if I stayed here."

"Me too. Andrew seems so far away – and Snob. But some of us will be seeing each other – perhaps not you or me – people who have shops, I'll be seeing again when I go buying. And Ian, the one I was talking to, we are thinking of running our own antique fairs."

Gilbert suddenly felt as though a great stone had anchored him to the floor. Barbara tripped against his foot. "Oh sorry," she said.

Gilbert asked: "Does he live near you, then?"

"Reasonably so. We live near Romsey and Ian lives in Kingsworthy. But Ian travels a lot in his job. He comes through Romsey every week."

"I see."

The music stopped. Barbara moved away from him and took her place at the table. She resumed her conversation with Ian. For Gilbert, any enjoyment had gone out of the evening. Barbara had agreed that they would not be seeing each other after tomorrow. When the band took their break for the food, Gilbert slipped away to the cloakroom. As he passed the hall, he decided to phone Myra. This time there really was no reply. He counted to fifteen rings – enough time to reach the phone from anywhere in their small house. When there was no reply, Gilbert replaced the receiver and took the telephone directory for the area. It included Romsey. Gilbert turned to the 'B's and ran his finger down the page until he came to Blaize. There were three entries: A M Blaize, A J Blaize and

G M Blaize. Gilbert made a note of the two numbers for A M and A J in his diary against the letter B. He wouldn't write her name in full in case Myra should one day look in his diary, though he suspected she wouldn't. For all her faults, Myra was straightforward. She didn't pry. But she was also no fool.

Gilbert didn't feel like eating. It had given him quite a jolt to hear that Barbara and Ian would be working together. Later that evening, when the dance as finished, Gilbert sat in the tea room with Barbara and the others, having a last cup of tea. This time he made sure she sat next to him.

"I'm going to miss you," he ventured.

"Once you're home, you'll hardly remember me," she said cheerily. She didn't want Gilbert to go home depressed.

"Maybe we'll run into each other sometime," Gilbert persisted. "For instance at the antiques fairs. I've decided to collect postcards."

"Why postcards?" Barbara asked. "Do you know anything about them?"

"A little," Gilbert said. "But they don't take up much room. We haven't much room at home, you see." He was also thinking that postcards were something that Myra would be bored by. In that case she wouldn't want to accompany him in search of them.

"I shall look out for you, then," Barbara said.

Gilbert felt a new hopefulness at last. Tomorrow would not be such a wrench.

"What are you going to call your new antiques fairs?" he asked.

Barbara didn't know. They had discussed possible names like Heirloom or Gemini – Ian's zodiac sign. But they had not reached a decision yet.

"There's a little café I often go to in Winchester called The Music Box – maybe they sold one to buy the cafe."

"Oh yes." Gilbert was mystified.

"I mean we could choose a name that way – from something one of us owns."

Gilbert had lost interest in the new venture. He had an anguished feeling inside him – like something gnawing away at his innards. It was something he had never experienced before. Gilbert decided it was the pangs of jealousy.

In his room that night, Gilbert lay awake for what seemed like hours. So he got up and packed his suitcase ready for the morning. He put on a chair-back the same blue shirt he had taken off that night – it would have to do. He took out of his pocket the diary and looked again at the two phone numbers. Then he felt in his pocket for his pen. It was Barbara's pen. Gilbert had borrowed it during the last lecture and had forgotten to return it to her. He could give it back during the morning. They were, after all, staying for early lunch. Gilbert put it back in his own pocket.

*

Myra wrestled the lawn mower out of the shed, glancing doubtfully at the sky, which was threatening rain. She lowered the cut on the mower, in defiance of Gilbert's strict instructions. He always said they'd have healthier grass if they left it a little longer, but Myra thought it looked messy. Anyway, Gilbert wasn't there to object. When she'd done about half the tiny patch of lawn, Roy poked his head above their neighbouring fence and she was forced to stop as she couldn't hear what he was saying.

"I've got a box of bedding plants left over, Myra love. Any use to you?" he said, nodding at the bare borders around the lawn.

"Well." Myra hesitated, unsure of exactly what you did with bedding plants, but before she could object, Roy had handed them over the fence.

"I'll come and give you a hand to put them in, if you want. Gilbert's car's not out the front, so I'm guessing he's away. I'll bring a trowel and some compost – get the kettle on, love."

She opened her mouth to tell him that Gilbert had been away for nearly a week, but she guessed Roy already knew that. He seemed to keep a close eye on their comings and goings.

*

Barbara went to bed with her mind extremely active. She had enjoyed the final evening enormously. The new idea of organising fairs with Ian filled her with enthusiasm. He had a transit van as well as his car. He would do the humping of trestle tables, the layout and the advertising and publicity. She would handle the bookings, take the money and pay for the hall. With travelling around each day, it was impossible for Ian to do bookings and paperwork. They would meet from time to time at Barbara's house to plan future fairs. Ian had suggested they ran a stall as well, since they both had a carful of stock each. Barbara could run the joint stall and Ian would be on the door. It was all basically worked out. They had to meet soon to discuss the best venues and to work out the economics of the scheme.

Barbara had asked Ian if Cass couldn't help out – and whether she would resent someone else. He'd replied that Cass had been urging him to start his own fairs but that she was tied up at weekends giving sculpture lessons to a small group, plus she'd have her pregnancy to cope with.

Tomorrow there would be little time to see Ian – he would be tied up with the rest of the committee. But they had exchanged phone numbers and addresses. Gilbert had not seemed to like Ian, Barbara thought. Would she ever see Gilbert again, she wondered. Would he stroll into her antiques fair one day looking for postcards? Sleep didn't come to her until almost four in the morning. She wandered down to the washrooms at 3 o'clock and saw Gilbert's light on under his door. So he couldn't sleep either.

Saturday morning brought rain – the first for a week. Barbara wore jeans and a loose top to travel home in. Just before lunch, she wandered around, coffee in hand, saying goodbye to those she'd met. Then she went into the writing room and had a last look at the gardens from the deep window alcove. It was here that Gilbert had kissed her. She smiled, amused at his sudden passion. It would be something he would not be able to tell his wife about, she thought. Something he would have to keep a secret all his life. Gilbert was not the type to talk to the boys about his conquests, but neither was he as discreet as he should be. Barbara was convinced that other people noticed that he wore his heart on his sleeve.

The lunch was a cold one, meat and salad, with fruit and coffee to follow. Gilbert shared her table. He was particularly quiet. Barbara had chatted on about the lectures, the lovely week, the other people she'd met. Gilbert was polite but bored, she was sure.

When it came to her leaving, she took her room key to reception and picked up her two suitcases. The coach had arrived and the driver stood outside the cab in the rain, smoking. Gilbert came down into the hall.

"My coach is here," Barbara said, extending a hand. "I'll say goodbye, Gil."

He took her hand, holding it rather than shaking it. "I don't want to say goodbye," he said.

"Perhaps it's not goodbye. We will probably both come here next year." She pulled her hand away and reached for the other suitcase.

"Let me," said Gilbert and walked with her to the coach.

The last she saw of him was as the coach turned out of the main entrance. He was still standing where they had parted. She waved but he did not wave back.

*

Gilbert's homecoming had been somewhat of a shock. Bracing himself for some sort of showdown with Myra, the reason for it unknown to him, he had stopped the car at an ugly parade of concrete shops in Bitterne and bought a box of Bournville chocolates for her. Then, at the very last possible moment, he removed the tiny gold spectacles from his tie and wrapped them in his handkerchief which he stuffed in the top pocket of his jacket.

Myra was determined not to ask Gilbert anything at all about his holiday. He could sense it. She had greeted him with her usual turned cheek for the obligatory kiss, then had disappeared into the kitchen to make a cup of tea. Gilbert had said how nice it was to be home, and Myra had made non-committal comments in reply. They were both being extremely polite to each other. Myra was neatly dressed as always, and today wore a print dress in blue with a cardigan that Gilbert had bought her for her birthday. Or rather, that Gilbert had paid for. Myra had gone into town to choose it.

Gilbert took his suitcase upstairs and then wandered down into the lounge. After the enormous proportions of Wendell Court, the rooms at 'Gilmyr' were claustrophobic. Gilbert took in the swirls of the patterned carpet and the orange cushions on the beige suite. The gas fire suspended halfway up the wall looked too big. Somehow the room made Gilbert feel breathless. Odd – he had never noticed it before. And the quiet seemed suffocating. He looked out at the small rectangle of garden. Myra had cut the grass so closely it looked like a carpet. The borders were newly planted out with summer annuals laid out in double rows like soldiers on parade. Gilbert sat down on the edge of his chair and saw Myra's half-finished list of extra jobs to add to his chores. She came in with the tray of tea and rock cakes. Years ago, when they had first met, Myra had baked him some rock cakes and looked anxiously at him when he took a bite. They were dry and brittle but he'd felt obliged to say 'rock cakes – my favourite!' He was thus was doomed to be served them on every possible occasion since, and every time Myra must have thought she was giving him a treat.

Gilbert wanted to talk about the holiday, to re-live some of the past week before he could adjust to being back at home. Of course he could never mention Barbara. He cast about for something neutral to say.

"I've decided to collect postcards. Used to, you know, as a boy. Somehow I let it all lapse."

"Stupid things, postcards," said Myra. "I can't see the point of collecting them – just sending them."

"People collect the oddest things. On this course there was a chap who collected menus – old ones, of course, from some of the transatlantic liners. He had some from the Lusitania."

Myra was picking at a loose thread in one of the sofa cushions. Clearly she had lost interest and was thinking about other things.

"I'll probably look for my postcards at the antiques fairs. More likely to find bargains than in the specialist shops."

And that was how Gilbert sowed the seeds for his possible future meetings with Barbara.

*

On Monday, back at the office, he took out his diary and dialled the first number he'd written down from the directory. As he listened to the phone ringing out, he trembled inside. What if she answered? Would he say hello? Then what? He would not know if she was alone. Besides, he was not alone either. Miss Green, the office junior, was within ear-reach at the filing cabinet, doing rather more yawning than filing. He waited with a finger poised on the button to cut himself off. There was no reply. He replaced the receiver, shuffled some papers on his desk and decided to dial the second number.

Before he had time to think, Barbara's unmistakeable voice was close to him. He listened, hardly daring to breathe, then guilty, replaced the receiver.

*

Barbara had settled back at home refreshed from her week away. The house looked lovely. Mrs H, her daily help, had put fresh flowers from the garden in each room. The house was cool and spacious and elegant, she thought and its proportions reminded her of Wendell Court. She took her coffee outside to the terrace and looked out at the very large sweep of lawn backed by mature shrubs. It was very secluded – that's what had drawn them to the house in the first place. Andrew had been noticeably pleased to see her and she'd prattled on about the course and the possibility of organising fairs with Ian Avery.

"I took some photographs," she told Andrew. "I'll be able to show you what the place looks like."

Andrew had eaten very few of the freezer meals. He'd been invited out to friends in Otterbourne twice and of course by his mother who had fed him enormous home-made meals. Barbara suspected this was because she felt Barbara didn't feed him properly. When they dined at his mother's, she always piled twice as much on Andrew's plate as on Barbara's, as if he needed building up. Andrew had also been to the cinema, having a meal at The Dolphin on the way. She felt vaguely resentful that he'd managed by himself so well. It made her feel superfluous.

Snob did not bother to greet Barbara, showing only its disdainful bottom and tail as it headed out into the garden, but at teatime it wound itself in and out of Barbara's ankles in figure-of-eight movements until Barbara got its fish.

By Wednesday, Barbara had almost forgotten Wendell Court. She wouldn't be hearing from Ian for a few days yet, and Andrew had gone up to Edinburgh on business and was not due back until the next day. She had also got the 'Fiona business', as she thought of it, out of the way. Her sister had left another two messages at Wendell Court reception and Barbara had ignored them both. She knew her sister's pattern. Barbara was but just one name on a long list of people who Fiona called every time she had a crisis. As her whole life seemed to consist of lurching from crisis to crisis, Barbara's name came up fairly regularly on the 'rota' of calls. When Fiona didn't get the advice or help she craved from one person on the list, she'd just call the next one. Those on the list were well aware of who the others were, and when Fiona went through particularly bad patches, they'd call each other to have a good moan about Fiona's needy ways. This time it was all about her job and how she was simply desperate to move from Aberdeen, where she was PA to the managing director of a textile design company, to follow a job-offer in London. Though she loved her sister, Barbara's first instinct was to discourage her, panicked by the thought of having her just a train-ride away and able to descend on Barbara without warning. The problem seemed not to be the lure of the new job, but feeling unappreciated in the current one, her affair with her handsome but married boss presumably having come to a nasty end.

After a 20-minute monologue from Fiona, Barbara finally managed to bring the conversation to a close, realising as she did so that not once did Fiona ask how Barbara was or whether it was a convenient time to call. She'd once said, while recounting some grisly episode in which a long-standing feud with a neighbour had ended with a spot of retaliatory tyre-slashing: 'oh, it's all right for you, Barbara. Your life just rolls on smoothly'. Though Barbara initially smiled at Fiona's complete ignorance of anyone else's life, let alone her own sister's, she did afterwards feel a pang of guilt. Had Fiona really got a raw deal? What was Barbara's life anyway? Just a round of housewifely duties, polite dinner parties, and a spot of antique collecting. A healthy bank-balance, a nice husband, a nice house, no children to worry about. What some people might call 'genteel'. Perhaps it really did just roll smoothly. And some of Fiona's problem were certainly real, even if they stemmed from Fiona's own stupidity in the first place, like imagining that marrying Malcolm, a Glasgow hard-man with a cast in one eye and no discernible source of income, was a daring and glamorous thing to do, undoubtedly only done to shock her undemonstrative father into some kind of reaction. Like the time Fiona was 15 and he'd taken in her morning tea and biscuit, just like he did every day, only to find two pairs of feet protruding from the bottom of the eiderdown. He'd said nothing: just turned straight around and gone back to the kitchen, returning with a second cup of tea, the sugar diplomatically placed on the tray. Despite the visceral cries for help, designed to lock straight onto Barbara's psyche, dealing with Fiona was strangely cathartic, and Barbara felt relaxed, even happy, after talking to her. She put the hang-up call that had happened on the Monday down to Fiona, not quite ready to pour out all her troubles. Not assembled a long enough list, perhaps? Or just a wrong number.

But on Wednesday at about five, several hours after she'd spoken to Fiona, the phone rang again. This time there was a long delay before the receiver was replaced. And on Thursday it happened again twice. Barbara felt ill at ease. She had the distinct impression that someone was listening attentively at the other end. She slept badly, her nerves jangled. When she did sleep finally she had bad dreams. By morning she was calm. If the telephone rang again before Andrew returned, Barbara decided she would ignore it. It was eleven-thirty when it rang. Barbara was arranging the flowers. She stopped, waited quietly without moving. It rang out loudly in the quiet house for a long time. Barbara's heart felt as if it was jumping in her chest. Finally after the fifteenth ring she could stand it no longer – she slipped out of the back door and made her way to the bottom of the garden, out of earshot, though she found herself straining to listen for the sound. What if someone was watching the house – a burglar trying to find out whether the house was occupied so he could pick his time to break in? With Andrew away, suddenly the house seemed too big, whereas before she had always revelled in its large rooms, its tree-lined drive, its shrubbery. What had been delightfully secluded had begun to feel threatening, every spot in the garden a potential hiding place. Andrew would be home in just a few hours: was it better to go out for a walk, where she would not be constantly listening for the phone, or would that simply give the burglar the opportunity he wanted? What if it was some pervert calling her number, enjoying the annoyance he was causing?

On the second call, after repeating 'hello' several times, Barbara had said 'I know there's someone there – why don't you speak?' and she was annoyed to hear the anxiety in her voice. The third time, she said nothing, just picked up the phone and listened to the caller's faint breathing, and the slight background noise that indicated he might be in a public place. She waited until he put down the phone before she replaced her handset. Twenty seconds. It felt like an eternity.

To kill time, Barbara phoned Janet, a middle-aged lady who lived in Pound Lane, and asked her around for tea. Janet was something of a bore, much concerned with her odious grandchildren who, as far as Barbara could see, had no redeeming qualities whatsoever, and with the conduct of the vicar, about whom she was relentlessly censorious. But Janet was also a Sunday painter of some talent, and liked nothing more than to talk about her latest watercolour outing. She would fill the gap admirably until Andrew returned – better still, she had a car so that if any would-be burglar was watching the house, a car in the drive would send the right signals.

*

Gilbert realised he was never going to be able to pluck up enough courage to talk to Barbara on the phone. He practised conversation-openers but was horribly struck by the thought that she might barely remember who he was, or that he'd phone while she was hosting visitors, or even that Ian Avery would be there and the two of them would laugh together afterwards at the fact he was obviously stuck on Barbara. No, it just wouldn't do. Besides, he couldn't keep on dialling the number like that – she'd actually sounded frightened the last time she answered and he was mortified at what he'd done.

On his way home from work, he bought the *Hampshire Chronicle* and set about looking at the advertisements for antique fairs. The following Sunday there were fairs at Winchester Guildhall, Petersfield Community Centre and the Ponderosa, a big pub a few miles outside Wickham that usually hosted country-and-western nights but now hosted a monthly antique fair. Barbara would surely be doing one of these fairs – Gilbert could go ostensibly looking for postcards and just bump into her. What could be more natural? He decided against phoning each organiser to see whether she'd booked a table. He'd just have to visit each one until he struck lucky. That gave him a week to mug up on postcard-collecting so that he have at least some idea of what he might specialise in – and a week to persuade Myra that he'd be out all day and wouldn't need the Sunday roast that he seemed to have eaten every week of his married life. She'd already queried the presence of the *Chronicle* in the house. Their usual was the *Evening Echo*, a Southampton-city paper where the main news on every page seemed to be who was in court for what offence. The *Chronicle* was a 'county' newspaper, and it portrayed a different world, one of hunting with hounds, society parties, protests about 'green belt' infringements, and a whole string of rather curious reports from villages of arcane decisions by parish councils and endeavours to make the latest Women's Institute meeting, at which there was invariably a speaker on 'growing cacti' or 'knitted toys', sound interesting. What Myra seized on were the property pages full of character cottages, Georgian rectories, or charming conversions, all at astronomical prices. She guffawed loudly as she read out some of the descriptions. He wondered whether Barbara took the *Chronicle* and what her house was like. Ampfield was well represented in the property advertisements by photographs of detached houses with sweeping lawns. There was even one with an ‘orangery’, whatever that was. He never had asked her what Andrew did for a living, though clearly it was lucrative if they could afford to live in such a village. It was all a far cry from Sholing.

Summer

Cass Avery was just as Barbara had imagined her. She was as tall as Ian, big-framed, with thick dark shiny hair that hung straight and loose almost to her waist. Her face was free of make-up but she was blessed with an olive complexion of enviable smoothness which gave her a slightly exotic look. The loose turquoise Indian smock she wore over her trousers disguised any indication of pregnancy. As she greeted her visitors with a warm and confident smile she looked, thought Barbara, like the sort of person to whom giving birth would be simply a brief moment of interruption to her life, a moment of inconvenience before resuming all those normal activities she'd been busy with the day before. Barbara found this rather depressing. Cass probably made all her own clothes as well as running sculpture classes, cooking for a dozen guests and looking after Ian.

Andrew handed over the bottle of Hirondelle rosé wine that he'd been clutching and they walked through the hall into the house. At other dinner parties she'd been to, mainly with neighbours or with friends of Andrew's from work, the main concerns seemed to be getting the table centrepiece, the starched white linen tablecloth and the matching crystal glasses exactly right. Food (coq au vin more often than not, or Beef Wellington if they were really trying to impress) waited politely in the Hostess trolley alongside, and courses proceeded conventionally through appetiser, main course and sweet, with coffee and After Eights usually taken in the lounge. Conversation was lively, but slightly guarded, avoiding the issues where the men might get carried away in too boisterous or hectoring an argument. Talk among the women was slightly distracted because they all kept one ear on what their husbands were saying, for fear of embarrassment. Barbara should know – she'd run plenty of that kind of dinner party herself – but it was clear that this was going to be very different.

As Barbara and Andrew walked into the lounge, a noisy discussion was already in progress between the two couples who had arrived before them. Before introductions could be made, one of the men, who had a shock of grey hair and startlingly blue eyes, took Barbara by the arm, drawing her into the group and asking her earnestly whether she thought that new ideas manifested themselves first in philosophy, music or art. Barbara laughed, nonplussed.

"Take no notice of Harry," said Ian, walking up behind her. "He's our resident Mad Painter. You'll get used to his funny little ways – and anyway, when he asks you a question, he never listens to the answer because he's always much too keen to spout his own views."

"Not true!" objected Harry, good-naturedly.

"Actually, I rather think it's music," ventured Andrew and was immediately sucked into the discussion. Barbara felt her eyes sliding away from the group to look at the room itself – an irritating characteristic she'd noticed in other antique dealers, constantly alert to the possibility that they might miss out on some wonderful bargain. The walls were painted a dramatic dark green, the perfect complement to the stripped-pine furniture, the pair of comfortable-looking white sofas and the numerous antique oil paintings. An elaborate French clock-set stood on the mantlepiece in front of an ornate mirror, and Barbara could see an all-white dining room reflected in its glass.

"This is MY room," confided Ian, as the others continued their conversation. "The rest of the house is strictly to Cass' taste. Except for that," he said, gesturing towards an abstract sculpture in the corner that looked like a series of granite ostrich eggs piled end on end. It went oddly well with the room and made Barbara want to go over and touch its surface.

"Did Cass do that?" she asked.

"No, that's one of her students' pieces, actually. A young chap called Dylan."

"After Bob Dylan, or Dylan Thomas?"

"Who's to say? He may even have made up the name himself. He's probably called something horribly conventional like Norman. Or Gilbert, even. Which reminds me – have you heard anything from your devoted little spaniel since the course?"

"I think I was a passing fancy," said Barbara lightly. "Besides, I was careful not to give him my phone number in case he swore undying devotion and I could never get rid of him."

By the time Cass called them into the dining room for supper, Barbara was beginning to feel a bit squiffy. Two large glasses of red wine were too much on an empty stomach and she heard herself rather foolishly joining in with a heated debate on the nature of eternity. How ever did these subjects arise? There seemed to be none of the tentative get-to-know-you openers that she was used to at dinner parties, with people asking what Andrew did for a living and how old their children were, the latter a subject that provoked an awkward silence when she said that they did not have any children. She realised she didn't know a thing about the people in the room on a prosaic level, but had somehow skipped this whole phase and become well acquainted with their views on David Hockney, the latest Martin Amis novel, LA drug culture and Marxist techniques for teaching history in university. It was hard to keep up. She resolved to switch to water for the rest of the evening.

Ian was right about the house – the contrast could not have been more stark between the dark, cosy feel of the sitting room and the white walls, stripped floorboards and startling modern paintings of the dining room. There were white rollerblinds at the windows instead of curtains and even the lampshades were white. A vast glass vase held an extravagant arrangement of white lilies. There was no tablecloth on the pine table and the plates and dishes were of a rough terracotta-coloured earthenware. Thick glass tumblers, almost like jam-jars, held the wine. Seemingly effortlessly, Cass produced an unending stream of delicious food, the casserole dishes covering the table, along with homemade bread, black olives, onion salads, chickpeas, cous-cous and a number of other things that Barbara couldn't quite identify. She glanced nervously at Andrew, a traditional meat-and-two-veg man, but what he would have rejected at home, he was happily tucking into here, quickly realising that this wasn't a please-would-you-pass-the-salt kind of dinner, but one where you just reached across the table to grab any dish you fancied and ate them in no particular order, while the conversation eddied and flowed around you. It was all curiously liberating and Barbara was astonished to find when she next looked at her watch that it was gone midnight.

In the car on the way back, she found herself reassessing her view of Ian, in the light of having met Cass and their friends, and seen him at home. Her mother used to say that you never know what people are really like until you've seen where they live and she was absolutely right. Barbara had expected Ian to have some nice pieces: antique dealers always used some of their 'stock' to furnish their homes, selling it on every few months and acquiring more – it was one of the perks of the trade. But it was all much more bohemian than she had anticipated, and she realised she had based her view on Ian's committee-work at the course, and on the efficient, business-like way he had discussed running fairs together. She had supposed that his friends would be the cravat-wearing, half-moon-spectacles types who sold expensive oil paintings and had little shops in market towns like – well, like Romsey. The auction rooms at Romsey were full of these types, braying loudly at each other in greeting and continually fussing with their catalogues, though Barbara had to admit that the real buying (vast quantities of what was called 'shipping furniture') was usually done rather more unobtrusively by people who looked more like didicoys, scruffy and unkempt and giving the impression that they didn't have two ha'pennies to rub together. Until, of course, they withdrew from their pockets a well-thumbed roll of banknotes thick enough to choke a horse. People always looked the wrong way at auctions, she felt, keeping their gaze firmly fixed on the auctioneer even when they were not intending to bid themselves. Only when the price of something reached astronomic proportions compared with its estimate, with two buyers locked in a war of attrition, did they swivel their heads around to see who on earth could be paying through the nose for a rusty pockmarked sword with half its handle missing – and what on earth they were going to do with it once they'd won it. Barbara found it much more enlightening to look around the room during bidding, seeing who was buying what, and whether the auctioneer was taking bids 'off the wall', that is from non-existent buyers, in order to push the price up. She tried to imagine Gilbert competing for a lot he'd set his heart on, but somehow he just didn't fit. He'd be impassive – always an advantage in the trade – but somehow too dogged. Not competitive enough.

She put him from her mind as Andrew swung the car into their drive and her thoughts turned to how she might make one or two changes to her house to give it just a little bit of the style she had so admired at Ian and Cass's.

*

Gilbert barely said a word in the car all the way to Eastbourne. Whenever Myra tried to get a conversation going he was monosyllabic. She hoped he wasn't going to be like this all weekend at her parents'.

"I know you don't really get on, but you will try to be sociable, won't you?" she asked him over the swishing of the windscreen wipers.

"I'll do my best," he said.

Myra was less than reassured. "You could ask him about his trains – he'd like that."

"Last time I even mentioned the word 'train' he gave me an hour-long lecture about something called the Box Tunnel. It was torture."

"Yes, but you can pretend a bit, surely?"

"I don't think so," said Gilbert, bleakly.

They lapsed into silence as the car continued at a stately 25mph behind a tractor laden with crates of cherries. The narrow road snaked between the downs and Myra noted the names of the villages – Chalvington and Ripe. They drove past the entrance to Charleston Farmhouse which Gilbert said had been the home of the Bloomsbury Set, the first thing he'd volunteered on the whole journey. Myra didn't know who the Bloomsbury Set were and was damned if she was going to ask Gilbert.

By the time they reached Eastbourne they were nearly an hour behind schedule and the rain was still bucketing down. Myra saw the net curtains on front-room window of her parents' house twitch a little as a hand was hastily withdrawn. She knew that her mother would have been looking out of the window most of the morning in anticipation of their arrival. Gilbert struggled with the latch on the wrought-iron gate as the wind whipped at his anorak.

"I thought you were never coming – the lunch will be spoilt." It was the same greeting every time, thought Myra, yet every time there was nothing to spoil, just the same plates of cold ham and salad, followed by tinned peaches, slimy-looking slices floating about in a viscous syrup in a bowl. And then the Mr Kipling cakes, straight out of the packet. All presented as it was the very first time they'd served up this meal. It was going to be a long weekend. She eyed the weather, hoping to see a break in the cloud, but the rain looked set in. After lunch they went up to the bedroom to unpack. It had been Myra's old room but every trace of her had been eliminated in somewhat unseemly haste after Myra left home to get married. Her mother had wanted to create a 'guest room' but Myra and Gilbert were the only visitors they ever had. The colour scheme had a lot of orange in it, a bit like at Gilmyr, and the rose-patterned eiderdowns which Myra had loved so much had been replaced by a continental quilt.

Gilbert took off his spectacles and began to clean them, a sure sign that he was about to make some pronouncement on which he did not want to be challenged.

"I'm going to take a turn around the block. I need some fresh air after that long drive."

"You'll get soaked," said Myra, knowing that he'd go anyway, that he just wanted to escape, but hardly able to blame him.

"I'll probably walk down to the front and look at the sea for a bit. I've got a slight headache."

When he got back, an hour later, his fair hair plastered to his head, making him look younger and more vulnerable, Myra and her parents were playing cards, sitting round the dining-room table with its green chenille cloth. Now that she and her mother had each drunk a large schooner of sherry, Myra was feeling more optimistic. Her father, who had an empty bottle of Guinness at his elbow, asked Gilbert if he wanted a drink, something he asked every time they met; Myra never knew whether he didn't remember that Gilbert didn't drink or whether he did it just to tease or provoke him. Her father nodded at the empty seat at the table, Gilbert sat down, and dealing began. Her father dealt the cards quickly and efficiently, a legacy – he always said – of having to dole out change on the buses all his working life. Gilbert was surprisingly good at card-games and Myra hoped that he would remember to let father win, otherwise he'd get grumpy. Of course, Gilbert would be good at cards: he had the classic 'poker face', expressionless and impossible to read.

That night, when they lay in bed, the rain rattling at the window and the draught moving the cord of the ceiling light back and forth, he lay on his back pretending to be asleep. Myra knew he was only pretending because his breathing was too quiet. She prodded his side.

"What?" he said, without moving.

"You did well tonight – chatting to Dad. He likes someone to talk to."

“Someone to listen to him, you mean”.

“Ssh – they’ll hear.”

“I should have got my own back and gone on and on about the antiques course. It’s called the ‘bore him before he bores you’ principle.”

Myra giggled and Gilbert turned towards her to give her a bear-bug. Perhaps the weekend wouldn’t be so bad after all.

*

Barbara borrowed one of Andrew’s sketching pads and started to draw the table layouts for her first antiques fair with Ian. She thought about the way the hall had been set out at the fair at Nursling: the tables had been rather too close together which meant that browsers could easily block the view of a neighbouring stall from other customers, who then tended to walk straight past. She would learn from this, she thought, and even though the hall at Midhurst was not as spacious as the one at Nursling, they could still lay it out attractively. And perhaps all the postcard stalls could be at one end of the hall as collectors – usually exclusively men – spent ages at each stall and that way they wouldn’t block one of the main aisles. It would also be good to make a portable sign, perhaps a big arrow, so that they could station someone outside the hotel on the street who could hold the sign and point people towards the conference suite at the back. Electricity might be a problem: they would need to invest in a number of cable-reels so that stallholders could set up spotlights because that always made the displays look more attractive, even though the hotel might kick up a fuss about the extra cost.

She sipped her coffee and doodled on the pad, trying out ideas for how their new name might look on the posters, and listening to the sound of Mrs H’s vacuum cleaner downstairs. She drew a little cartoon of Mrs H, a skinny figure, arms akimbo and with a downturned, disapproving mouth.

*

Next morning, a weak sun had broken through the clouds and after breakfast Gilbert escaped his in-laws' house for an hour on the excuse of having a stroll and getting the papers. Myra's mother was fond of the *News of the World,* though she had always hidden it inside the *Sunday Express* when Myra was a child, believing that Myra would never spot the subterfuge. She was disappointed these days at the decline in frequency of stories about vicars running away with female members of their congregation. She couldn't decide whether this was because it no longer happened, or whether the paper had just got bored with these stories unless the people involved were famous. Gilbert wondered if this had perhaps been one of her own fantasies, instead of being stuck with a Guinness-drinking train-spotter whose idea of excitement was a day at Clapham Junction.

He walked down to the front and watched the sea, a long line of turgid grey. He remembered a science fiction story he'd read once, about a couple who were allowed to return to their home as long as they didn't roll down the car windows on the way. They disobeyed: and instead of the lively town scene they'd been watching through the windscreen, when they rolled down the passenger window, the scene disappeared – all that was out there was just a grey fog. He leant on the rail and gazed down at the bandstand, an Art Deco extravagance with a dome and a circle of steps down to the stage. At least, he thought, he knew to call it 'Art Deco' now. Before his week at Wendell Court, he would have had no idea. He'd slipped in that comment about the Bloomsbury Set on the way down, too – he'd been proud of that. He was appalled at his own ignorance. He thought of Barbara again – her kindness to him, her elegance, her beauty – the way her hair hung down her back in a ponytail. Last night, when he made love to Myra, Barbara's face had come, unbidden, into his mind and he had almost cried out her name. He'd opened his eyes then and stared resolutely at the top of the pillow, just above Myra's head, implanting its creases, its texture, into his brain in order to drive out the much more alluring image that kept beckoning to him.

*

The following Sunday, Gilbert set out early to make his first foray to an antique fair in the hope that Barbara would be there with a stall. In the hallway of the Ponderosa was a black-and-red poster with cowboy-style lettering: 'Coming soon – The Test Valley Hobos featuring Hank Wesson, plus the Tenor Cs.' At the centre was a picture of Hank, a thin man wearing a stetson and a bootlace tie and holding an acoustic guitar. He was clearly supposed to be American, though Gilbert knew that his name was actually Derek Fry and that he lived in a council house in Shirrell Heath with his wife and about six children. The insurance firm he worked for had the Test Valley Hobos as one of its clients, which is how Gilbert also knew that the guitar was new – last year a fellow band-member had reversed the van straight over Derek's guitar which he'd absentmindedly put down just behind the rear wheels while he smoked a rollup. As for the 'Tenor Cs' the pun was so awful that Gilbert couldn't begin to imagine what their music was like. He'd never been a great country and western fan, and he always watched with a certain bemusement as his neighbours Roy and Anne got dressed up in full western regalia every Friday night to go to the dance at the Bricklayers' Arms in Swanmore. They were particularly fond of a dance called the 'slosh' – the wife had given him a quick demonstration one day as she stood on Gilbert's front path having borrowed some sugar from Myra. It seemed to require the entire length of the path to perform and he wondered how a roomful of 'slosh' dancers avoided treading on each others' toes. She was always urging Gilbert to join them one evening – "it would take you out of yourself," she said to Gilbert, eyeing him in a meaningful way. Gilbert was unsure whether this meant it would take him away from Myra, or whether Anne thought there was an 'inner Gilbert' longing for release via the dancefloor.

He had hung about in the Ponderosa's foyer long enough. It was time to brave the hall. All the time he'd been standing looking at the poster, trying to gather his courage and adopt the right air of nonchalence for his grand entrance, a swarm of people had been pushing past him, anxious to get to the bargains. Inside the hall it was hot and stuffy and packed to the gills. People stood three deep at every stall, jostling for a better look. He was carried along on a tide of bodies. "Look at that!" he heard one woman cry as she spied a pine-framed washboard. "We used to have one of those but we threw it away." He moved at shuffling pace down the hall, craning his neck to see if Barbara was behind one of the stalls, at once excited yet fearful of seeing her, especially when he recalled the embarrassment of his silent phone-call. At last he spied her stall, tucked just in front of the stage, and caught a glimpse of her red hair as she bent forward to show a customer a porcelain figurine.

Quickly he dropped his eyes and veered off towards the postcard tables. His plan was only to approach her once he'd done some buying, then she would never suspect that he'd gone there specifically to meet her – it would be just a chance encounter. It was easy to spot the postcard tables. There was no crush: just a line of middle-aged men in anoraks patiently thumbing through boxes and boxes of cards. Each wore a rubber thimble on their index finger to make flipping the cards easier. Gilbert made a mental note to get one – it would clearly mark him out as a serious collector. Half an hour's quiet trawling brought him 23 postcards depicting generals and statesmen, a respectable haul for a first attempt. He tried out a phrase that he'd heard Ian Avery use: "what's the trade on that?" he asked each dealer in turn, and was rewarded with a decent discount.

Taking a circuitous route to Barbara's stall, Gilbert took advantage of a lunchtime lull in the crowd to stop by a table specialising in 1920s ladies accessories – evening bags, embroidered shawls and enamelled powder compacts in striking designs. From here he could clearly see Barbara and he felt his heart leap as he saw again just how beautiful a woman she was.

"Can I interest you in anything?" asked the stallholder. "That's a lovely colour, isn't it?" Gilbert realised he had been fiddling unconsciously with a silk scarf while he observed his quarry. On impulse he picked up a jade green beaded bag at random from the stall.

"I'll take this," he said, thrusting it at the dark-haired woman who, he noted, was sporting a distinct moustache. He endeavoured to raise his eyes to hers before she thought he was staring at her upper lip, and handed over £15. It was rather more than he could afford but the deed was done before he could change his mind and before he could think to ask for the trade price. As he walked over to Barbara, he began to feel a sharp pain behind his eyes, the harbinger of one of his headaches. He willed it to go away and fixed a tight smile on his face as he waited for Barbara to notice him.

"Gil! How wonderful to see you! I was just thinking about you."

It was exactly the greeting he had been hoping for but somehow he couldn't shake off the residual tension and his expression barely changed. He did however in a single glance take in every detail of Barbara's appearance – her russet-coloured lipstick, long hair caught back in a tortoiseshell clip, her cream blouse with its full sleeves. There had been a subtle change and Gilbert identified this as her jewelry. She had seemed to have a conventional taste in necklaces when she was at Wendell Court, usually wearing some simple pearls, but today she had a striking ethnic-looking string of large pottery beads with a bracelet to match. Slightly hippyish, thought Gilbert, who actually had very little concept of what a hippy looked like, never having been one himself or associated with any.

They made somewhat stilted conversation, or at least stilted on Gilbert's part, and rather fragmented on Barbara's part as she had to keep breaking off to attend to customers. One middle-aged woman picked up a teaspoon from the stall and examined the price-tag attached to its handle. It was one pound.

"What can you tell me about this teaspoon?" she asked in somewhat aggressive manner, waving the spoon in front of Barbara's face.

"Well, it's a teaspoon," responded Barbara reasonably, rolling her eyes at Gilbert when the woman put it down again and tut-tutted off.

"I feel like making up a story about how it originally belonged to Winston Churchill and how he'd always used it for his breakfast marmalade. Honestly, what do they expect? I tell you what – I'll ask Margery to look after my stall for a few minutes and we'll go and have a cup of tea. At least we can talk in peace."

*

It had been strange seeing Gil again. He looked out of place at the antiques fair, just had he had looked out of place on the course. His clothes were too formal and his manner was strained. She wondered exactly what might be his 'real' milieu, or even if he had one at all. Perhaps at work he fitted in better, though she could hardly picture him bantering with the tea-girl or being the life and soul of the office party. Part of the problem was his face. It was a smooth, bland face, pale. An unlived-in face. It was a face that had apparently gone through the years without a trace of his character of emotions being etched on it. His hair too, was pale and straight, and his eyes cool blue and remote behind the gold-rimmed glasses. Only his mouth showed something of what might have been going on inside. She noticed straight away that he had not been wearing the tie-pin that she had given him and felt curiously relieved at this. It somehow let her off the hook. But then he had surprised her by the gift of the evening bag – a beautiful bag that she had already had her eye on earlier in the day on Irene's Art Deco stall. She'd never been bought a handbag by a man before – Andrew would never have dared to guess her taste in bags, even after all these years. It was, all at the same time, an intimate and a detached kind of gift and she hoped that she had received it graciously enough.

She'd been brought up to pay much attention to manners: even if the person who showed up on your doorstep was the last one you'd want to see in the world, Barbara always greeted them effusively, and if she was given a present, she always wanted them to think it was precisely what she had always wanted. It was therefore a continual irritant to her that other people did not behave in this way. Andrew's parents for example. Some years ago, they'd bought his parents a TeasMade. For years Andrew's father had traipsed down to the freezing-cold kitchen every morning at 6.30am to make the tea. Now he had retired, he deserved a little luxury and the TeasMade would mean he could stay in bed and have the tea all ready for him. Their faces when they opened the package were a picture. "Oh," was all they said, in clear and bitter disappointment. Barbara and Andrew made it worse by gushing about how wonderful these machines were while his parents sat glumly, surrounded by the packaging. In the car afterwards, Andrew said that it had obviously been an affront to his father's manhood – that he was not thought capable any more of looking after his wife, or doing things around the house. That he had been put out to grass.

"Yes, but he could have pretended just a little," Barbara had said. "You know, said how lovely it was and then put it in a cupboard and forgotten about it."

"People are not all like you," he'd replied.

Gilbert showed her the old postcards he had bought, including a set of photographs of famous military leaders. Barbara found what was written on the reverse much more interesting that the photographs themselves, the copper-plate handwriting faded and difficult to interpret. People seemed to use postcards as they would telephone calls today. One of the cards simply said 'I look forward to seeing you at tea tomorrow' which also, Barbara thought, reflected favourably on the Victorian post office and the speed at which it delivered. These days if you sent holiday postcards, they generally arrived long after you'd returned home and thus seemed faintly ridiculous. 'Surreal' would be how 'mad artist' Harry would describe them, though Barbara still only had a hazy idea of what it meant. The only recollection of surreal art she had was those strange paintings by Salvador Dali, all melted clocks and elongated figures. As she handed the cards back, she was about to comment on the fact that all these power-mad generals were rather short but she remembered in time that Gil was rather short, so closed her mouth again. He was not easy to talk to. He had a discomforting habit of staring too long and too intently into her face. She fingered her new beads, newly acquired from one of Cass' art students, and tried to bring the conversation to a close. Then an odd thought struck her. She remembered the ringing phone and the silence on the line when she had picked up the receiver.

"What exactly is it that you do, Gil?"

"Do? You mean work? I work in an office."

"Yes, I gathered that from your perpetual suit and tie. What kind of office?"

"It's in Southampton. Above Bar. It's over a building society."

Barbara raised her eyebrows slightly at him. She said nothing in the hope that this would make him feel he had to continue but Gil appeared to be oblivious of such techniques.

*

Myra was having a good day. Gilbert had been out of the house for hours on one of his stupid antiques quests. Quite where he derived this interest from was beyond her. They didn't have a single thing in the house that pre-dated the 1960s and nor did she want anything. She had rooted out all that junk years ago, including the stuff he'd insisted on bringing over from his parents' home after his mother died. A 1930s oak sideboard he'd wanted to have – great bulbous-legged thing that would have taken up half the dining room. She had put her foot down about that one, but kept the china dressing-table set for a while because it was rather pretty. Gilbert would have kept the whole of the old house as a shrine if he'd had his way, of course, but it had to be sold to help them reduce their mortgage. His salary was pathetic, but that was because he would never push himself forward for promotion. Myra kept telling him but after the third time she'd raised the subject, he had a panic attack and had to retire to his room to lie down. Confrontation was not his strong point, which was a constant irritation to Myra who enjoyed a good ding-dong. Whenever there was a row, he'd just walk away leaving Myra up in the air. It's no wonder I suffer so with my nerves, she thought, as she heaved the mattress onto its side for its monthly turning. Out of the window, through the net curtains, she could see Roy and Anne from next door getting into their rather flashy yellow Ford Granada. It had a confederate flag draped over the top of the dashboard, a dent in one door and a wire coat-hanger instead of an aerial. They were laughing their heads off about something and Myra felt a momentary pang of envy. She watched them drive off, the stereo – one of those old eight-track things – blasting out cowboy music. She turned the Jimmy Young Show up a bit louder and moved over to the wardrobe to give it a good sort-out.

She wished they had the kind of built-in wardrobes around the bed that she'd seen in *Ideal Home* and not these ludicrously cramped ones in the corner of the room. She tided her clothes as best she could considering that there were three or four items on every hanger, sorting out a couple of skirts for the dry cleaners and earmarking some things she never wore any more for the Oxfam shop. Gilbert's side of the wardrobe was sparse but immaculate, his shoes neatly lined up along the bottom and his spare suit hung inside a plastic cover. The trouble with men, thought Myra, is that they go on and on wearing the same stuff for month after month and never think to get it cleaned. Gilbert's clothes often stank of cigarette smoke from all the people in the office who smoked. The only time she'd visited him there she was appalled to find him returning from the newsagents with a carton of 200 cigarettes. Not for me, he explained – it's for the boss. Myra ticked him off for allowing himself to be used as an errand boy. As he went into the boss' office, she caught a glimpse of an ashtray on the desk, full to the brim with fag-ends. A fat hand with rather hairy fingers reached into the ashtray and stubbed out another one as she watched.

Myra decided to add Gilbert's suit to the dry-cleaning pile, and before bagging it, she fished through the pockets removing a button, a paperclip, a petrol receipt and a compliment slip from Wendell Court and a small unused envelope containing several pieces of torn-up paper covered in Gilbert's fussy handwriting. She threw it all in the bin, grabbed both suit and bin and headed downstairs. Outside the wind was gusting around the house and she had to fight the kitchen door to get it to open properly. As soon as she upended the bin over the metal dustbin, the wind whipped half of the stuff out and across the lawn. Myra pursued the first piece of paper and might have been inclined to leave the other bits had something not caught her eye. In Gilbert's handwriting the fragment said 'one as lovely'. She reached for another piece which had wedged itself under a rose bush: 'presumed too much', it said. It was clearly not a business letter and sounded more like poetry. He'd written a poem for her once, back when they were first courting, the usual sort of moon-and-june stuff, but she'd been deeply touched at the time. She had pictured him sitting at the kitchen table biting the end of his pen while he struggled to find the right words. Not that he'd been a particularly romantic type really, so the poem was quite out of character. It may have been that he felt more comfortable expressing his feelings in writing rather than to her face, as she couldn't recall one sentence he'd uttered to express his devotion other than 'I do' at the altar. It was only now that it struck her that it had probably been his mother who had written the poem on his behalf.

Myra retrieved a number of other pieces of the papertrail and headed back to the kitchen, spreading out the torn sheets on the table. It was like a jigsaw puzzle, though most of it was missing and quite a few of the pieces were entirely blank. Moving them around, she managed to assemble two more phrases: 'please forgive' and 'Dear Barbara'. Myra stared hard at this last fragment. She could not think of a single Barbara among their acquaintances. A knot of anxious fury began to form in her stomach. Carefully she put the salvaged pieces of paper in one of the pigeon-holes of the bureau, slotting them in between some old bills. She wasn't entirely sure why she had done this but she was very certain that she would say nothing to Gilbert about her discovery. Forewarned is forearmed, she said to herself. And you never know with Gilbert when you might need some ammunition.

*

"I think we've made a really good start," said Ian, putting down the sheaf of papers onto the walnut coffee table. "We can't expect to make a profit right from the word 'go'. But we were at 80 percent capacity in terms of table rentals and the advertising certainly pulled loads of people in. I know Ron thought we should have done more, but Terry Smith said he thought it was good, and if we can please an old hand like him, it's not bad. If the hall had not been quite so expensive, we might even have afforded more than a curry each at the

Tundoor Mahal out of the takings. It didn't even stretch to a naan bread, as I recall."

Barbara laughed. "I don't think you're going to be the next John Paul Getty, but it wasn't bad, you're right. I quite enjoyed being on the door, taking all their money."

"Bit arduous though, to do it for four solid hours. Couldn't you persuade Andrew to lend a hand next time?"

"Andrew? You've got to be joking. He thought setting up 40 trestle tables was the hardest work he'd ever done in his life. He was hardly going to hang around after that. Tell Cass she'd better hurry up and have her baby, so we can recruit it to the team."

"I thought Andrew was the practical sort – you know, woodwork and all that?"

"He likes to think he is, but it's really only a ruse so that he can escape to his workshop and sit about drinking tea or re-arranging his tools. He's been making the same set of architectural models now for about six months. As soon as he finishes another bit of it, he finds something else wrong and takes it all apart again."

Barbara was unsure what made her say that she'd enjoyed being on the door. She'd hated it: all those greedy-eyed people in their wet coats and anoraks, shoving each other to get in, and all claiming to be 'trade' so they could be admitted half an hour early. The entire four hours she'd endured a litany of complaints about the entry charge, which as she smilingly pointed out, was less than the price of a cup of coffee at the rather upmarket hotel where the fair was being held.

"Same strategy for next time, then?" said Ian. "Only let's put the flyers in all the local antique shops this time – and in the library."

She picked up the advertisement that Ian had sketched out. She had still not got used to seeing her name in huge letters: 'Blaize Antique Fairs'. Ian had chosen a script typeface and the 'z' was a dynamic zig-zag which reminded her of *The Mark of Zorro*, that old 1940s film with Tyrone Power in it.

"Are you sure about the name?"

"Quite sure," he said. "Anything else would have sounded too twee. Anyway, it has nice connotations – Blaize. You know, 'blazing a trail' and whatnot. Mind you, we could have combined our names. Do you know the old story about Sam Goldwyn?"

"I know he was the man who said 'a verbal contract isn't worth the paper it's written on.'"

"I have a feeling all those famous lines were written by his pet hacks. They're just too good. His real name was Goldfish, of course, and he teamed up with a man named Selwyn. They combined their names and called the firm 'Goldwyn'. But if they'd used the other half of their names, it would have been 'Selfish.'"

"Much more accurate," said Barbara.

"Exactly. And what would ours have been? 'Barbarian'." He whooped in delight, picking up one of the scatter cushions from the sofa and twirling it in the air, narrowly missing a green-shaded Tiffany lamp on the side table.

"No need to live up to the name, Ian."

"Sorry. I'll turn back into a sober businessman. Though just saying that word 'sober' makes me thirsty. What time is it?"

"Gin and tonic time," said Barbara. "I think we've earned it."

"Attagirl!" said Ian, planting a large kiss on her cheek. "Don't stint on the ice."

*

'10.30am,' wrote Gilbert carefully in his blue notebook, propping it up on the steering-wheel. 'All quiet'. He used a fine ballpoint pen and his writing, always neat, was small and cramped. He took up the binoculars again and trained them on the driveway, adjusting the focus to bring what he assumed might be the drawing-room of the house into view.

The sash windows were elegant, painted white against the mellow hand-made bricks and there seemed to be a big vase of flowers on the sill. He could actually see very little: the rain that had been pouring down all morning had streaked the car windows and the windscreen was continually steaming up. In a way, the rain was good because it made his Austin, parked in a lay-by on Beresford Hill, less noticeable. He watched as the green single-decker bus toiled up the hill taking shoppers into Romsey. As it went past, it splashed up muddy water from a puddle over his car: he'd have to clean it before Myra saw it. He'd have hardly got it this dirty on his commute from Sholing into Southampton. Perhaps next time he could say that he had to go out investigating a claim. A blue Rover swished by and, a few moments later, turned into the drive. '11am,' wrote Gilbert. 'He arrives.'

A slight movement caught his eye and he swung the binoculars up, catching sight of Barbara at an upstairs window. She seemed to be looking directly at him. The binoculars trembled slightly in his hands, and they clicked against his spectacles. He wondered if this was what police surveillance must be like, though presumably it was different for them – they were emotionally detached. As he must be if he was going to do a professional job. Once Barbara had let Ian into the house – the door was only open for a couple of seconds – there was nothing else to see. Gilbert felt he was burning up and wished he had the courage to go right up to the house and confront them. After all, why not? He only wanted to protect her. She'd understand. She'd be grateful, surely?

While he was rehearsing what he could say if he could ever summon up the courage, the Georgian front door swung back and out stepped Barbara in a dark green coat. The loathsome Ian Avery was immediately behind her wearing a stupid leather jacket that was too young for him. As they headed for the Rover, Ian reached an arm around Barbara's shoulders and gave her a hug. Gilbert couldn't stand it any more. He started the engine, put the car into gear and turned around in the lay-by, heading back towards Southampton, his hands gripping the wheel too tightly.

*

As Ian Avery got into the driver's seat he said to Barbara, without turning: "By the way, your friend was parked up on the hill this morning."

"My friend? What friend?"

"Gilbert. He was there when I went up to Frank's to collect the leaflets. I wasn't sure at the time but the number plate looked familiar."

"But why?" Barbara was clearly astonished. "Why sit up there and then drive away? It couldn't be him."

Ian turned the car at the crossroads and headed towards Salisbury. "Oh it was him all right. I had a good look. I recognised him."

"You've only met him a couple of times."

"Yes, I know, but I had reason to study him carefully."

Barbara didn't reply immediately, wondering exactly what Ian meant by 'having reason' to study Gil. "I don't like it," she said after a while. "He's up to something." She felt a cold finger of fear stroke her spine.

Ian smiled. "Forget it. He isn't worth bothering with. He's a nutcase."

"Perhaps I should invite him round for coffee or something. Clear the air. Let Andrew check him out."

"I really wouldn't bother. He'll eventually get fed up and latch onto someone else."

"I think I will, though, just to resolve things. Actually, I don't have a phone number for him. Would you have the number in your Wendell Court file?"

"I may do. I'll take a look if you insist. Anyway – what did we decide to do about that venue at Brighton?"

Barbara made an effort to take her mind off Gil. "I think we should go for it – after all, there's enough trade there to buy. The place is full of antiques dealers."

“Yes, but there are also plenty of fairs – will it take yet another one?”

“We need to find an edge: some angle on it that no-one else has thought of.”

They were reaching Salisbury now and Ian slowed down at the lights.

“If I’m quick I can get out here,” Barbara said. “I’ll give it some thought,” she called as she scrambled out of the car. “Pop in when you’re passing. Thanks for the lift.”

He’d gone and she was left in the rain. There was a shop she especially wanted to browse around. She’d found several fairings there before, and some pretty figurines. But they were closed for lunch until 2pm. Barbara escaped the summer rain by nipping into the nearest coffee shop. She had about ten minutes to waste.

She tried to concentrate on the pros and cons of doing a fair in Brighton. It was a big step up. Their first fair had been reasonably successful, but once you took into account the rent for the hall, printing flyers and posters, paying for advertising, and all the hundred and one admin tasks, it barely broke even. Then there was that problem with Ron, the silver dealer, whose table rental they had had to refund after a big argument about whether there had been the amount of advertising promised. The hotel in Brighton wanted five times as much in rent for the room, though the table fees could go up. She scribbled down a few figures on her paper napkin but no matter how many times she tried to do the sums, she kept getting them wrong. It was Gil: his face kept swimming into her mind, blank-eyed and serious. Ian must have been wrong. It couldn’t possibly have been Gil who Ian had seen. Why would he be sitting in his car up the road? If he was visiting, he’d come and knock the door, surely? Although, come to think of it, she had been careful never to mention where she lived. He’d obviously taken the trouble to find out. She began to feel uneasy.

She drained her coffee cup and was just about to leave the cafe when the door flew open and in walked a large rangy man, grey hair awry, wearing a vast and rather wet tweed overcoat held together at the front with what looked like a piece of string. His glasses had a large wodge of masking tape stuck on the front and Barbara took in his appearance before it registered in her mind who he was. Harry, the 'mad artist', who she had met at Ian and Cass' dinner party. He spotted her almost immediately and insisted on buying more coffee.

"What brings you to Salisbury?" asked Barbara.

"I've come to see a gallery about some of my paintings."

"How exciting."

"Not really. They hum and haa, and suck their teeth, and then take a few pictures as if they are doing you an immense favour. Months go by and then when they sell, they take most of the money. It's for the glory, really – getting my name known and all that. How about you?"

Barbara explained she was on an antique-hunting trip, then inexplicably found herself telling him about Gil and how Ian thought he'd spotted him parked in a lay-by near her home.

"Just stuck on you, I expect. Not surprising really. Shy chap, is he?"

"Yes, very shy, or rather, very repressed. He behaves rather like a faithful dog whenever I see him, just waiting for me to throw a ball so that he can fetch it and I'll praise him. I think his wife's a bit of a tartar: he went to the antiques course just to get away. He's not even interested in antiques. He latched onto me the second I arrived. I felt rather sorry for him actually – so out of his depth. Not at the course, in his life I mean."

"I have heard the mermaids singing, each to each / I do not think that they will sing to me."

"What's that?

"It's T S Eliot. The Lovesong of J Alfred Prufrock. Do you like Eliot?"

Barbara, never having picked up a book of poetry since she left school, was slightly flustered and began to say something about never really finding time to read anything other than the *Telegraph*.

"Don't apologise. Never apologise. I just thought it sounded like your Gilbert."

"It does."

Later, her bag stuffed with half a dozen excellent fairings, negotiated at a good price, Barbara headed for the railway station, but hesitated as she passed a secondhand bookshop. Two more minutes and she was the owner of a Faber hardback of T S Eliot's collected poems 1909-1925. The pages were yellowed and the cover scuffed, but that hardly mattered. On the train, she turned straight to The Lovesong of J Alfred Prufrock. She read it over and over, so absorbed that she almost missed getting off at Romsey.

*

The music festival was exactly the same as in previous years, but Barbara felt slightly different about it this time, perhaps partly because she had had a week away on her own at Wendell Court so felt less resentful that what could have been a 'proper holiday' was being spent being an appendage to Andrew's own interests. After the Wendell Court experience, she found she was able to approach people – and escape from them – more confidently and that helped her to skilfully avoid the real bores. She also felt brave enough to say to Andrew that she wanted a bit of free time to herself to explore Oxford, so while he went to a lecture on Baroque music, she explored the sidestreets and back alleys, browsing in the antique shops and walking along the river by Christ Church College.

She did consider going round the Ashmolean, but when she reached the entrance hall, she realised that she had been thinking mainly of how it would impress Andrew that she had done something 'cultural' with her afternoon and decided that she didn't really want to go there at all. Instead she went to Blackwells in Broad Street, where she bought a book on Georgian antiques, full of sumptuous colour photographs, then took herself off to Marks and Spencer to buy a couple of new summer dresses.

There was no Gil-like person at the music festival and in a curious way she missed his solicitous manner. Andrew could never be described as solicitous – he was always slightly distracted. He had, however, been excited to have his sheet music signed by Rostropovich, after which he had bought Barbara a glass of champagne to celebrate and had even noticed – a major improvement – that she was wearing her new dress that evening.

By the time of the farewell dinner on the last evening, Barbara was surprised to find she was actually quite enjoying herself. She had linked up with Angela, one of the other wives, who had also been brought along by a husband convinced that he was giving her the treat of a lifetime. The two women formed a happy alliance, exchanging wry grins at the more eccentric behaviour of their menfolk and rolling their eyes whenever the men descended into nerdy talk about the latest headphones or the advantages of hi-fi separates. Barbara and Angela just enjoyed the music, which was surely what it was supposed to be about.

*

It was still dark when Gilbert woke up, his throat dry and parched. He reached for the glass of water on the bedside table, then picked up the clock and peered at the dial, which was supposed to be luminous but seemed to have given up the ghost. He could just make out the hands: it was four-fifteen. He sank back onto the pillow grateful that there were another three hours to go before the alarm went off. The room was hot and Myra seemed to be taking up much of the bed. Gilbert tossed and turned trying to get comfortable. When he turned the pillow over to the cool side, he finally drifted off to sleep. Not a happy sleep though. Within minutes the dreams had started again.

He'd heard it said that you don't actually keep dreaming the same thing over and over, and that it's just a trick of the mind – the dream itself tells you that you've dreamt this before. Gilbert could put the scientists right on that one. For years now the same two dreams had recurred. The first took place in a huge terminal – an airport perhaps, or a big railway station. Gilbert was carrying luggage down a long dark-walled corridor, at the end of which he had to get onto a silver-coloured escalator with his suitcase. But as he approached, he saw that the escalator was going much too fast and he was wracked with fear. Sometimes he'd actually be on the escalator already when it began to speed up, with suitcases whizzing past him and the handrail impossible to hold, snaking away from him as if it was alive.

The other dream was worse because of the appalling sense of dread that it engendered. He was walking across a floor – sometimes it was a thick greeny-glass transparent floor, sometimes he was walking on stepping stones. Because he was familiar with the dream, he was always careful to look straight ahead, but out of the corner of his eye, he could still see them, almost feel them, beneath the surface in the water below – monstrous creatures, unrecognisable, prehistoric. All crowded in to that one stretch of water, and all just calmly swimming back and forth an inch or two below the surface. They never leapt out of the water, never reached for him with their reptilian mouths, never wound themselves around his ankle, trapping him as he walked. The horror came from the fact that they were there, ever-present, timeless. Whenever he woke after this dream he felt sick with shock.

*

Gilbert parked the car neatly and crunched up the gravel of the drive towards the red front door. Leaves were scattered across the front lawn, evidence of last night's summer storm. The wind had still not abated and Gilbert smoothed down his hair and adjusted his tie. He had been surprised to get the call at the office from Barbara because he knew he had been careful to avoid saying where he worked. She told him she'd got his number from Ian, from when he'd registered at Wendell Court, so that Gilbert was torn between being pleased that she had called and being annoyed that Ian had had anything to do with it.

"Gil – how nice to see you," said Barbara as she opened the door, standing back to allow him to pass by her into the hall, which was paved with black and white tiles and had a circular table in the centre with a large vase of fresh flowers on it.

"Do come in. I've got the kettle on for coffee already so it won't take a second. I've just got to give Mrs H her money."

A sprightly older woman appeared in the hall as if on cue, carrying a dustpan and brush which she stowed in a cupboard under the stairs. She wore a flowered, though rather faded, dress and was thin and wiry with a heavily lined face and a shrewd expression, all of which made the dress look incongruous, as if borrowed from a prettier sister. She pocketed the money Barbara gave her without comment, nodded to them both and strode off through the still-open front door.

"A woman of few words, but all of them sharp," said Barbara, steering Gilbert into the sitting room. "Sometimes I think she's in charge of me, rather than the other way around. I even clean up before she comes in case she thinks we are completely slovenly."

Gilbert remembered that he was still clutching, rather tightly, a box of Tartan shortbread which he then handed over, Barbara accepting it graciously.

"I'll just go and put these on a plate. Make yourself comfortable."

Worried he might sit in Barbara's favourite armchair, Gilbert hovered in the middle of the room, taking in the creamy walls, the elaborate flounces of the curtains, the oil paintings and the effortless look of elegance and comfort that the room exuded. He noted that they had numerous table lamps with fringed shades, rather than the single central ceiling light that Myra favoured and which cast such harsh shadows that it made everyone look ill with dark rings under their eyes. Anticipating Barbara's return, Gilbert moved towards the bookcase so that he would not look as if he'd been afraid to sit down, but had been drawn by the books. Perhaps he could even make an intelligent remark about them. Much of the shelves were taken up with volumes on antiques and architectural history – he recalled that Barbara's husband was an architect. There was a fair bit of hardback fiction too: Barbara seemed to collect Monica Dickens, who he'd heard of, and Barbara Pym, who he hadn't. He turned as the door swung open behind him and Barbara came in, bearing a tray with a willow-pattern coffee service and a large matching coffee pot.

"Real coffee," said Gilbert. "How marvellous. At work we only have the powdered rubbish."

He was about to ask about the Barbara Pym books when he saw that there were three cups and saucers on the tray.

"I'll just call Andrew," she said. "He'll be pleased to meet you – he's working at home today while the car's being serviced."

"Oh, jolly good," said Gilbert, feeling a sharp stab of hatred and jealousy. So he was not to be alone with Barbara after all. As she left the room, a smooth-coated black cat slinked in, turned its large yellow eyes on Gilbert's face and stared for several seconds, before jumping daintily onto the table, landing on the tea tray but miraculously avoiding the china. It licked the sugar expertly off the top of one of the shortbread pieces and leapt down again, hurrying away through the door just as Barbara returned. Gilbert debated whether etiquette dictated that he say anything – or nothing – about the cat's behaviour, but he was distracted by the arrival of Barbara's husband.

Andrew was tall and lanky, with fine brown hair that fell in a lock across his forehead. He wore corduroy trousers and a tattersall shirt and looked, thought Gilbert, like an absent-minded professor, though Gilbert had never actually met one – in fact, Andrew looked the way absent-minded professors were portrayed on television. He was good-looking, with even features and strong eyebrows. He clasped Gilbert's outstretched hand with a firm but brief grip. "Good of you to come," he said, flashing a vague smile as if he'd already forgotten exactly how Gilbert fitted in to Barbara's life. He made straight for a large G-Plan reclining chair and put his feet – he was wearing suede shoes, Gilbert noted – on the footstool. Barbara busied herself with the cups.

"So – are you an antiques buff like my wife seems to be turning into?"

"Hardly," said Gilbert, stirring his coffee. "She's much more knowledgeable than I am – I'm just starting out. She's been very helpful." He glanced over at Barbara who had taken the adjacent chair.

"Gil is a postcard specialist," she said. "He's building a collection of cards of the world's great military leaders."

"What do the captions say? 'World-famous for sending young men to their deaths?'"

Gilbert felt the smile fade from his face.

"Sorry," said Andrew, "Only joking. I'm sure it's a fascinating hobby. You're not interested in the business side of it all then, like Barbara?"

"Running antique fairs you mean? No, I don't really have the time – work and all that."

"What is it that you do?"

"I'm a claims handler for an insurance company. Just a cog in a rather large machine, I'm afraid." He wished he hadn't said that. He was also conscious that when Barbara had asked him what he did for a living, and indeed had pressed him for an answer, he'd avoided saying anything. So why exactly was he admitting it to Andrew?

"Well, you must be a fairly important cog if you can come out all this way just to have a cup of coffee with us."

"No – I had to drop something off in Romsey for the firm, so it fitted in well." He could hardly tell them he'd had to invent a dental appointment in order to escape the office for an hour. He was sure Old Harding could tell he was lying, and that stupid junior with the lank hair had sniggered when he said he'd be back by lunchtime.

There was a slightly awkward silence as if they expected him to entertain them, or to declare some purpose to his visit. Gilbert stared hard down at his coffee cup wondering what to say next. He kept seeing himself handing over the green antique handbag to Barbara at the fair and felt it was strange to now be sitting opposite her husband, a person whose existence he knew about but had somehow managed to deny or put out of his mind until now. Barbara, ever the skilled hostess, quickly moved to fill in the conversational gap and started chatting happily about her forthcoming fair in Brighton and about how wonderful Ian was to work with. Gilbert heard himself promising to come along on the day to help boost the numbers. Andrew bit into the last piece of shortbread, the one the cat had licked, put his coffee cup back on the tray and levered himself out of the reclining chair.

"Well, it was nice to meet you, Gilbert," he said, "and do stay to talk to Barbara, but I must go back to my study and get some work done."

"Andrew – don't let Gil go without showing him your workshop," said Barbara. "He constructs the most marvellous architectural models out of bits of card and balsa wood," she said, turning to Gil. "I insist that you go and admire them. In the meantime, I'll look out that copy of Miller's Guide that you said you were looking for."

Gil dutifully followed Andrew out into the hall, Andrew striding ahead. As they passed the hall table, Gil saw there was a pair of door-keys on a red leather fob lying on the table-top. He quickly palmed it and dropped it into his pocket, unconscious of exactly why he was doing this, or what possible use the keys would be to him. Andrew led him through a stained glass door that led to a quarry-tiled conservatory whose glass roof was barely visible through the flourishing grape-vine that twined and twisted across its entire width. The workshop proved to be a white-painted wooden summerhouse at the bottom of the garden. It was clearly his territory. Its interior was modern and uncluttered – Gilbert had heard the term 'minimalist' and imagined that this is what it meant. A worktop of black ash ran the entire length of the room with a series of matching plan-chests underneath, each neatly labelled with the contents of the drawers. At right angles to the worktop, placed to catch the best light, was Andrew's drawing board and high stool, a half-finished design for the elevation of a Georgian style house taped to the surface. A coffee table held a neat pile of architectural magazines, the top one, Gilbert noted, seemed to be in Japanese.

Andrew clicked on a white Anglepoise lamp and beckoned Gilbert over to where there were half a dozen models laid out – each a miniature group of buildings like the set for a Lilliputian play. Though every detail of their design had been carefully modelled, down to the fancy ridge tiles on the roof of one of the buildings and the curved line of a staircase, they had an unreal quality. They reminded Gilbert of the time he had woken up as a child in his parents' house in Totton to see the entire street covered in snow, the outlines of the houses smoothed and blended, the trees perfect spheres of uniform white, and the parked cars hunched under their white blankets like sleeping shell-backed creatures. The snow had hidden the dirt, the shabbiness, under its purifying caress. Perhaps, thought Gilbert, that was why he found the architectural models so appealing.

At Andrew's instigation, he picked up each one in turn, holding it carefully underneath its baseboard and turning it back and forth so that he could see it from every angle. Ready to dislike Andrew from the moment he learnt of his existence as Barbara's husband, Gilbert now felt his animosity seeping away. Andrew explained each model: he specialised, he said in designing perfect Georgian townhouse replicas, whose exterior belied the modernity that lay within – open-plan spaces, electrically operated vertical blinds, Swiss underfloor heating, clever false ceilings that held dozens of downlighters, and cable ducts to each room to be ready for the time when homes had their own computers. At this, Gilbert raised his eyebrows slightly in disbelief, recalling the bulky beige VDU which connected his insurance branch to head office.

"Some people call this architecture 'pastiche'," said Andrew, "but I find that rather insulting."

"Quite," said Gilbert, conscious that he had no clear idea of what 'pastiche' might mean.

"Well, we'd better get you back to Barbara before she thinks I've kidnapped you. She regards all this" – he gestured with his hand in a sweep that took in the whole room – "in much the same way as I regard her antique fair ventures. Thinks it's all a bit puzzling."

"You don't share her interest in antiques, then?"

"The bric-a-brac is a load of old tat, most of it. But it's not that exactly – I just can't see why on earth she wants to go traipsing around the country, collecting 50 pence pieces off queues of the great unwashed in some ghastly church hall."

"I think they're a bit more upmarket than that," said Gilbert. "Hotels and so forth."

"Well she's never expressed the wish before to go into business – she used to be quite the contented housewife. Now she doesn't even have time to come to see the Bournemouth Symphony Orchestra with me any more. Always off out with Ian Avery. What do you think of him, by the way? My mother thinks Barbara's gone off her head and says I shouldn't allow it."

Gilbert was so astonished that Andrew had volunteered an opinion of his mother's, that he did not react immediately to the question about Ian Avery. Gilbert's own mother would neither know nor care what Myra was doing and at 38 he certainly would not have countenanced soliciting her advice on marital matters, never mind telling a complete stranger what she'd said.

"Barbara has a very good head for business," said Gilbert, "and she does it wonderfully. That is, she's a wonderful person." He looked down intently at his hands, holding them so he could inspect his nails, short, clean and scrubbed. He was annoyed to feel his face flush. "It's just that Ian Avery – well, you asked me what I think and ...."

He tailed off, unsure what he had intended to say, but aware of the tension that his unfinished sentence had produced. Glancing up, however, he saw that Andrew was grinning broadly. He clapped Gilbert on the shoulder.

"I think Barbara can take care of herself. So don't worry – and you can be her knight in shining armour if she needs rescuing."

Her knight in shining armour: Gilbert thought about the phrase all the way back to Southampton in the car. Instead of going straight into the office when he got back, he walked up to the first floor and went into the men's washroom there, well away from any possible encounter with one of his own colleagues. He leant with both hands on the edge of the washbasin in order to bring his face closer to the mirror. It stared back at him expectantly, the gold rim of his glasses shining from the glare of the fluorescent striplight. He straightened the knot in his already-straight tie and adjusted the tie-clip that Barbara had given him. His face had resumed its usual pallor but, inside, Gilbert felt exultant. He took a deep breath, left the washroom, and headed for his desk.

*

"And this is Dylan," said Cass as the approached a slim figure bending over a grey bucket in which he was making papier mâché. "Dylan – meet Barbara."

"Enchanté," he said, taking Barbara's hand in his rather damp palm and bending over to kiss her knuckles. As he did so, a lock of his unruly blond hair fell across his forehead. He flicked it back.

"I've seen some of your work," said Barbara, regaining her hand, and slightly embarrassed at Dylan's gesture. "I thought the eggs were wonderful."

"I'm flattered," said Dylan, shoving his hands in the pockets of his plaster-spattered dungarees and grinning at Barbara.

"You're not here to have your head turned by flattery," said Cass. "If that papier mâché is ready, you can show Barbara how to apply it to the armature. She's our newest recruit."

Barbara felt less like a new recruit than a visitor from the Townswomen's Guild. Everyone in the room apart from her seemed to have mohican haircuts, pottery earrings, or – like Dylan – the authentic look of a working artist. Barbara's slacks and denim smock suddenly felt all too new and too stiff, like a child's dressing-up costume. But Dylan accepted her with an easy grace and she was soon absorbed in helping him to create the head of an African woman, pressing the mulched paper around the wire frame.

"Cass is a brilliant teacher, you know," said Dylan. "I guess she'll give it up when she has the baby, so I'm trying to learn as much as possible from her before that happens. I like the organic stuff, or figurative sculpture – I'm not really into all this new installation stuff which is all they are teaching these days at art school. What kind of sculpture are you going to be doing?"

"I don't really know yet, to be honest," said Barbara. "My only experience is in antique restoration – plaster of paris mouldings and that sort of thing. But that's only dabbling, really. It will be small-scale, though, whatever I do," she said, thinking of Andrew's undoubted horrified reaction if she started bringing home large or aggressively modern pieces. There had already been a row about it. Andrew seemed to think that wives should be allowed one interest – in Barbara's case, the antique fairs which Andrew marginally tolerated – but that two interests was beyond the pale. She'd argued that she'd done a pottery evening class a couple of years before and he hadn't objected to that, but he said it was completely different to a Saturday school. This was Winchester School of Art, not the local community centre and everyone was going to be more serious about it. She'd remembered how condescending he'd been when she had brought home her first efforts from the pottery class, a slightly lopsided vase and a plate formed by pressing a tulip-tree leaf into the clay. Sometimes she wondered why on earth Andrew had become an architect – he hated anything modern and had a deep suspicion of anyone who, as he term it, seemed 'arty farty', equating it somehow with effeminacy. She suspected he had inherited these prejudices from his mother – occasionally a more open-minded Andrew peeked through from behind these preconceptions. He had enjoyed the company of Cass and of Harry at the dinner, though their very different outlook on life was something he had clearly treated just as a 'diversion'. For Barbara it was becoming something more than that. It wasn't envy exactly that she had felt – more a feeling that she had been living a half-life – and all this time had been unaware that other possibilities might be open to her. As she worked on the sculpture with Dylan in comfortable silence, she smiled to herself at the thought of Ian – how different he was from Cass, yet how matched a pair they were. So many of the people she knew in Ampfield and Romsey were completely hidebound – stiff, formal, unable to relax. Ian was a breath of fresh air: the way he'd immediately called her 'Babs', would give her a hug on the slightest pretext, and seemed to think her every utterance was worthy of intense consideration. It wasn't that Andrew didn't listen to her, it was just that his vaguely abstracted air was a permanent feature, used when the Village Bore was droning on about people from the pub parking on the grass verges, but equally when Barbara was trying to talk about the profit margin calculations on the next antique fair, or whether they should replace their three piece suite with the pair of sofas she had seen in *Homes and Gardens*.

The only time he really came alive, really seemed focused, was when he was talking about music. He'd told her that architecture had once been described as 'frozen music'. Barbara thought this was a beautiful metaphor but was frustrated that she couldn't remember where the quote was from. It was German, she was sure.

"All done," said Dylan, jolting Barbara out of her reverie. "The hard bit comes next week with the top layer, but you'll be working on your own piece then. Cass has asked me to help you make the armature. You need to do some sketches of what you've got in mind and we'll work from that. Any ideas yet?"

"As a matter of fact, I have had the germ of an idea," she said, telling Dylan about the 'frozen music' quote she had remembered.

"Schiller," he said instantly. "The poet. A true German Romantic. He wrote a lot of philosophical pieces too – and he thought beauty had a moral quality – that it wasn't just about aesthetics. Mind you, a lot of people think he stole that phrase about frozen music from Goethe, his friend. Might be a trifle ambitious for a first piece. Symbolism and all that."

"My husband is an architect – he may be able to help me with the sketches."

"Until next week, then, gracious lady," said Dylan, bowing.

Barbara was buzzing with excitement as she left the studio and walked up the tree-lined road to the bus stop. Maybe even Andrew would approve of her project, especially if she could get him involved in it. His main objection seemed to be that she had cheated him of his usual weekend routine by being at the class on Saturdays and spending most Sundays doing the antique fairs.

"I'll hardly ever see you," he'd complained. She had refrained from pointing out that it was his choice to commute to London for work when he could quite easily have found a position with a firm of architects in Southampton or Winchester ("provincial minds," scoffed Andrew) and on the days when he worked from home he was locked away in his workshop, emerging only for a brief lunch-break. Now, instead of waiting for him to come and talk to her to break the solitude of her day, she could be sketching ideas for her sculpture.

She suddenly saw herself as a different person entirely – a serious person, a person with a mission. A person that perhaps even Harry would find interesting to talk to. She'd need to read some books on art, of course, but she could ask Cass to recommend some.

As she boarded the bus by the statue of King Alfred, a movement caught her eye. Outside the Guildhall was a pale-faced man in a grey suit. She thought for a moment that it was Gil, but when he turned to watch the bus go past, she could see that she was mistaken. This man was older and bigger-built. He was laughing about something with his companion. She realised she had never seen Gil laugh.

*

Getting Andrew alone at home would be difficult, Gilbert decided. The only opportunity would be at the weekend, and then he'd have to wait until he was sure Barbara was out of the house before making his move. Barbara and Andrew usually went out together, shopping in Romsey or out to the New Forest for a walk. Sometimes they went for a ploughman's lunch at a pub called the Royal Oak. It was hard keeping tabs on them in these remote places, as Gilbert was fearful of being spotted. He could wait until Barbara was doing the next antiques fair with Ian, but he had his own plans for that day. No, to approach Andrew, it would make sense to call at his office. Neutral territory too, which had its advantages. It wasn't hard to arrange. Gilbert booked a day's leave, drove early to Winchester station, bought his ticket and then retreated into the small station café where he could keep an eye on the platform. He'd told Myra that he had to go up to town for the company, concerning a claim: she had expressed mild surprise but not questioned him further. He pretended to browse the magazines, feigning an absorbing interest in caravanning journals, when he saw Andrew pass the window. Gilbert moved quickly through the shop doorway and down the platform in the opposite direction. Not until he was fifty feet or so away did he turn round and look to see where Andrew was standing. He need not have worried. Andrew had placed his briefcase between his feet and was studying the front page of the *Daily Telegraph*. They boarded the train five carriages apart.

All through the journey, Gilbert was tense: his throat felt dry but he could not risk walking down to the buffet car to get a coffee in case he bumped into Andrew. Opposite him, two women conversed non-stop, full of excitement at the prospect of a day out in London. They were loud, rather cheap-looking he thought, not like Barbara with her elegance and good taste. At Waterloo he was so anxious not to lose sight of Andrew that he forgot to hand in his ticket at the barrier. The guard called him back and Gilbert had a second of irrational fear that they knew he was up to something. He handed over his ticket and rushed for the Underground, seeing Andrew far below him on the escalator.

At Green Park, Gilbert emerged into the clear crisp autumn air, the escalator disgorging its passengers right next to the park railings, through which he could see dozens of people walking on the paths, presumably on their way to work, some even on rollerskates weaving through the crowds. Andrew set out at a brisk pace, never glancing over his shoulder. He crossed the road in front of The Ritz, where a richly uniformed doorman was hailing a cab for an elderly woman in a fur coat, and headed down a side street. Gilbert hung well back, speeding up only once Andrew had disappeared through the front door of an elegant terraced Georgian building with a cream facade and a first-storey bow window. He read the name on the discreet brass plate: Elkington Shaw, Architects. The door was black and glossy, the only eccentric touch being the brass doorknocker, which was in the shape of a T-square. The whole place smelt of money.

Satisfied, Gilbert retreated back onto Piccadilly, walking aimlessly along, just killing time until Andrew was settled at his desk. He passed the open door of a church and, on impulse, stepped inside. It was so dark compared to the low-angled sun-dazzle of the street that his eyes took a moment to adjust. There was much oak panelling, a faint smell of incense and rows and rows of pews facing a rather plain altar. There were just three isolated figures in the pews, bent forward in silent prayer. Gilbert made his way over to a niche in front of which a number of candles on a black iron stand were flickering. He was conscious of the sound of his shoes on the tiled floor. The niche contained a large plaster statue which a plaque identified as St Anthony of Padua. Gilbert was fairly sure that Padua was in Italy, but could not recollect anything about the saint: though he had been forced to attend Sunday School as a child, he had stopped going to church when he became a teenager and could now recall little other than the most popular Bible stories or the tales of St George and St Francis rewritten as 'ripping yarns' in order to excite the interest of small boys. He had the feeling that Roman Catholics had a different set of saints anyway from Protestants – perhaps St Anthony was one of these?

He looked up at the statue: the face bore a serious yet kindly look and as Gilbert met its steady gaze he realised that he had not once, in the tension and stress of tailing Andrew to

London, planned exactly what he was going to say. He began to sweat despite the coolness of the church, and took off his glasses to wipe them. As he put them back on, he noticed a series of little scraps of paper around St Anthony's feet. Each contained a handwritten message asking the saint to intercede for them. 'Please help Marie,' said one, 'who is sick in heart after the loss of her husband'. 'Pray for a good outcome to my exams,' said another. Gilbert reached for a blank slip of paper from a pile on the votive stand. Taking his pen from his jacket pocket, he wrote carefully 'Please protect Barbara from those who mean her harm' and tucked the note close to the statue, just where St Anthony's bare toes protruded from beneath the hem of his robe. He turned quickly and left the church, opening the heavy door onto the noise and bustle of Piccadilly.

Autumn

"I thought perhaps Torquay," said Myra leafing through a brochure on coach holidays, "the Cornish Riviera."

"Looks more like Cannes, all those palm trees," said Sandra, a square-faced stout woman who was dressed as if she believed she was still a sylph-like 19-year-old. She put her gin and tonic back onto the teak coffee table and reached for a Thomas Cook brochure that had a laughing family on the cover, playing idyllically and harmoniously on the beach. "What about Spain? Or Crete?"

"There's no way Gilbert will go abroad," said Myra. "In fact, I don't think he ever got around to renewing his passport, so I've a fat chance of getting some Mediterranean sun."

She walked over to the MFI bureau in the corner of the sitting room, pulled down the flap and rummaged through the nooks and pigeon-holes until she pulled out two dark blue, stiff-covered passports.

"Just look at my photo in this," she said, handing one over to Sandra. "What was I thinking of, having my hair done like that?"

"Very trendy at the time," said Sandra, attempting to be polite but being overcome with giggles. "That's surely not an Afghan waistcoat you've got on? It is, isn't it? I can't believe it!"

Myra snatched it back. "Very funny, I'm sure. Wait until you see Gilbert's if you think I look a sight."

She checked the date on the inside page of Gilbert's passport. "Yes, it ran out three years ago."

"Let's see, then," said Sandra, snatching it out of Myra's grasp. She opened it eagerly to the first page and examined the black and white photograph, partly obscured by the embossed stamp of the Passport Office. Gilbert was wearing a shirt and tie with a V-necked pullover, his expression serious but somehow absent.

"He looks exactly the same as he does now," said Sandra, disappointed.

"His glasses are different," said Myra, defensively.

"Everyone wore those heavy dark-rimmed glasses then. You know, the Michael Caine look."

"You don't have to go on holiday with Gilbert. Leave him here with his stamp collection and we'll go off together: we'll have a high old time."

"Postcard collection," corrected Myra. "Nice thought, but there'd be hell to pay if I went on my own. It'll have to be Torquay."

She would like to have told Sandra how different Gilbert had been since he went on his own to the antiques course, and about the scraps of letter she'd found in his pocket, but as she was thinking how to phrase it, Sandra got started on one of her interminable monologues about Gerald, her divorced husband, in whom she seemed to take more interest than when they were married. She was just telling Myra for the third time about how they were thrown out of their honeymoon hotel for skinny-dipping in the pool at midnight, when Myra heard Gilbert's key in the latch. She stiffened, and put down her gin and tonic, even though she'd hardly taken a sip but had replenished Sandra's glass twice.

She knew every sound in sequence. The click as he shut the door, the rattle of the keys as he hung them on the hook, the rustle of his mac as he hung it on the oak hatstand, the muted thud of his briefcase hitting the floor. The timing of the sounds, and their volume, determined what mood Gilbert was in. Tonight, he seemed furtive, the movements muffled, as if he didn't want her to know that he was home yet.

"We're in here!" she called, more cheerily than she had intended, but still challenging.

Gilbert came in, sliding through the gap between door and frame, as if not to disturb the house. He looked dispiritedly across at Sandra. "Ah, Sandra," he said.

"We were just talking about you, Gilbert. I told your lovely wife here that she should leave you."

Gilbert, stricken, stared blankly, wondering how Myra could have found out so quickly.

"What's the matter – someone walked over your grave? I only meant leave you for a holiday. Sunny Spain, just us girls – what do you think? Sangria and flamenco: we'd be in our element."

As relief flooded in, Gilbert pondered what possible element it was that Myra was designed for. Mars, perhaps.

"Don't take any notice of her," said Myra. "You're coming with me – to Torquay. A coach holiday."

"Fine," said Gilbert, backing out of the room. "I'll have to check how much annual leave I've got left, though," He thought with awful clarity of all the days he had taken secretly as leave in order to follow Barbara around.

"You must have loads – we've not been anywhere this year, and all you've had is that week at the antiques thingy."

"Yes, but we're terribly understaffed at work. They may not let me go." He gave a half-wave to Sandra and retreated into the hall.

"Honestly!" he heard Sandra say. "What a wet blanket!"

*

Barbara and Ian had a good early run down to Brighton, the weather fine and the roads clear. Barbara felt nervous and excited: only their second fair, and already they were into what she thought of as the 'big time'. Ian drove along the seafront and up past the Royal Pavilion.

"Have you been inside?" he asked, gesturing at the rather absurd onion-domes, looking like a wedding cake plonked down in the middle of a careworn junk shop.

Barbara shook her head. "It's a catalogue of bad taste, so don't bother, said Ian. "I don't know why people rave about it. I'm quite a fan of chinoiserie, but it's over the top even for me. Still, it gets a lot of visitors, and every single one of them will have seen our posters. He slowed down past the noticeboard alongside the Pavilion, crammed with advertisements for poetry readings, jazz nights, new museum exhibits and nightclub DJs.

"Damn it – where's our poster?" He jammed on the brakes, pushed open the car-door roughly and leapt out. "Some bugger's taken it down."

"Just too much competition for space, I expect. Don't worry about it – there's plenty more."

"Annoying, though, when it's our first time." He pulled into the hotel's circular driveway. "I'll just nip out and make sure they've unlocked the back entrance."

By 8am, everything was set up: the tables arranged around the room, the cashbox and tickets by the door. Stallholders would not start to arrive for another thirty minutes.

"I'll just have a little walk around, if that's all right," said Barbara. "I could do with stretching my legs."

"Go ahead," said Ian, amused that Barbara, who had just helped him haul about 50 trestle tables around the hall, would still feel the need to 'stretch her legs'. He suspected she wanted a quick look in the windows of the shops in The Lanes before they started. "I'll get stuck into the coffee while you're gone."

Barbara walked through Reception, past the concierge at the door and out along the street that sloped downhill toward the sea. It looked a grey, flat smudge in the distance. Only a few dog-walkers were in evidence. She struck out briskly, hoping that she was heading in the right direction for The Lanes, only having been to Brighton once before, to put up all the posters during the previous week. The lamp-posts alongside the hotel still bore the black plastic ties that had held their notices, but not one of the posters was still there. In the gutter, she saw one of them torn in half, a dirty shoeprint disfiguring its surface. Incensed, she strode on further, turning inland towards The Lanes where she knew there were two big noticeboards where they had advertised the antiques fair. Even from fifty yards away, she could see the posters had gone. Four drawing pins framed an empty space. She spun around, looking for the culprit, but there was no-one about, just a couple of old drunks sitting on a bench, oblivious to her and to the rest of the world. What seemed like an accident with the first poster, clearly was no such thing. Someone was sabotaging their fair.

She strode back the way she came, walking much faster now and seeing nothing of her surroundings, her mind churning through the possibilities. When she got to the hotel, Ian was supervising a small crowd of stall-holders, some carrying cardboard boxes, others with plastic crates stacked on luggage trolleys, all eager to set up.

"A word, please. Alone." Ian looked up, startled at Barbara's angry tone. He extricated himself from the dealers, grasped Barbara firmly by the elbow and steered her into the coffee lounge.

They stood in the corner, under a large reproduction of a Dufy painting, all jaunty sails and highly coloured buildings. Ian was still holding Barbara's arm. "What's the matter? Is it me? Because if it is, can I apologise later, after we've got everyone in and organised? This isn't a good time, right now."

"No, of course it's not you. It's much worse." Ian could not restrain a smile, but it faded when he saw Barbara's face beginning to crumple. She explained what had happened, swallowing hard and taking refuge in anger rather than tears.

"OK, here's what we'll do," said Ian. "We'll see the hotel manager first, to see if he knows anything, then we'll think about who could possibly have done this, whether it's spite – someone with a grudge – or whether it's just kids tearing the posters down for the fun of it. But we can't do any of that until afterwards: there's just no time. So we'll go back in, look confident, put on great big grins, and act our heads off."

"It's Ron, isn't it? Who else could it be? He was so nasty last time, saying that he wanted his stall-money back, that there wasn't enough advertising. Then when I tried to sell him a stall for this fair, he gave me a real mouthful."

"I think it may well be Ron. But put it out of your mind for now. I tell you what: ask the concierge if there's anyone who can stand outside the hotel for an hour or so, handing out some of our flyers. That will help. Bribe him if necessary. And

I'll see you back inside." He took a couple of £10 notes from his pocket and handed them to Barbara.

"Are you always this good in a crisis?"

Ian smiled. "I had a boss once who said that, when something goes wrong, 'don't get mad, don't get even: turn it to your advantage.'"

"I'm still on the 'getting mad' phase."

"Me too – though 'getting even' is also fairly appealing, especially if it turns out to have been that obnoxious git Ron."

He patted Barbara on the arm and went back into the hall. Barbara grabbed a handful of flyers and set off to charm the concierge.

*

On the morning of the fair, Gilbert decided that he wouldn't go to Brighton. Myra was spoiling for a fight and insisting that he do some work around the house. Besides, it would mean talking to Barbara with Ian hovering constantly at her side, and he felt sick at the very thought of it. And perhaps she would be more grateful for his protection if he stayed away from time to time.

Brighton never appealed to Gilbert, its mix of money and shoddiness. There were always down-and-outs hanging around the railway station, and the road down to the beach seemed to consist of betting shops, gaming arcades and cheap sandwich bars. The Lanes were quite nice, but the prices were sky-high. He'd once seen two men walking towards him: they were holding hands, and Gilbert didn't quite know whether to look at them or to pretend he hadn't noticed.

His train of thought was broken by Myra's shout from the kitchen: "Could you pop to the hardware shop and get some more magnolia emulsion? This wall is looking very scuffed. We'll need a new brush, too."

Gilbert sighed. "Are you sure you want magnolia? You wouldn't prefer orange?"

The sarcasm was lost on Myra.

Gilbert took his car keys off the hall stand and went out to the car. On the way down the drive, he pulled out a few odds and ends from his coat pocket – a receipt, a paper tissue and a railway ticket – lifted the metal dustbin lid, and threw the rubbish in.

*

Ian put the phone onto loud-speaker and Ron's voice with its strong Hampshire accent echoed around Ian's sitting room.

"I thought we'd been through all this, Ian. Yes, I was unhappy about Midhurst: you said you're be putting up a banner across the High Street and that never happened. You also said you'd have a display ad in the Midhurst and Petworth Observer and instead it was a little titchy ad tucked away at the back that I shouldn't think anyone saw."

"I know," said Ian, placatingly. "In the end, as you know, the Council wouldn't let us put up the banner – and we've really had no control over where the Observer put the advertisement on the page."

"And the result was that I only took £15 all day. It was a disaster, basically. And that nipper you had outside – every time I went out there, he'd gone off to the shop or something to get a Coke. Worse than useless."

"But we did refund your money," Ian reminded him.

"That's what I don't understand – I thought it was all settled. So why are you calling me now?"

"Well, to be honest Ron, I wanted to make sure that you didn't bear us any ill will. We had a bit of trouble at Brighton with someone sabotaging the fair, tearing down our posters and so on."

"And you're accusing me? You've got a bloody cheek! You really think I'd drive all the way down to Brighton and waste a whole day just to put the boot in at your poxy fair? I've got better things to do with my time. Anyway, I couldn't care less about your fairs – I'm sticking with Kingfisher Fayres in future. They've never let me down."

"I didn't mean to accuse you, Ron," said Ian in what he hoped was a sincere voice. "I just wondered whether perhaps you'd complained to other stall-holders about Midhurst and one of them has decided to take action on your behalf."

"Absolutely not. The only person I complained to was Terry Smith and he seems to think the sun shines out of your arse. Actually, I don't think he cares much about the fairs – he's got the hots for your Barbara. I don't think I'd exactly turf her out of my bed, either."

Barbara put her hand over her mouth to suppress her guffaw and the unwelcome but comic image of Ron – bald and with a belly that made him look six months' pregnant – in her bed. He probably wore a string vest. She doubled over with laughter.

"She sitting on my knee at the moment, Ron," said Ian.

"Get away with you!"

*

The grocer's boy, Bert (75 if he was a day but still designated a 'boy') had just put Barbara's two cardboard boxes of groceries in the kitchen when the phone rang. She signed the chit, mouthed 'sorry' and went into the hall, distracted from saying the number – Ampfield 23510 – by the sight of Bert's brown-overalled back retreating out the front door and crunching over the gravel to his Morris van, which surely should have been retired in the 1960s.

"I'm just throwing myself on your mercy," said the voice in Barbara's ear.

"Fiona? What's up? You sound strange."

"Stunned is what I am. He's only told his wife about me. I mean, whatever for? Catholic guilt or something?"

Barbara mentally shuffled through all the men Fiona had been involved with over the last couple of years – most of whom had had wives – and retrieved the image of Nigel, the smarmy, suited-and-booted but rather red-faced man who was both her boss and her latest entanglement.

"Well I just had to flee – simply no choice," said Fiona. "Can't risk handbags at dawn with that old cow."

"What's that noise?" asked Barbara as an echoing, indistinct voice in the background was erased by a roaring sound.

"I'm at the station. They're making an announcement."

Barbara had been to Aberdeen station, so could immediately picture it, the vast span of its glass and iron roof, the huge and echoing concourse.

"Can Andrew be a darling and pick me up?"

Barbara went cold. "Where are you, exactly?"

"Winchester of course. It's taken bloody hours to get here and I'm desperate for a shower and a G&T, and this sodding suitcase is pulling my arm off. Andrew's there, isn't he?"

"Yes, he's here. How long were you planning to stay?"

"God, I haven't even arrived yet and you're asking when I'm going – you're just like the Aged Parents."

Barbara was silent.

"Sorry, sorry – I'll be no trouble. You'll hardly know I'm there. Just need to lie low for a day or two."

Andrew was less than pleased at having to drive into Winchester on one of the few days he didn't have to go there to catch the London train.

"Bloody woman," he said, slamming the front door behind him, while Barbara went upstairs to make up the spare room.

*

Fiona didn't exactly look as if she was suffering emotional trauma. She thumped her suitcase down in the hall, shrugged off her camel coat, letting it drift onto the nearest chair, and then went into the sitting room, throwing herself into Barbara's favourite armchair, spreading her arms out dramatically across its chintz, rose-patterned covers. She wore, Barbara couldn't help noticing, a very expensive skirt suit with padded shoulders and a flounced jacket over a frill-necked blouse. Her auburn hair had obviously been very recently cut at an expensive salon and her silver earrings looked custom-designed. She kicked off her black patent court shoes. "God, I could murder a drink," she said. Barbara always felt like some poor rural peasant compared to Fiona. It was only when Fiona visited that Barbara noticed things about her house that singled her out as an uncultured provincial. That curtain pole, for instance, she saw should have been hung a few inches higher so the top of the window frame was not visible through the tab-tops. And that bisque ornament on the mantelpiece spoiled the symmetry. Barbara was dismayed with herself for noticing these things that at all other times contented her.

For one so completely traumatised, Fiona also proved to have a very healthy appetite, scraping the bowl clean of peanuts and even avidly sucking the lemon out of her gin and tonic. On that first night, when Barbara was congratulating herself at managing to stretch the steak and kidney pie to three, Fiona pulled a face. "Darling, I couldn't possibly – the very thought of meat makes me think of those poor animals. Just give me the vegetables – I'll be perfectly happy with those". This reminded Barbara of that old Jewish joke: how many Jewish mothers does it take to change a lightbulb? None – just one to sit there saying 'no, I don't like to cause a fuss. Don't worry about me. I'll be fine sitting in the dark'. The next morning, a large slice of ham had disappeared from the fridge.

It took three hours and three gin and tonics before Fiona remembered to ask Barbara how she was, by which time 'fine' was the only possibly answer.

Her sister had not always been like this. As children they had been close, uniting against their dominant father. They'd had a secret language, a tree house with a password for entry, and a cocoa-tin intercom between their bedrooms. This closeness seemed inconceivable now.

Just as Barbara was convinced that Fiona was doing her prima donna act only to get attention – the attention that she never did get from their father – it happened. Barbara got back from a coffee morning in the village to find Fiona lying on the floor of the hall, with Mrs H standing over her, telling her to 'buck up' and 'stop being hysterical'. Fiona was lying on her side, her right arm twitching. When Barbara bent down and touched her, she felt stiff. She did not meet Barbara's eye but stared fixedly at the wall as if looking inwards to watch some ghastly film unspooling inside her head. Barbara could see her teeth, like a dog with its fangs bared.

"For goodness sake, Mrs H, call an ambulance."

*

Andrew dropped Barbara outside the main entrance of Southampton General Hospital. A line of dispirited-looking men and women stood outside the sliding doors, every single one smoking a cigarette and a number of them attached to drips on wheeled stands. They all turned to look with incurious eyes at Andrew's car, like a herd of cows.

"I'll be back in exactly one hour to pick you up," he said, leaning over to kiss her as she opened the passenger door. "It's murder parking here on a Saturday – I'd never find a space."

Barbara translated this as meaning that Andrew found her sister hard enough to bear in normal circumstances, let alone in hospital where he was supposed to show some measure of sympathy for her plight. Clutching a box of chocolates and a slew of women's magazines, she headed through the doors, past a noisy cafe and a reception desk and along the main corridor, which was painted in two depressing shades of grey with a grey lino-tiled floor. A man in an overall was buffing the floor with a machine, swinging it to and fro as he moved along. Signs hung down on chains from the ceiling giving directions to different wards, some with letters that had peeled off, making it even harder to navigate. The lift lobby, when she eventually found it, contained three extra-large steel lift-doors and a complicated sign explaining what was on each floor. Barbara didn't recognise half of the terms used: what, for instance, could 'maxifacial' possibly mean? She knew that 'oncology' meant 'cancer' and supposed that you couldn't very well have a sign reading 'cancer' in a hospital. Too direct, too plain-speaking.

When the lift arrived, it was as big as a room, presumably because they wheeled entire beds into it to move patients from floor to floor. She remembered visiting her grandmother in her council flat in the 1960s – on the tenth floor of a newly built high-rise block with its own laundry room and (the latest innovation) a rubbish-chute on each floor. Nan thought it was wonderful. Travelling up in the somewhat claustrophobic lift with Nan, Barbara had noticed that one of the screws on the back panel of the lift-compartment had worked loose and the panel was flapping. She remarked on it. 'Oh yes, Nan had said. 'Must have been the undertakers yesterday.' When Barbara looked puzzled, Nan explained that the lifts were too small to fit a coffin in, so had been built with a special removeable panel that gave access to extra space. 'Otherwise the corpses would have to be stood on end,' she said cheerily.

The hospital lift was packed, everyone silent and resolutely facing the doors like the Undead, each clutching their spray of flowers or paper bag of grapes. Barbara got out at the third floor and headed for Ward F35. As she rounded a corner, she almost collided with a blond young man in a white coat, a stethoscope around his neck, carrying a clipboard. They both apologised and dodged around each other. It wasn't until he had gone by that Barbara realised it was Dylan. He went up in her estimation for juggling a busy career as a doctor with such dedication to art.

Outside Fiona's ward, two nurses were chatting at a desk, looking through lists and rotas but talking at the same time about last night's episode of Coronation Street. They directed her smilingly to Fiona's bed, next to the window in a ward with seven other beds in it. Barbara was horrified to see that it was a mixed ward: doubtless Fiona would have a lot to say about that. As she walked across the room, her mustard-coloured skirt making a slight swishing noise, she noticed that all three men turned their heads to watch her – clearly they were on the road to recovery. Fiona was sitting up in bed, propped up by a huge pile of pillows. She looked, as she would term it, 'peaky', the impression mainly conveyed by the fact that she was not wearing her customary heavy make-up. She wasn't entirely devoid of glamour, however: a mauve cashmere shawl was wrapped around her shoulders and she was wearing a gold watch and a number of thin gold bracelets. Barbara was tempted to lift the bedclothes to see whether she was also wearing her gold ankle-chain.

"Thank goodness you're here," she croaked, reaching out both hands towards Barbara. "I can't possibly stay here, it's too inhuman. Take me somewhere more suitable. Take me home."

"I'm not sure I can do that yet. It's rather up to the doctors. You're only 'under observation'. I shouldn't think you'll be here long." Barbara contemplated the image of Fiona having a long recuperation at Ampfield. It was not one to dwell on.

"An hour is too long with these Neanderthals," she said, gesturing at the men in the other beds. They looked interested, as if a TV drama might be about to unfold, but not exactly ashamed. "The nurses are slovenly and the ward is filthy. And they don't even have brown bread for breakfast, just Mother's Pride."

"Keep your voice down," whispered Barbara, knowing that Fiona's treatment would get infinitely worse should the nurses overhear, a bit like complaining in a restaurant and knowing that the kitchen staff would spit in your soup. Not that Barbara had ever complained, always operating on the theory that you just ate it quietly, didn't make a fuss, but never went there again. “Anyway, I’ve brought you some goodies.” She put the chocolates and magazines on the side table next to the bed.

“Where’s Andrew?” Fiona asked petulantly.

“He’s got a bit of business to do in town.”

“The phone has been ringing off the hook for me, as you can imagine. They’re constantly wheeling the phone trolley over. Nigel is desperate to have me back: said I was the one person who could take his company to the next level and that without me, he’d be sunk.”

Barbara wondered whether everyone in Fiona’s life really did gush in this style about her, in which case Barbara felt rather peeved that no-one ever did it for her, or whether Fiona just made it up in order to feel valued. Stung by the injustice of this, Barbara decided that Fiona was not going to have it all her own way. She started to tell her about the fair in Brighton and the sabotage of the posters.

“Have I met Ian?” Fiona zeroëd in on the one aspect that was not relevant to the story.

“I think you might have seen him when you first arrived. He’d just dropped me off.”

“In the blue Rover? Handsome? Droopy moustache? Rather nice leather jacket?”

Fiona had a photographic memory for any male between 18 and 60. Her radar must be constantly sweeping, issuing beeping sounds when any eligible man hove into view and storing his characteristics on a complex card-index system.

“I suppose he is quite handsome. I hadn’t thought about it. He’s just ‘Ian’.”

“Don’t be ridiculous.”

“I’m married – I don’t tend to eye up every male that passes, unlike you.”

“Married, yes, but not brain-dead surely? Why would he be interested in running you around to all these antique fairs? Don’t tell me it’s your business acumen he’s interested in.”

"That's exactly what he's interested in. Besides, Ian is married and his wife is about to have a baby."

"I rest my case," said Fiona, mysteriously.

Fiona then embarked on a series of anecdotes about handsome men she had known, all of whom – of course – had treated her abominably. Barbara glanced at her watch and was relieved to see that Andrew would be picking her up in ten minutes.

"Of course, if I'm boring you ..."

"No, no. But perhaps I'll go and see if I can have a quick word with one of the nurses, to find out when you're being discharged. And I need to be outside when Andrew arrives so he doesn't have to park the car."

"Honestly, the way you kowtow to that man," said Fiona, opening the box of chocolates and picking out the coffee creme. "Let him wait a while. Come to think of it, having the gorgeous Ian around might be no bad thing. Keep Andrew on his toes." She held the box out to Barbara, who shook her head. "Maybe it was Andrew who tore down your posters in a fit of jealousy. Maybe it'll be antique pistols at dawn."

Barbara smiled, shaking her head. "You're quite impossible. Though all this speculation does seem to have perked you up a bit."

Remembering that she was supposed to be dangerously ill, Fiona put the chocolate box back on the bedside locker and collapsed back against the pillows, sighing. "If I'm supposed to be 'under observation' when exactly are they going to start 'observing' me? I've barely seen anyone except the ward-maid since I've been here."

"I think you'll find that all the doctors go home at the weekends. You may have to wait until Monday. I'll see what I can find out," said Barbara, kissing her sister on the cheek and heading for the nurses' station, her progress across the ward tracked once again by the eyes of the male patients, bored and visitorless.

*

“What’s the verdict?” asked Andrew, moving a number of carrier bags off the leather passenger seat so that Barbara could get in.

“I don’t think there’s a thing wrong with her other than her usual neuroses. That collapse was entirely of her own making. One minute she thinks she’s having a stroke, the next she’s on and on about Nigel and how often he keeps phoning her.” Barbara was about to relate what Fiona had said about Ian, but something stopped her. No sense in putting ideas in Andrew’s head.

“Please tell me she’s not coming back to Ampfield to stay when she’s discharged. I think I’d be the next one to be hospitalised if she stays even one more day.”

“No, they said she’s quite well enough to go straight home. Anyway, what have you been buying? I thought you were calling in on your mother, not ransacking the menswear department of Tyrrell and Green.”

“She wasn’t in. Anyway, it’s not all for me. There’s something for you in the little bag. You can look at it now if you want.”

“A present? How lovely.” Barbara reached over and opened the bag, to reveal a turquoise bracelet, thick and smooth-textured. She slipped it onto her wrist.

“I thought it might match that art deco handbag you bought yourself a couple of months ago.”

Barbara remembered with some discomfort that she had not told Andrew that the bag had been a gift from Gil. “It will go perfectly. Thank you darling. Oh – guess who I saw in the hospital just now? Dylan, that friend of Ian and Cass, the one who did that amazing egg-sculpture.”

“What’s he in for?”

“He’s not in for anything – he works there. He’s a doctor.”

“I don’t think so. I distinctly remember Cass saying what a disappointment Dylan has been to his father because he never got any qualifications. Works in the docks, loading cars onto container ships.”

"But he was wearing a doctor's white coat. Looked most official."

Andrew raised his eyebrows. "Sounds like he might have some explaining to do."

*

Gilbert couldn't stand it any longer. This time he drove the car straight into Barbara's drive, not caring whether she heard him, pulling up alongside Ian's blue Rover. He raised the brass knocker on the front door but placed it softly back when he heard the music. A brass band was playing a stirring tune: the music was loud and a man's voice was singing above the music and thumping something in time to the beat. Softly, Gilbert inserted his key in the door and turned it.

The music was coming from the dining room, towards the back of the house. He crossed the hall and pushed open the panelled door with the tips of his fingers. At the large oval dining table, Barbara and Ian were seated with their backs to him. The table was covered in papers, but they weren't paying much attention to business. Ian was pounding the edge of the table and singing: 'Fiddle, cello, big bass drum / Bassoon, flute and euphonium'. He had a sprig of flowers stuck into the top of his hair and Barbara was laughing.

They didn't hear the door open. Gilbert, rigid with fury, said: "Oh, I'm sorry. Don't let me interrupt your cosy scene." And he closed the door loudly. He caught a glimpse of Barbara's stunned expression, echoed on Ian's face, before the door banged shut.

Gilbert strode back out the front door and was getting back into his car when Barbara appeared on the drive. She tugged open the driver's door and grabbed at Gilbert's arm.

"Come back here!" she shouted furiously. "What on earth do you think you're doing? And how the hell did you get into my house?"

Gilbert stood up, white-faced, tight-lipped. “The front door was open. I did knock, but you didn’t hear. Too engrossed.” His voice had taken on a smug tone now.

“Rubbish,” said Barbara, referring to the front door, but she faltered uncertainly. Perhaps she had forgotten to take it off the latch. “Anyway, how dare you embarrass me in front of people like that!”

"People? Is that what you call him? I thought he was rather more than that.”

“For goodness sake. Ian Avery is a business partner of mine and we were sorting out a business arrangement.”

“I see you find it necessary to explain.”

Ian appeared by Barbara’s side. Gilbert nodded curtly to him.

“Time to go, old man,” said Ian, shoving him back into the car. “Keep your bony nose out of our business. And next time, wait for an invitation before coming round here bothering Babs.”

Gilbert gave them a wintry smile, but his hand was shaking as he tried to put his key into the ignition.

“Wait!” said Barbara. “Just wait here and don’t you dare move!” She walked back into the house and emerged about a minute later. Gilbert saw with horror that she was carrying the jade-green beaded handbag that he had bought her.

“Here!” she said, thrusting it at him. “Take this with you because I don’t want it any more. I never want to see it, or you, ever again.”

Gilbert didn’t put out his hand, so she threw the bag onto his lap and slammed the car door shut.

*

They waited on the drive until his car had disappeared from sight. Barbara said: “Do you mind, Ian, if we finish this some other time? I’m afraid I’ve lost my concentration.”

"Of course. No hurry. I'll be passing by on Friday." He went back into the dining room, gathered up the papers and stuffed them into his briefcase.

"I'm sorry about that," Barbara said. "I did tell you what he was like."

"Forget him. He isn't worth thinking about. How you could ever have become mixed up with somebody like that, I'll never know."

"I can't forget him. He won't let me." She turned away to look out at the garden beyond.

"What got into him today, do you think?"

"Oh, it's stupid really. He thinks ... well, it's obvious he thinks we're having an affair."

"Ha! And what? He's jealous?"

"It's not quite that – not that simple. He seems to have appointed himself as my protector or something. Do you think I was too harsh with him? I'm sure he means well really."

Ian rolled his eyes. "Babs, you just can't help thinking the best of people, can you? The guy is a sad nutter and you were right to send him packing. Let's hope that's the last we see of him."

*

The church was dark inside and smelt of incense, but the light coming through the stained glass windows gave it a warm, soft glow.

"I read the poem – about the mermaids," said Barbara to Harry as they sat alongside each other on the pew, looking at the east window. "In fact, I bought a T S Eliot collection and read the lot. Not sure I understood them all, though. At school, we only did Browning and Tennyson."

"Understanding is rather overrated in my view," said Harry, fiddling with a button that was about to fall off his jacket. "Comprehending is all you need – anyway, Eliot was a terrible thief, raiding other people's poems and patching them all together. When he did it, they called it 'homage'. If I paint a picture and borrow other people's figures, they sneer and call it 'derivative'. You can't win. By the way, as we are surrounded by saints in all these windows, by the magnificent William Wyllie, I note that there's a distinct absence of female saints. What do you know about your namesake – St Barbara?"

"Nothing at all."

"Her symbol is a tower. To punish her for her Christian beliefs, she was walled up in a tower that had two windows, but she put in an extra window so she could pray to the Trinity. She was killed by her father."

"A cheery little tale."

"Quite – shall we stroll in the churchyard? John Keble's grave is just outside the south door."

"My own father ..." Barbara started to say, but was interrupted by the opening of the door. A woman bustled in carrying an armful of flowers. She looked surprised to see anyone in the church, and gave the ill-kempt Harry a deeply suspicious look, probably thinking that he was a tramp. Barbara almost expected her to ask 'is this gentleman bothering you?' But Harry gave out a cheery 'good morning' and then, to the woman's alarm, burst into a loud rendition of the first verse of 'Sun of My Soul'.

"You realise she thinks you're completely mad?" said Barbara as they closed the door behind them and strolled down the path.

"Oh good. I do so like to disturb these bossy Christian women. They are convinced that God is an Englishman, you know. I once recited the Lord's Prayer in French to one of those women, and they were horrified to think it existed in another language. Anyway, Sun Of My Soul is very appropriate – written by Keble, you know."

Curled up in the long grass alongside Keble's modest tomb, made of pink granite, was a fat tortoiseshell cat. It opened one eye when they approached, satisfied itself that they were no threat, and then closed it again.

Harry sat down rather awkwardly on the sloping top of the tomb and examined his outstretched boots, fiddling with the frayed laces. "You were going to tell me something," he said, not looking up at Barbara.

"Was I?" asked Barbara, too brightly.

"About your father."

"Oh, it was nothing really."

"Well, tell me what the nothing was, in that case."

Barbara put her hands in her pockets and turned away from Harry slightly, looking down the path towards the lychgate with its pretty flint-faced cottage attached.

"It's just that when you were talking about St Barbara being shut in the tower by her father, I thought about her defying him – by making that third window – and I felt that perhaps I should have defied my father more. He was a bit 'old school', you know."

"Is that a euphemism for 'tyrant'?" asked Harry.

"I suppose it is. You know: having to keep silent at mealtimes, being sent to your room for the slightest transgression, being forbidden to have certain friends because they 'weren't suitable'. Never feeling you were worthy to be his child. And of course not one word of praise or affection. I can't even remember him putting an arm round us. I thought that must be how all fathers were, so I just put up with it. My sister had a different way of dealing with it – she ran away at every opportunity to avoid confronting him – yet everything she does is still aimed at desperately trying to earn his praise."

"And you?"

"I don't know. I don't think it's affected me. Not as an adult."

"What time are you due home?" asked Harry, looking at his watch.

"I told Andrew 6.30. Gosh, that only ten minutes away. We'd better go back to the car."

"I've got news for you, Barbara Blaize. It has indeed affected you. You're too dutiful. I've never done anything dutiful in my life, and look at me. I live a golden existence."

Barbara laughed, taking in Harry's scruffy clothes, his jacket with a button missing and his dishevelled hair.

He linked her arm through his.

"We are now going over to the King's Head to have a leisurely gin and tonic, after which I just might consent to drive you home half an hour late. It's a minor act of defiance, I know, but you've got to start somewhere."

*

"Barbara! Telephone!" shouted Andrew.

Barbara walked across the hall to the phone, giving Andrew a questioning look as he handed her the receiver.

He put his hand over the mouthpiece. "Ian," he whispered. "Some crisis or other."

"Ian? Is everything OK?"

"Babs, I'm sorry to call so early, but we've got a problem. I was all ready to come and pick you up but when I went out to the car, all four tyres were flat. The van's at the garage having a new exhaust fitted, so I'm stranded."

"How can all four tyres possibly be flat?" asked Barbara, realising even as she said it what the answer was.

"Looks like they've been slashed with a penknife. It must have happened last night, though I never heard anything. I don't know who's got it in for me but if I get hold of the bastard I'll throttle them. It's not just the fair, because I'm sure we'll find a way around that, even if we have to spend the profits taking a taxi to get there. But it's Cass too – with her being pregnant, to leave us stranded out here is not just vindictive – it's inhuman."

"Do you think it's Ron again?"

"No, I can't see him doing this and I believed him when we talked to him about Brighton. Anyway, he lives miles away – why drive all the way out to Kingsworthy to slash my tyres? It could possibly be the miserable old git who lives next-door-but-one, I suppose. He is always complaining about my van being parked out front."

"Have you called the police?"

"Yes, though a fat lot of good that'll do. Cass will stay here to deal with them while I get a taxi over to pick you up. We're really tight on time now if we are to arrive before the stallholders."

"No need for a taxi – I'm sure Andrew will help out, won't you darling?" said Barbara, smiling winningly at her husband.

"It's Sunday and I'm having my breakfast," he shouted. "Bloody Ian can get a bloody taxi."

"Sorry about that," said Barbara to Ian, as Andrew stormed off back to the kitchen. "He's been a bit on edge lately. I'm sure he's not getting at you specifically."

"He's right, though," said Ian, sighing. "I'll be over to you in half an hour and we'll take the taxi on from there to the Marlands. Bye now."

Barbara put down the phone and went into the kitchen, where Andrew was buttering toast and Snob was watching balefully from the worktop.

"You could have been a bit more sympathetic," she said. "It's hardly Ian's fault that someone slashed his tyres."

"Maybe it is his fault," said Andrew, slamming the marmalade jar back onto the table.

"What do you mean?"

"I don't like Ian and I don't like what he's doing to you."

"What on earth do you mean 'what he's doing to me'?"

"You've changed beyond all recognition since you met him. I hardly ever see you. We use to have weekends together but now you're either off at your sculpture class or out doing fairs. Every bloody evening you're sketching or you're hunched over your accounts book. Or you're not even here when I come home from work because you're out at some pub with Harry; and then you want to spend half the evening telling me all the wonderful things that Harry said. Or Ian's still here when I come home, both of you laughing your heads off over some private joke and drinking my best burgundy. I've had enough, Barbara. I just want things to go back to normal."

Barbara silently contemplated what used to be 'normal' in the Blaize household.

"Maybe it would be better if I learned to drive?" she said. "Then I wouldn't be reliant on you or Ian ferrying me about. I could be home quicker. Harry's offered to teach me."

"That just about takes the biscuit," said Andrew, getting up from the kitchen table and throwing his napkin down.

"I thought you enjoyed that evening with Ian and Cass," said Barbara, trying to divert him from the obviously provocative subject of her learning to drive.

"I've changed my mind about him. He's a wrong-un and you'd do well to sever ties with him or you might have to suffer the consequences."

He swept past her.

"I'm going to my workshop. I'll see you when you get back tonight."

"Are you not going to wish me luck with the fair?"

The door slammed and Andrew was gone.

*

Gilbert put the binoculars back into their black leather case, stowed them under the driver's seat and pulled the car slowly out of the layby. He drove down the hill towards the house, keeping in third gear and watching for the farm track that he'd spotted on an early stake-out. It was a single-track lane banked by high hedges. About a hundred feet along it was a muddy pull-in opposite a rusty five-bar gate. He tucked the Austin in as close to the bank as he could. Attracted by the movement and noise, three cows came to the gate to stare across at him, plastic identifying tags dangling from their ears like a strange form of jewellery. Gilbert locked the car and stood in the lane, wiping away every trace of mud from his slip-on shoes. Then he pushed his glasses back against the bridge of his nose, patted his suit pocket out of habit to check his notebook was still there, and set out. He did not go straight to Barbara's house but crossed the main road further down, doubling back so that he did not have to pass by Barbara's only neighbour, a Victorian flint cottage with tall chimneys in an elaborate swirling design all made of red brick.

Turning into Barbara's front gates, which stood open, Gilbert avoided the crunching gravel drive by skirting around a garden path leading to the side of the house. He walked briskly so that he would appear to any passers-by as if he was on official business of some kind. He deliberately did not look at the windows of the house. The side-gate was unlocked and he closed it carefully behind him, walking past the conservatory and up to the kitchen door. As he approached, there was a sudden noise from within. Gilbert stood paralysed: surely he'd seen the cleaning woman leave fifteen minutes earlier? Then the catflap opened with a rude clacking sound and the black, sleek, arrogant head of Barbara's cat appeared, its yellow eyes meeting Gilbert's for a moment before it jumped through the flap and shot off into the shubbery, the flap banging shut behind it.

Gilbert reached in his pocket for the keys. They almost slid out of his grasp, so sweaty were his hands, and initially he tried to open the door with the wrong key. He swapped them over, fumbling slightly putting it into the lock, but it turned smoothly. Gilbert pressed down on the handle and opened the door without a sound. He stood just inside, holding his breath. A clock ticked peacefully on the wall and light from the window fell on a dark green Aga and white kitchen units. In front of the Aga was a cat-basket with a cushion inside, covered in clots of black fur. A painted stencil of ivy leaves wound around the walls just under the cornice and Gilbert imagined Barbara standing on a stepladder, carefully spraying each stencil in turn, with her hair tied back and perhaps wearing a smock to protect her clothes.

"Hello?" he called out, at first tentatively and quietly, but then as he crossed the kitchen, he called a little louder and more confidently. Next to the door that led from the kitchen to the hall was a wall-mounted blackboard topped by a stylised illustration of chickens pecking outside a barn. 'Courgettes Beef Cat food' was chalked in Barbara's handwriting. Underneath, someone else had written 'vacume bags'. He stepped into the silent hall. Familiar territory from his last visit. Thinking of that visit and how he'd mishandled it made his mouth dry and he licked his lips and swallowed. The centre table now had a bowl of red tulips on it, the tulips opened out and drooping gracefully. One petal lay on the table and Gilbert picked it up carefully and balanced it back on the nearest bloom so that the arrangement looked perfect again. He glanced quickly in at the sitting room and ran his hand along the spines of the books on one of the shelves, their dust-jackets bright and glossy, and the fronts neatly lined up along the shelf edge. He took out 'A History of Meissen' which had a pink jacket illustrated with a classic Meissen design tureen, and opened the first page. There, in black ink, on the flyleaf, was Barbara's signature. 'Barbara Blaize', the letters rounded and flowing, the 'l' looped, the capital 'Bs' with little curlicues, and the tail of the 'z' dropping below the line. A modest writing style, a signature designed for clarity. Gilbert closed the book and replaced it on the shelf, lining it up meticulously with the others in the row. He glanced at his watch. Not much time.

He went back into the hall and up the stairs. On the landing were four panelled doors, all of them closed. He tried them one at a time, heart pounding, convinced that he might have made some terrible mistake and that Andrew, or even Barbara, would be inside. The first led to a guest room wallpapered in a flower-sprig pattern that Gilbert recognised as being Laura Ashley. There was a pink washbasin in the corner and twin divan beds with what seemed an overabundance of cushions. The room was impersonal: he could not feel Barbara there. He closed the door and passed on.

Next was a small room that Barbara clearly used as her antiques workroom. Cardboard boxes were stacked everywhere, full of china wrapped in crumpled newspaper. On a table lay a fairing, a cute depiction of three little piglets in a green basket. One of the heads of the piglets had been broken and, judging by the various pastes and brushes alongside, Barbara was attempting an 'invisible' repair. On the wall above the table was a cork noticeboard with a calendar, a typed schedule of fairs with many handwritten amendments, and a number of business cards from antiques dealers, none of whom Gilbert recognised. Three polaroid photographs occupied the centre of the noticeboard. He leaned closer. The first showed a laughing Barbara unloading a box from the back of Andrew's car. The second was a distant shot of a crowded antiques fair. The third was a close-up of Ian, holding a lollipop and pulling a comic face for the camera. 'Who loves ya, baby?' was written in felt-tip pen on the white border underneath. Gilbert felt sick. He stumbled from the room, back out onto the landing, his jaw rigid. He tried the next door and found the bathroom, where he leant over the sink for a moment until his breathing slowed. He ran the cold tap and held his hands under it, letting the water play on his wrists. He could already feel the onset of a sharp headache just above his eyes. He turned to the towel-rail but all the towels looked pristine and freshly ironed, arranged symmetrically, so instead he pulled out his white handkerchief and dried his hands on that.

He hurried from the room, down the stairs and out through the kitchen, locking the door behind him. As he went through the side-gate, he heard the distinctive sound of crunching gravel. He pressed himself against the side of the house, inching forward until he could see around the corner. It was Barbara walking up the drive, carrying a bulging shopping bag. He cursed himself for not having listened out for the bus.

Barbara took her keys from her handbag and opened the front door. The very second that Gilbert heard it shut behind her, he sprinted from his hiding place across the front garden and out of the gate, running all the way back to his car. Once inside, he spent a good five minutes with his head resting on the steering wheel, his glasses clutched in his hand. He would have stayed there longer, but a mud-caked tractor lumbering slowly along the lane stopped alongside him.

"Are you all right?" asked the driver, leaning out from the tractor-cab. He was young, with a reddened face and wild blond hair.

Gilbert sat up. "Thank you, yes. Thank you," he said, and the tractor moved on.

*

"It's not Ron," said Ian in the taxi on the way into Southampton. "It's not any of the stall-holders. It's not the miserable git next door. It's not that eccentric woman who lives up the lane from me who once called the police because she was convinced I was dealing in stolen furniture. It's not some rival antique fair organiser. I think we know exactly who it is, don't we?"

"You're frightening me now," said Barbara.

*

"Mr Smart?" The lank-haired junior put the phone back on the hook and looked questioningly over at Gilbert who was busy sorting out the paperwork from a suspicious insurance claim about jewellery theft, the owner seemingly having given three different accounts for how it had gone missing. "Mr Harding wants to see you in his office."

"Now?"

"You know Mr Harding. It's usually 'now', isn't it?"

Gilbert sighed, picked up his notebook and pen and went out into the corridor. He suddenly thought that maybe he ought to take his desk diary with him as well, in case Old Harding wanted to discuss any appointments. He doubled back through the glass doors, just in time to hear the junior repeat the word 'now' in an exaggerated whiney imitation of Gilbert, with everyone else hooting with laughter. They went through only a token effort to suppress the laughter once they saw Gilbert re-enter the office, smirking down at their desks, the junior making pig-like grunts and letting her hair fall across her face like curtains.

Old Harding's office stank of cigarette smoke. The window, its white paint yellowed, was tightly shut, and the glass ashtray on the centre of the desk was already piled high with stubs. Harding smoked menthol cigarettes in the vain hope that they smelt fresher. Gilbert recalled the television commercial that said something about 'cool as a mountain stream'. He'd been in the boss's car a few times to go out to appointments. It stank as well. The furniture in the office was old and all came from MFI. His secretary had attempted to get him to replace it with new stuff from Tyrrell & Green, but Harding dismissed it as 'that shop for posh people'. He had a cocktail cabinet in his office, though whether anything as sophisticated as cocktails was ever served from it, Gilbert doubted. It too was made of that shredded-wheat material beloved of MFI, veneered with a photograph of wood. It had a flap that pulled down to reveal the ranks of gin and tonic which Harding seemed to exist on. As Old Harding stubbed out his cigarette, scattering ash across the desk-top, he leant back in his chair, his feet off the ground, his little fat legs dangling. Gilbert remembered something Tony in the office had said about Harding: 'so close to the ground, it's insanitary'.

Gilbert sat on the edge of his chair, notebook and diary poised, his face expectant.

"How are you getting on?" asked Old Harding. "Managing to sort out that Droxford claim?"

"I've just passed it to the investigations team, sir. Looks very like fraud to me."

"Good, good," said Harding, doodling on his pad. "Another one we won't have to pay, with any luck. What about those cases deferred from last year?"

Gilbert briefed Harding, who lit another cigarette before thumping his chair back down onto its four legs. He leant across the desk and smiled in a vacant way, fixing his pale blue eyes on a spot just above Gilbert's head.

Just as Gilbert was wrapping up his report of the deferred cases, Harding interrupted him. "The thing is, Mr Smart, you're hardly ever in the office any more. I'm wondering why. I asked Shelly last Monday to send you in. You were out at the dentist. I asked her on Wednesday and you'd got a day off. On Friday they said you'd gone to Totton to talk over the RD Fittings claim. Now I find you've got another two days' leave booked this week."

Gilbert sat immobile. He could feel sweat beading on the bridge of his nose, where his glasses rested.

Old Harding spun a pen round and round on the desk.

"How can I know what you're doing when you're never here? You're supposed to be an office-wallah. That's why I hired you." Harding was given to these quaint turns of phrase, referring to his sales area as his 'bailliwick'.

"I'm sorry, sir."

"You're horribly predictable, if you don't mind me saying so, Mr Smart. This chopping and changing is not like you at all. You've always been content to sit there at your desk all day poring over all the wretched paperwork, not gadding about the countryside."

Gilbert had a strong mental image of sitting in his car in the layby above Barbara's house, looking down across the hedgerow and being distracted by the sound of a skylark high above. He had swivelled the binoculars upwards but could not locate the small speck that was the bird.

"I was just trying to be a bit more pro-active." The word sounded strange on Gilbert's lips: it was an American phrase he'd heard a number of people in sales using recently.

"Pro-active? Yes, very commendable." The silence lengthened. Old Harding toyed with the ballpoint pen again.

"And I did fill in the holiday leave forms. It's just that we, that is my wife and I, we don't go away on a proper holiday much any more, just on outings really, or long weekends, so I'm trying to take a couple of days at a time, to suit her, you know. And I'm doing some postcard collecting and it's nice to have time to go around the antique dealers on a weekday when it's a bit quieter." He was aware he was babbling.

"Myra, isn't it?'"

Gilbert nodded.

"Well we don't want to upset Myra, do we?" Old Harding put on his vacant smile again.

*

"No Dylan today?" asked Barbara as she set out her equipment on one of the long wooden tables in the studio.

"I don't think we'll be seeing Dylan for a while." Cass turned so that her back was to the other students and lowered her voice. "I'm afraid he's been arrested."

"Good grief – what on earth had he done?"

"He was caught impersonating a doctor at the General. Which would have been bad enough, but apparently he'd been getting away with it for weeks before anyone even noticed. Doing ward rounds, being charming to the old ladies and so on. He even fooled the nurses, a couple of whom protested to the police when they took him away."

"I saw him there, in a white coat, striding along the corridor when I went to visit my sister. It never occurred to me that it wasn't all entirely above board. I wish I'd mentioned it to you at the time. I just thought that's where he worked. Why on earth would he want to impersonate a doctor, anyway?"

"Dylan likes to be at the centre of things. I think the problem is that he doesn't actually need to work – his father is very well off and Dylan gets an allowance. He doesn't know that I know this and in fact he's told me on a number of occasions that he was orphaned when still a child. I manage each time to put on a suitably mournful face. It's not his first arrest, incidentally – last time they nabbed him he was done up in a clerical collar and had just conducted some old boy's funeral."

Barbara burst out laughing. "You've got to hand it to him for bare-faced cheek."

"It's a shame, really," said Cass, "because he has the potential to be a first-rate artist if he set his mind to it. Poor Little Rich Boy syndrome, I call it. Now – how's your piece coming along?"

*

As he went upstairs to hang up his jacket, Gilbert reached into the pocket of his suit jacket for the gold tiepin. It wasn't there. He tried the other pocket. Perhaps he had put it back in his cufflink box, though that was unlikely because he had always been careful to remove the tiepin before he got home, as such an unusual item would be bound to arouse Myra's suspicions. It was hardly the kind of thing he would have bought himself. He shuffled through his cufflinks, though it was obvious at a glance that it wasn't there. Tutting with annoyance, he went out to the car and checked the seat-wells and the glovebox. He must have dropped it – at the office, maybe. Then a horrible thought struck him. What if he'd dropped it in Barbara's house when he broke in? He started to sweat with anxiety, trying to recall exactly what route he'd taken through the house and whether he was sure he was still wearing the tiepin when he left. He contemplated, then immediately dismissed, the idea of returning to try and find it. Too risky. But what if Barbara asked him why he wasn't wearing the tiepin when she next saw him? Worse still, what if he had indeed dropped the tiepin at her house and she had found it? There were, of course, areas of the house where he might quite legitimately have dropped it when he had gone round for coffee – on the drive, in the hall or the sitting room, but what if it was on the stairs, the landing, the bathroom or Barbara's workroom? Then she'd know. Or what if that awful cleaner, Mrs H or Mrs M or something, had found it – she might show it to Andrew.

He got in the car, drove rather too fast to Bitterne Park where, on Cobden Bridge, he flung Barbara's house-keys over the parapet and into the Itchen. A woman on the deck of a houseboat below the bridge looked up at him curiously, but the deed was done. He immediately felt calmer.

*

Myra had just put the roast into the oven when the doorbell rang. Gilbert must have forgotten his key. But the shape just visible through the obscure glass of the front door was much taller than Gilbert. She hoped it wouldn't be a door-to-door salesman, or the Jehovah's Witnesses again, though they tended to go round in pairs. She pulled off her apron and swung the door open, ready with her 'repel all boarders' face. Standing on the step, very close to the door, was a lean, dark-haired man whose good looks quickly dissolved any animosity on Myra's part. He was wearing denim jeans and a dark blue polo shirt with 'Blaize' embroidered on the pocket and was jangling a bunch of keys that he held loosely in his right hand. Beyond him, parked at a funny angle to the kerb, was what Myra supposed was his car, the kind of low-slung sporty model she'd always imagined herself being a passenger in. Definitely not a salesman, then.

"Have I got the right address for Gil Smart?" he asked.

Without waiting for an answer, he put one foot inside the front door, on the mat. He wasn't smiling and there was an urgency about his manner that was making her nervous. She moved to block him from entering the hall.

"Gil? Oh, you mean Gilbert? He's never called 'Gil'. That's my husband. He's not here at the moment – he's gone to the newsagents to get the papers."

Beyond the man, Myra could see Gilbert rounding the corner of Forest Close, a copy of the *Sunday Express* tucked under his arm. As he came within sight of the sports car, he stopped and stared, then turned on his heel and walked back off again at high speed.

"Do you want to wait or can I give him a message?" asked Myra, hoping that the man would not turn around and see Gilbert hurrying away, though she was consumed by curiosity as to what business he had with Gilbert. A debt collector maybe? Myra had only a hazy idea of the state of their finances. Could Gilbert have got behind on the mortgage payments? But surely they wouldn't send someone round on a Sunday. Something to do with work, then?

"You certainly can give him a message. It's a simple one – I'm sure you'll remember it OK. Just tell him not to come near me or Babs again, to leave us alone. If he tries to sabotage our business again, he'll be sorry because I will be back with a very different kind of message, the sort that leaves a permanent mark. Have you got that?" He was leaning into her face, little drops of spittle landing on his moustache as he spoke.

"You must have got him mixed up with someone else," said Myra, backing away a little.

"There's no mix-up. I wish to God I'd never laid eyes on the man. Be sure and give him the message."

He turned and strode off down the path, leaving Myra, somewhat stunned, still standing in the open doorway. At the car, he banged his palm down hard on the roof, swore loudly and then walked back up the path. Myra managed to jiggle the security chain onto its catch, her fingers sweating. He put his face to the gap between the door and the frame.

"I'm sorry – it's quite wrong of me to shout at you," he said in rather calmer tones. "It's Gil who's the problem here. It's just that I'm so angry with him: that tyre-slashing and the scene he made at Bab's place – it was just the last straw. I can't take any more of his nonsense."

Myra said nothing in reply.

*

Barbara slid into the driver's seat and put her hands on the wheel, at '10 to 2', as Harry instructed. The driving position was high and the interior of the car bore no resemblance to Andrew's Audi: the 2CV looked as if it would not be complete without a crate of live chickens in the back or maybe a bale of hay. The front seat was a 'bench' seat and Harry slid over to sit close to her.

"Where's the gear-stick?" she asked.

"It's that thing protruding from the dashboard that looks like an umbrella handle, the thing you've just hung your handbag on, Barbara," said Harry. She laughed. "You have to remember that this is an anti-car," he said, "a car for people who don't really like cars and are a bit embarrassed at having one."

"I've seen the advertisements – 'a camel designed by a committee'."

Harry flapped up the side-window. "But it's very practical as well as being eccentric," he said. "And if I need to transport large paintings, I can simply roll back the roof and stick them in through the top. Of course, it's a French car, so I should really be instructing you in French, otherwise the car might not understand. So – *allons-y*!"

And so began Barbara's first driving lesson, round and round the deserted car-park of the Carrefour hypermarket at Chandler's Ford.

"Why did you never learn to drive when you were first old enough to get a provisional licence? I couldn't wait to get a bit of independence: when I was seventeen I bought some clapped-out Beetle where you could actually see the road through the floor of the car as you were driving. And it had a six-volt battery, so the headlights were like little candles barely illuminating a few feet of road in front of you. You had to lean forward and peer over the steering wheel into the stygian gloom. But I loved it."

"I'm not really sure why I never learnt," said Barbara. "I suppose I always had boyfriends to drive me around, so I got lazy."

"And then a husband," said Harry. "What does he make of this sudden wish to learn to drive?"

"He can't understand it. He thinks I'm turning into a feminist. I suggested that it would take some pressure off him if I could drive myself around, but he harrumphed, so I've not mentioned it again."

"Deception is the better part of valour," said Harry. "Now – let's see if you can get as far as third gear."

*

'Liquid Leaf' the product was called, though it might have been called 'liquid gold' considering the price they were asking for it at the art shop in Romsey. Barbara unscrewed the top carefully, revealing a tiny brush fixed to the lid. The 'antique gold' shade looked about right, though much of it was in the form of sludge at the bottom of the jar. Screwing back the lid, she picked up the post from the hall table and carried everything to her workroom which, she noted with pleasure, was neat and tidy following the ministrations of Mrs H. She took the picture frame down from the hook where she had hung it to dry, having carefully moulded and glued little balls of plasticine to replace the missing bits of moulding. She ran her finger over them – a little uneven, but they should do the trick. She shook the bottle of Liquid Leaf and began to careful paint each one, humming the chorus of Neil Diamond's 'Sweet Caroline' under her breath, a song she had had on her mind for days now. As she moved the brush over the last piece of moulding, it fell off, rolling across the workbench and straight off the end, trailing a smear of gold as it went. 'Wretched thing,' she muttered, stooping down under the noticeboard to pick it up, where it had acquired a layer of fluff sticking to the paint. Clearly a spot that Mrs H had overlooked, though Barbara doubted that this was something she could mention, being slightly afraid of Mrs H. As she reached for the piece of plasticine, she noticed something else gleaming, wedged between the wooden floorboard and the bottom of the skirting. Perhaps a brass picture-hook? She slid it out, holding it between finger and thumb and stared at it uncomprehendingly. A tieclip in the shape of a tiny pair of gold spectacles – exactly like the one she had bought Gil. Before she was conscious of the implication of what she was seeing, her hand, her arm and then her whole body turned completely cold and she swayed slightly, almost as if an abyss had opened at her feet and she was trying to balance on the edge.

*

"Gilbert Smart, please," said Myra, twirling the cream-coloured phone lead idly around her finger.

"I'm sorry, but he's not in today," said a bored voice.

"Oh – out on a job, is he?"

"No – a day's leave. Who's calling? Can anyone else help?"

"No thank you," said Myra and quickly put the phone down in case they might recognise her voice. She imagined them giggling and gossiping in the office – 'just think – his wife not knowing he had a day's holiday'. The humiliation of it.

She thought back to that morning at breakfast: Gilbert had put on his suit and tie and gone off at the same time as he did every morning. He'd even taken his briefcase. He'd not said a word about having a day off, she was sure, even though she'd got used to tuning-out much of what he said, especially when he was droning on about antiques or the claims he was working on. So – he'd clearly set out to deceive her. She went through to the sitting room, opened the bureau and retrieved the envelope she'd found – the one with the torn-up note inside it. It must be a woman. This Babs or Barbara woman. There was no other explanation. She gave a bark of laughter, amazed at the thought of Gilbert having a 'fancy woman' – or that some woman might actually find Gilbert attractive.

She made a cup of tea then settled down to wait for him. She was sure he'd return at precisely his usual time.

*

Barbara put Gil's tiepin in the lower compartment of her jewelry box, next to a gold brooch in the shape of a lizard which Fiona had given her the previous Christmas. Andrew would never see it there. She never once thought of telling Andrew that she'd found it upstairs in the house, though she was unsure why she felt unable to tell him. On several occasions she had sat down, determined to work out in her mind what had happened and what she should do about it, but she found that her mind was completely paralysed. She simply went over and over the same anxieties. She remembered the vicar, in one of his sermons, describing worrying as being like sitting in a rocking chair – you go back and forth, but you never get anywhere. That's exactly what it felt like. She forced herself to be logical. On neither of Gil's visits to the house had he been upstairs – he'd had coffee in the sitting room and he'd gone with Andrew out to the workshop. Before he left, he had asked to use the cloakroom, but that was the downstairs cloaks. He'd had no opportunity to sneak upstairs. She went through other wild imaginings, such as the tiepin having got caught up on something and her inadvertently having carried it upstairs, but even as she thought it, she knew it was nonsense.

Perhaps she should just ask him straight out the next time they met, if he'd lost the tiepin? No, that was impossible. The man was so devoted to her he clearly wore the wretched thing every day – he must be aware he had lost it. He would either be too embarrassed to mention it, because it had been a valued present, or he would know very well where he lost it, but couldn't say without giving himself away.

Barbara still couldn't bring herself to think that all this meant that Gil had been in the house when she had been out. There were only two possible explanations: either Andrew had let him in, or he had broken in. But if Andrew had seen him, why wouldn't he have mentioned it? No, he must have broken in. Then Barbara remembered with ghastly clarity the argument she had had with Mrs H about the missing keys.

*

When Barbara got back to the house after the coffee morning at church, she went straight through to the kitchen, calling out a 'good morning' to Mrs H over the whine of the vacuum cleaner on the stairs. She plonked the plate of left-over cakes down on the kitchen table and tried to shake off the feeling of irritation at a wasted morning. They were such a dreary lot – Barbara must have been the youngest there by about 30 years – and always moaning that no-one every volunteered to do anything, though of course if someone new was to volunteer they would then be outraged at their own fiefdom being taken away from them. You couldn't win. A cough from behind her made her wheel round. Sitting in the corner of the kitchen, by the Aga, was a young mousy-haired man with a spotty face. He was in stockinged feet and had placed his large and rather smelly trainers in front of the Aga. He looked to be about 16 years old.

"Who on earth are you?" asked Barbara, knowing, as soon as the words were out of her mouth, exactly who he must be.

"I'm Bernie, ain't I? Came with mum while she does her cleaning. She said you wouldn't mind." He plucked absently at the gold stud in his ear, his head on one side. He didn't meet Barbara's eye.

"Did she, indeed? Have you finished that bottle of Coke?"

"Yeah. Ta," he said, handing it to her and burping slightly. The bottle was warm and sticky.

"I'll be right back," said Barbara.

She went out into the hall and shut the door behind her. Her heart was banging in her ribcage. She forced herself to breath deeply and slowly. Maybe she should just forget it – after all, what harm was Bernie doing, really? It wasn't as if Mrs H brought him along every day, so surely one day could be overlooked? Then she thought of all the times she had chosen to ignore Mrs H's little transgressions, her rudeness, her general condescending air, as if she was doing a favour cleaning for Barbara, rather than a paid job. Barbara had been creeping around Mrs H for two years now, cleaning up before she arrived in case Mrs H sniffed in that critical way that indicated she thought Barbara's housekeeping skills were less than adequate. And then there was the incident with the missing keys. Barbara strove to remember whether, out of Mrs H's large brood, it was Bernie who was the petty criminal: if so, perhaps this wasn't the first time that Mrs H had brought him along with her. It was ridiculous – a grown woman frightened of her own cleaner. She walked to the foot of the stairs and called up.

"Mrs H?" She was annoyed to find her voice quavering a little.

Mrs H's sharp features appeared over the top of the banisters on the landing. "Yes?"

"Could you turn off the vacuum cleaner for a moment?"

The noise subsided. Barbara walked up the stairs, unwilling to risk Bernie overhearing their conversation. Mrs H was standing, arms akimbo, in front of the bedroom door.

"I was rather surprised to find Bernie in the kitchen. I don't recall you mentioning that you were bringing him with you today."

"I didn't know I was bringing him, Mrs Blaize, until this morning. He was moping about the house something chronic, picking on the little ones when I was trying to get them ready for school, so I thought it best to keep him under my wing, stop him getting into trouble."

"I'd really rather you had asked me first. Has he been with you here before?"

"I don't know. Perhaps once or twice. Not regular."

"When I wasn't in the house?"

"If you've not seen him before, then it must have been when you wasn't here." Mrs H bent down and picked up the hose of the vacuum cleaner, clearly feeling that the conversation was over.

"Only, you'll recall we had a pair of keys go missing."

"I told you at the time – I don't know what happened to your keys and now you're trying to put the blame for it on me again, or on Bernie," she said, brandishing the hose at Barbara in a rather alarming manner. "Bernie might be a bit rough-and-ready but he wouldn't thieve nothing."

"No, of course not," Barbara protested, rather unconvincingly. A little voice inside her head told her she was deceiving Mrs H because she was well aware that neither Bernie nor Mrs H had taken the keys, but she silenced it.

"Because if I'm not trusted here," said Mrs H, "then I don't think I want to work for you no more."

This was Barbara's cue to reassure her that she was indeed trusted and that Barbara would be lost without her, a reassurance she had been pressed into giving several times in the past. But something shifted in Barbara's brain and almost before she'd even thought about it, she heard herself saying: "Very well then. I can pay you a fortnight's money in lieu of notice, of course. I don't want you to be out of pocket. We can settle up when you finish this morning."

Mrs H said nothing, staring at Barbara in disbelief. She struck the 'on' switch of the vacuum cleaner with her foot and, as it roared into life, the end of the hose she'd be holding grabbed at her skirt and sucked at the material. In the confusion, as Mrs H sought to disentangle the skirt, Barbara escaped down the stairs.

*

Barbara was trembling with rage. She'd never been that confrontational before and although it had been upsetting, she had also been conscious of the rush of adrenalin it had brought with it. Fresh from sacking Mrs H and without thinking clearly about the wisdom of what she was doing, she strode into the hall, dialled Gil's office number and was put through almost immediately.

Gilbert said: "Claims department."

"It's me – Barbara."

"Oh. Hello." Smug or guarded?

"Will you ring me back," she said calmly, "from a call box?"

She was not risking evasive answers just because others were listening in. He sounded surprised yet apprehensive. "Yes, of course. Would lunchtime do?"

Barbara glanced at the clock. "It's twelve now – what time will you call?"

"About twelve-thirty if that suits you," he said.

"All right. Goodbye."

Barbara slammed down the phone. It was unfortunate, she thought, that she wasn't able to demand an explanation from him immediately. There was no way she wanted to cool down or count to ten.

At 12.30, he phoned. Barbara heard the coins drop and the pips.

Gilbert said: "hello – this is rather a surprise."

"It won't be a pleasant one," Barbara answered, "when I've said what I have to."

"Oh?"

"I told you before and I will tell you again: I don't ever want to see or hear from you again, you odious little snoop."

He sounded affronted. "What do you mean, snoop?"

"You know perfectly well what I mean."

She resisted filling the silence, but tears stung the back of her eyes and she was worried that her voice would shake.

There was a muffled sound on the line. He's crying, thought Barbara. Let him. Let him cry.

Silence.

"Are you still there?

"Yes," he said at last. "I'm still here."

"Why are you stalking me? Why are you watching my house? What exactly are you hoping to achieve?" Be relentless. Keep asking. Make him answer. Don't let him get away with it.

"It was not for me," he said. "I can't say anything else without implicating another person. I won't do that. You must believe me."

Barbara thought he was trying to get out of it. "I'm sorry, I don't believe you."

"I must see you," he said, "to explain."

"I don't need explanations and I don't ever want to see you. Just leave me alone."

"Please, Barbara, can I come and see you? Now?" He was choked again. Barbara thought that maybe seeing him just once would be better, would close it off. Face to face, he would have to tell her the truth.

"All right, if you must."

Gilbert said he'd be on his way. Before he came, Barbara had a glass of brandy and sat quietly in the chair trying to calm her nerves.

When he arrived, she felt more in control of her emotions. They stood facing each other across the sitting room. She did not ask him to sit down. Gilbert hung his head. She saw, with a certain feeling of triumph, that he was not wearing a tie-pin and she wondered just how much he had tortured himself about where he might have lost the one she had given him.

"It was you, wasn't it? It's been you all along. I don't know why it took me so long to realise."

"What was?"

"Slashing Ian's tyres. Sabotaging our fair. Spreading lies about me. Watching my house through binoculars."

"None of that's true." He rubbed one toe of his shoe back and forth on the carpet, looking down at it intensely.

"So let me ask you something. Why aren't you wearing the gold tie-pin which I gave you? I thought you always wore it."

"I do. It's just that I forgot to put it on today. I'm sorry." He did not meet her eye.

"No you didn't forget. You're lying. You lost it, didn't you? Would you like me tell you exactly where you lost it?"

She took it out of her pocket and brandished it at him. "Shall I give it back to you, or shall I just hand it over to the police?"

He went white. He reached out one hand towards the bookcase as if to steady himself.

"There's a perfectly good explanation ... I must have dropped it when I was here."

"Upstairs? In my workroom? And when precisely was it that you went upstairs? Because I don't recall it. Or perhaps I wasn't here when you went upstairs."

He didn't answer.

"You're shielding someone, aren't you?" she asked coldly.

"Shielding?"

"You said as much on the phone," she said.

"May I sit down?" His face, always pallid, was grey and troubled. He sat on the edge of Andrew's relaxer chair, looking incongruous in his tension.

"What are you trying to do?"

"I can't explain without saying too much." He looked miserable.

"You insisted on coming here to explain."

"I was doing it for someone else."

"I see." Barbara didn't see at all, but it seemed the only thing to say. Suddenly, a terrible thought struck her. "Gil – was it Andrew?"

*

There was something strange about the sitting room when Gilbert walked in. At first, he thought Myra was doing a jigsaw, then he saw that what was spread over the coffee table in front of her were little pieces of white paper, all carefully arranged to form an oblong shape. She looked up, a strange smile on her face.

"Hello, Gilbert – good day at the office?"

He had just opened his mouth to give the usual non-commital reply when he recognised his own handwriting on the pieces of paper. Horrified, he realised what it was that Myra was assembling on the table.

"Who is Barbara, exactly?" asked Myra.

Gilbert didn't answer, still trying to work out how Myra could possibly have got hold of his letter to Barbara, the letter he never sent. Surely, he had thrown it away? Then with awful clarity he remembered putting the pieces into an old envelope and hiding them in the pocket of one of his jackets, intending to throw the envelope into a litter-bin on the street on the way back from Wendell Court.

"You've been through my wardrobe," he said, unconsciously reaching out to straighten one of the corner-pieces. His fingers felt icy.

"Let me read you some of the choicest bits," said Myra in a gloating voice. "Of course, there's some words I can't quite decipher because of how it's been torn up. But I get the general gist. 'The most beautiful woman I have ever met' ... 'I could not believe you would be interested in me' ... 'I only wanted to protect you' ..."

Gilbert took off his glasses, polished them on his handkerchief, and put them back on. Still, he said nothing. Myra stood up, took a huge breath and then blew the pieces of paper off the surface of the table, scattering them across the carpet like wedding confetti.

"You'll be in the spare room tonight," she said. "I'm going round to Sandra's now for a little girl-talk."

The next day, when Gilbert arrived home from work, he found all his clothes, along with a number of cardboard boxes full of his books, neatly stacked in the drive. All the curtains of the house were drawn. Somehow, it was the neatness that really unnerved him: this wasn't the reaction of an angry woman – she hadn't strewn everything over the front lawn. This was calculated, planned, a strategy in a war-game. He had no way of dealing with it. Unable to put his car on the drive because it was full of his things, he carefully executed a three-point turn in the road. As he looked over his shoulder to reverse, he saw the neighbours' net curtains move: that stupid, smug couple, no doubt having a laugh at his expense. He got out of the car, leaving the door swinging open and the engine running. He took nothing from the drive, but walked over to the neighbours' Ford Granada, pulled off the coat-hanger aerial and threw it down into the gutter. He got back in his car and sat immobile, staring into the distance.

*

The road back into Southampton was quiet, with all the commuters heading the other way. Gilbert pulled up by East Park and got out to check the parking meter – no charges after 6pm. He checked his watch: 6.10, and headed across the park towards the office, glancing up at the first floor windows. A figure wearing a blue tabard was moving back and forth across the window wielding a feather duster.

He positioned himself out of sight of the windows, but just two paces from the front door and, leaning against the brick wall of the building, settled down to wait.

At 6.30 the cleaner, a young blonde woman, emerged from the door, carrying a big refuse sack, and turned away from Gilbert to the side alley where the dustbins were kept. As she came back around the corner, Gilbert made his move, striding purposefully towards the door.

"Oh, Mr Smart," she said. "Back for a bit over overtime? I was just about to lock up."

"No – I forgot my briefcase," he said. "Don't worry – I'll lock up when I go."

"Right you are then. Don't stay too long. You know what they say, don't you?"

Gilbert looked blankly at her.

"All work and no play makes Jack a dull boy," she said in a sing-song tone.

"Quite," he said. What on earth was the woman on about? He stuck his foot in the door, raised one hand, in a stiff gesture of farewell and watched her hurrying towards the bus stop, shrugging off her tabard as she talked. How could she possibly do the cleaning in those high heels, he thought. Gilbert clicked the latch shut on the front door and headed upstairs. It was the first time he'd been in the offices on his own – it all looked tattier, somehow, papers strewn everywhere and the whole place stinking of a mixture of Old Harding's stale cigarette smoke and some chemical spray that the cleaner had used to attempt to disguise it.

He sat down at his own desk out of habit. He knew he should think about Myra, and about the confrontation with Barbara, but his mind was too restless.

He got up again and prowled around, careful to keep away from the windows. Perhaps he could make a cup of tea. He went into the tiny kitchen and looked at all the mismatched mugs linked up on the draining board. 'Boss' said Old Harding's in large black type. Miss Green's had some pop group pictured on the side, and the others were an assortment of chipped oversized mugs with everything from Mickey Mouse to slogans like 'underwriters do it with care'. Gilbert's mug was plain blue.

He picked up the Boss mug, sniffed it, and put it down again. The cleaner obviously used bleach to clean the mugs. Maybe a cup of tea was not such a good idea. He should have brought in his flask.

He left the kitchen and wandered into Old Harding's lair, shuffling idly through the papers in his in-tray but finding nothing of interest. He drew down the flap of the bureau and looked at the array of bottles inside – mainly Scotch and gin. The metal filing cabinet was locked. He tried out Old Harding's chair, a huge black leather thing that tilted back at an alarming angle when you pressed a lever. Just as he'd tilted it back to its reclining position, he heard a chilling sound – the unmistakable click of the Yale lock on the front door being opened.

He sprang from the chair and from downstairs came Old Harding's voice: "The Chubb lock wasn't on – that stupid women must have forgotten it. Good job we came back."

"But that's not what we came back for, though – was it?" said a female voice in a teasing tone. She then squealed in mock-horror. "Wait until we get upstairs, you naughty man."

Though Gilbert had never heard the junior, Miss Green, be anything but sullen, he recognised the voice immediately. There was no time to be astonished.

He tiptoed onto the landing, desperately trying to think of a place to hide. The kitchen? The toilet? No, they might come out there. He crept into the main office and ducked behind his desk. There was just room to squeeze underneath, between the pedestals. He edged the grey metal wastepaper bin out of the way with one hand, being careful not to knock it against anything, and then scrunched his body into the gap. A 'modesty board' obscured most of this view – and hopefully hid him effectively. He was sweating and his glasses kept sliding down his nose. He looked through the narrow gap – two pairs of feet walked across the landing towards Old Harding's office. As they walked, there was a loud slapping noise and Miss Green squealed delightedly again. It was only when they shut the door behind them that Gilbert realised he had been holding his breath all that time.

What do do next? Try and make his escape? What if they heard him? Wait it out? He then realised his wasn't an option because when they left, they would double-lock the front door behind them and Gilbert – who was far too lowly an employee to be granted a set of keys – would be locked in until morning. He'd had the vague idea that he'd sleep on the office floor, then wake up early and go and find somewhere to have a shave, returning at 9am as if he'd just come from home. The rumbling of his stomach reminded him of another snag – he should have bought something to eat before he came back to the office. He'd be starving by morning.

No, the only thing to do would be to make his escape, go for something to eat and then sleep in the car. He strained to hear what was happening in the other room. There was the clinking of glasses and the clunk of the bureau's flap. Suddenly the door opened and Old Harding emerged. Gilbert tried to squeeze himself into a smaller immobile ball. Harding's stockinged feet crossed to the kitchen and Gilbert heard the squeak of the fridge door. When he'd been a small child, they had had a guinea pig who had learnt that the squeak of the fridge door meant food, and at every squeak had hurled himself against the bars of his cage. There was the sound of ice rattling onto a bowl and Harding crossed the room again.

After ten minutes, the noises from the office changed. If there was going to be a right moment to escape, then Gilbert knew it would be very soon. He uncurled from the under the desk and crept across to the landing, ready to dart behind the door if he needed to. But Old Harding and Miss Green were oblivious – he felt he could have danced the hornpipe on the landing and they still would not have noticed. The door was open just a crack, but Gilbert resisted the temptation to look: it was quite gruesome enough in his imagination, without seeing it.

Carrying his shoes in his hand, he tiptoed downstairs, released the door and then – in a fit of bravado – slammed it behind him. He smiled to think of the fright this would give them as he turned round the corner of the building and out of sight.

The brief moment of satisfaction evaporated when he realised that he'd not even begin to think about the Myra situation – or even about Barbara – and that he had nowhere to go but home.

*

It was getting dark when Myra came home the following afternoon, walking up the hill from the bus-stop and turning into Forest Close, swinging her Marks and Spencer's carrier bag. She always wondered what flight of fancy had led the developers to name the road Forest Close – there was barely a tree in sight and even the grass verges had a dispirited air. She saw the Austin parked on the other side of the road and straight away saw Gilbert scrunched down in the driver's seat. The boxes were still exactly where she had left them.

She pretended not to notice Gilbert and went straight up the crazy-paving path to the front door and let herself in. She turned on the light in the hall and walked into the lounge, unbuttoning her coat as she moved over to the window to shut the curtains. She expected to hear Gilbert follow her in almost immediately. Or perhaps he wouldn't let himself in with his key – if he was going to do that, he'd have been sitting her already when she arrived. No, he'd probably ring the bell. A penitent.

After ten minutes, there was still no sign of him, so Myra went upstairs to their bedroom and, without switching on the light, peered carefully round the curtains so she could see the street. He was still there. Itching for a confrontation, rather than this standoff, Myra went back downstairs and out of the front door, walking briskly over to the car. She tapped on the window and Gilbert, startled, wound it down.

"Are you coming in, or what?" Gilbert looked tired and unshaven.

"I thought you didn't want me to come in. You've thrown all my stuff out."

"What I want is a proper explanation."

"Well I'm not sure I can give you one."

"That's that, then," said Myra, heading back across the road.

"No wait," said Gilbert, climbing out of the car. "It's not what you think. Please listen."

"Not here," said Myra, catching a glimpse of the neighbour's curtains parting slightly to reveal Anne's animated face pressed to the glass. "Inside."

Suddenly she was tired of the whole thing. "Look – help me with these boxes. If we leave them here another night, those little herberts from the estate will strew them everywhere. Where have you been, anyway? With Barbara?"

Gilbert sighed. "I slept at the office," he said.

They worked in silence, ferrying the boxes from the driveway up to the boxroom.

"Thank you, Myra," said Gilbert, awkwardly.

"For what, exactly?"

"For taking me back."

"After what you've done, I must be a saint to take you back."

"I've not done anything. It's all been a misunderstanding."

"So you say. There is one thing, though."

"What?"

"I tore up your postcards. You know, your antique ones. Well, I was angry."

"Oh." Tears sprung to Gilbert's eyes. "It's OK – they're not important."

"And I'm only taking you back on one condition – that you stay away from this Barbara person. I don't care how 'innocent' it all was – I don't want you going near her or communicating with her in any way. If you do, I'm going straight to the solicitor to ask for a divorce."

"I promise," said Gilbert.

*

"I'm sorry, Mr Smart, but I'm afraid we have to let you go."

"Let me go? What do you mean?" said Gilbert, holding onto the sides of the chair as if he was about to be swept away.

"Your attendance record," said Old Harding, leaning forward over the desk to stub out a cigarette. "I've spoken to you about it before, or rather I've tried to speak to you about it, but you've had one excuse after another and I fear you're just not admitting to yourself that there's a problem. Is it things at home?" he asked gently, knowing what a tartar Myra was. Old Harding rocked back on his chair and as always Gilbert was distracted by the realisation that his boss' feet were dangling in the air.

"No, no – everyone is fine," he said, fiddling with his notebook. "I've been – I've been out of the office a lot, I know, but it's all been quite legitimate."

"I'm sorry, Mr Smart. It's not up for debate. We are aware that you've not always been where you said you'd been. You have been, shall we say, observed."

Gilbert pictured himself looking through the binoculars at Barbara's house, unaware that perhaps someone had been watching him. It was like a hall of mirrors, or perhaps like those Russian dolls that fit one inside the other. He began to feel queasy and reached out to clutch the edge of the desk for support.

"There's no need to work out your notice, old chap. We'll pay you for the coming month. Miss Green will give you a box so you can clear your desk and gather up your personal effects. Best of luck," he said, reaching a hairy hand across the desk for Gilbert to shake.

Stunned, Gilbert walked back into the open office, expecting everyone to stare at him, but they all seemed to suddenly be intensely occupied with paperwork or typing. He sat down at his desk and realised that he had been holding his breath through much of his meeting with Old Harding. He took a few deep breaths and began to feel steadier. As he took his glasses off to clean them, Miss Green slouched over and put an archive box down on top of his blotter without saying anything. Gilbert began to go through his desk drawers, straightening up the memo pads, the box of carbon paper, the pens and bulldog clips. There was nothing to put in his box, not a single personal item. He left the empty box where she had put it, picked up his briefcase, went over to the coat stand to collect his mac and headed for the double doors, past desks crowded with framed photographs, hideous plastic trolls with purple hair, signs saying 'you don't have to be mad to work here, but it helps' and personalised coffee mugs.

No-one looked up. No-one spoke.

When he got to the car park, he realised that if he went home now, Myra would ask why he was so early, and then for the rest of the day, he would have to explain over and over, inventing some lie about why he'd been fired. He couldn't face it. It would be much better to go home at the usual time and tell Myra when he was good and ready – after dinner, perhaps.

He took his sandwich-box out of his briefcase, dumped the sandwiches in the nearest litter bin and headed along Above Bar towards the Bargate. He could while away an hour or more in the café at Owen Owen. The headache which had begun when Old Harding told him he was being fired started to recede and Gil felt he'd soon be able to think about what had just happened. But not yet. Not yet.

Gilbert didn't tell Myra that night that he'd lost his job. He just couldn't find the right moment, the right words. So the next morning, he got up as usual, took the sandwiches that Myra had made for him, put them in his briefcase, kissed her goodbye and drove off in the car. When he got to the end of the road, he wasn't sure where to go, so he idled the engine for a minute or two while he decided. There was a honking behind him and he looked in the mirror to see his neighbours' Ford Granada. He waved vaguely and moved off. He could always go to Barbara's, he thought. He may not have paid employment any more, but he had an important purpose to fulfil, one which would certainly benefit from his having more time to devote to it. Perhaps he might bring things to a head soon, he thought, though what this 'head' might consist of, he had not really articulated in his mind.

*

Gilbert's days began to fall into a predictable pattern. He would leave the house every weekday at 8.20am, clutching his briefcase and his Tupperware sandwich box. He drove to a car park just outside the town centre which offered a cheaper all-day rate, then walked down Bedford Place towards the Guildhall. The library didn't open until 9.30am, so for about half an hour he sat on one of the benches in the rose garden at the front of the Guildhall, watching the fountain. The Guildhall clock chime played the tune of 'O God Our Help in Ages Past'. Gilbert felt he could have done with a little help in the present. Once the library doors opened, he walked in and straight up the stairs to the reference library, his stride deliberately purposeful. There were ranks of large wooden tables and the atmosphere was quiet and restful. Gilbert took the *Daily Express* out of the rack and sat down to read. The only other occupant of this section of the library was an elderly Chinaman who read the *South China Morning Post* in minute detail every day, making notes in neat Chinese characters on a small notepad.

It didn't take long for Gilbert to read the paper from cover to cover. He occasionally looked at the *Daily Telegraph* too, just to break the monotony of the morning, but it didn't capture his attention. He found his mind wandering: he fretted about not having told Myra yet that he'd lost his job, but there never seemed to be quite the right time. On several occasions he had opened his mouth to say something, but she'd asked him to take the bin out or lay the table and the moment had passed. He knew he couldn't leave it much longer. There was enough money for next month's mortgage payment, because he had received four weeks' pay in lieu of notice, but after that, they would be in real trouble. If he could get another job, of course, he need never tell her he'd been fired – but with unemployment figures topping two million, it seemed unlikely.

At lunchtimes, he ate his sandwiches in the park if it was fine, or in a café if it was cold or raining: he'd buy a cup of tea and surreptitiously remove his sandwiches from their container, holding it under the table so the owner wouldn't notice.

The afternoons were the hardest to fill. He bought the *Southern Evening Echo* as soon as it came out, from the paper's own offices in Above Bar, and combed the Situations Vacant columns, circling any possible ones. Then he'd head for a phone box and start calling. Almost everyone asked whether he had references, and when they heard he hadn't, they'd tell him they couldn't offer him an interview.

After a few days of this, he could feel the anger surging inside him. It was all the fault of Ian Avery – the whole situation. If Avery would only leave Barbara alone, there would be no need for Gilbert to have gone through all this. What's more, having to look for a job was distracting him from protecting Barbara. He hoped that Andrew would appreciate the lengths he'd gone to. Perhaps he could ask Andrew for a job, or a letter of introduction to a potential employer? As an architect, Andrew would surely have plenty of influential contacts. But perhaps it was best to finish his task once and for all – then Andrew would certainly be in his debt.

He was jolted out of his reverie by a large, fat woman plonking herself down on the bench next to him. Gilbert was annoyed – there were plenty of other benches that were unoccupied, so why invade his personal space?

The woman sighed ostentatiously as she put down three bulging carrier bags. Gilbert inched away towards the other end of the bench and tried to make himself invisible.

"Such a relief to sit down!" declared the woman. Gilbert made a non-committal grunt and glanced briefly at her. She was a blousy woman in her 50s with dyed blonde hair and was wearing a puce-coloured mac which was belted unflatteringly around her waist. Gilbert found himself imagining her going into a dress shop and actually choosing his hideous garment to buy. It seemed so unlikely. He never liked shopping for clothes himself; he tended to leave most of that to Myra. He thought of Barbara and her sense of style and elegance. Maybe he ought to take more interest in what he wore. Coloured shirts with contrasting white collars were all in fashion – maybe he should buy one of those? But then he remembered that he hadn't got any money: certainly not enough for any non-essential purposes.

"Cheer up, love, it may never happen!" said the fat woman.

Inexplicably, Gilbert found tears springing into his eyes. He turned away to hide his face, but she put a hand on his arm and patted it.

"There, there. I'm sorry, love – I didn't mean to upset you. I'll leave you in peace – my bus is due in a minute anyway." She thrust a card into his hands. "I have the gift," she said.

Gilbert looked blankly at her.

"I'm a psychic, dear. If it's someone who has passed to the other side who you're grieving for, I can help."

He clutched the proffered business card, embarrassed.

"No, it's nothing like that."

"Well, perhaps a reading then. I like to put my gifts at the service of others. It's £20 for a tarot reading, or I could do a palm reading now for £15. I don't mind – I can get a later bus."

Gilbert got up off the bench, self-consciously putting his hands in his pockets as if she might be able to read his future if his hands were exposed for just a second longer.

He mumbled something about having to do to a business meeting and hurried off. On the way back to his car, he took out the card and studied it: 'Serenity Peters – Psychic'. He could not imagine anyone less likely to have a name like Serenity. The phone number was a Southampton one. He went to throw the card into a rubbish bin, then changed his mind and put it in his briefcase instead.

Winter

Gilbert decided that a spade would be the best implement. He'd gone to the big hardware shop on Shirley Road, the one where they put most of the goods outside on the pavement – galvanised buckets, brooms, rope and chain sold by the yard, and garden troughs. He'd looked at the hammers for a while and held one in his hand to feel its heft, tapping the end of it lightly against his palm. He put it back on the rack and moved over to the garden tools, turning his face away from the forks when an unbidden image of a body with the tines embedded in their chest came to his mind. Weren't pitchforks what the villagers carried aloft when they were pursuing Boris Karloff in Frankenstein? A mediaeval implement, bloody, horrifying. The row of black metal spades looked more promising. Businesslike. Practical. As Gilbert was eyeing them, a small man in a brown cotton overall approached him and asked if there was anything he could help with.

"Just browsing," said Gilbert and hurried out of the shop.

He realised that where he bought the spade was crucial – it needed to be somewhere big, somewhere anonymous, where he would not draw attention to himself. He'd already eliminated knives as a possible tool – too visceral, too bloody. He started to sweat at the very thought. He could buy a gun, of course, but where on earth from? In the pictures, they made it look so easy – you just hung around on a street corner and the local gangsters showed up almost at once. Money changed hands and suddenly you owned a gun. No, a spade was the right thing, easy to acquire, not attracting suspicion. He decided he would go out to the garden centre in Eastleigh, just far way enough for no-one to recognise him. He'd pay by cash, not cheque. He'd buy a few seed packets at the same time, to make it look like he was just another Sunday gardener. Did gardeners buy seeds in the winter, though? Gilbert knew little about gardening. Their own postage-stamp sized back garden was given over to a patio and a square of lawn which Myra made him mow every week throughout most of the year. There was little in the way of plants or flowers: Myra said they were more trouble than they were worth.

*

When Barbara got to the Gallery at the School of Art, the finishing touches were being put to the displays. She was amazed to see Cass there: the woman was clearly going to work right up to the very day she produced the baby. Barbara's sculpture was on a white plinth, alongside a large installation made out of rusty old bicycle parts, but before she could admire her own work, Cass came over with a pile of printed cards and a roll of double-sided tape.

"Thanks for coming early. Could you be an angel and stick all the cards alongside the relevant pieces? They are all numbered, so don't have to worry about getting them muddled up. I'm just going to make sure the lads setting out the wine are doing it properly. There's a string quartet coming – did you know? I thought it would add a touch of class to the event."

At that moment, a couple of young men in cutaway jackets hurried past carrying instrument cases. Barbara was pleased: even Andrew might enjoy the music, even if he wasn't excited about seeing the sculpture.

"Doesn't quite seem the same without Dylan, does it?" she said to Cass as she stuck the card carefully on the side of the plinth of which was displayed his polychrome head of an African woman. "Will he come back to the class eventually, do you think?"

"I don't know. He might well move on somewhere else, otherwise every time he looks at us, he'll remember that we know he was a fraud. An amiable fraud, though." She stood back and appraised Barbara's Frozen Music sculpture. "You know, your piece turned out very well indeed -you've definitely got an eye for shape and form. Your drawing skills are really coming along, too."

"I don't think Andrew will want me to continue next year, though. He's made such a fuss about me doing this."

"Because it takes up your Saturdays?"

"Yes and no. Because I'm becoming more independent, I think. He's not used to it. He's used to having all my attention."

"Is he coming tonight?"

"Oh yes. I said that as he'd put up with me being preoccupied with this sculpture for weeks and weeks, then the least he could do was see the finished result. What about Ian?"

"Yes, he should be here in a minute."

At this point, Harry burst through the doors, wearing some ancient mis-shapen tweed jacket, a rather grubby silk cravat and a dashing fedora. He embraced Barbara and Cass.

"OK I'm here, so you can open the bar now."

"You're too early," said Cass, laughing. "So you'll just have to preview the show and get into the wine later. Barbara will give you a guided tour."

Harry took Barbara's arm.

"I'll look at the rest of the show after I've had some wine, because I feel I will need it if I am to comment politely on all these exhibits, but first of all, I want to see this Frozen Music piece of yours."

Barbara was embarrassed and as they approached it, she started to make excuses for it.

"My dear girl – never apologise for your work. In fact, defend it with your last breath. Tell me how the idea came to you."

She gave a halting explanation. He squeezed her arm. "So, I can see that the buildings are also notes – they drip and hang and they march across a kind of stave in the form of the telegraph wires. Tell me: why did you choose white?"

"Andrew's model buildings are always white. I thought it might please him if I used the same technique."

"Would you really have preferred to use colour?"

"Yes, I suppose it would – I thought of the musical notes as coloured. Warm colours, almost like a rainbow from start to finish, to indicate the emotion of the music. But I wasn't quite sure how to achieve it."

"I'd suggest going with your instincts next time. But you're definitely on to something here. Have you tried painting, or just sculpture?"

"No, I've never done anything like this before. Not since school."

"Come round to my studio sometime, why don't you? We'll have a painting session, just you and me."

The gallery filled up with visitors and the hum of conversation grew to a roar. The string quartet could hardly be heard above the chatter. Attractive young college girls dispensed the wine and Barbara began to feel quite squiffy. She put down her glass and ate a few crisps out of the bowl on the side table. It was only as the evening began to wind down that she realised Andrew had never arrived.

*

"Is that Serenity?"

"Hang on, I'll get her. Mum! It's for you!"

He recognised her voice when she came to the phone and explained that he had been the man on the park bench.

"I remember you, love. Now, how can I help?"

"I'd like to arrange a palm reading, please."

She fixed an appointment and gave him directions to the house. Just before she rang off she said: "By the way, what's your name?"

He hesitated slightly too long. "It's Andrew," he said, finally.

The house was on a side-street in Woolston, close to the new Itchen Bridge, in a row of identical bay-and-forecourt Edwardian houses. A set of wind-chimes hung outside the porch, giving off an eerie Eastern atonal sound in the breeze. A sign over the door said 'I believe in fairies' and the ludicrousness of this dispelled any fears that Gilbert might have had about having his palm read. He would treat it as a joke, he decided, though in his heart he knew that his quest was a serious one, even a desperate one. He hungered to know what was to happen to him, yet he also dreaded knowing.

Serenity looked rather more like a psychic than when he had seen her in the park. She was wearing a dark purple dress, over which she had draped a pale grey fringed shawl, and she had fluffed up her blonde hair. She ushered him into a room at the back of the house. The curtains were drawn and the room lit by a Tiffany lamp in the corner.

"Sit down, dear, and make yourself comfortable. And, if you don't mind, please could you pay the fee now, before we start?"

"Yes of course," said Gilbert, fumbling for his wallet. Perhaps she asked for the fee in advance in case she told people bad news and then they refused to pay?

He placed his hands, palms up, on the table and she held them gently, though for more than a minute she did not look at them at all, but looked directly into Gilbert's eyes.

"Are you right-handed, Andrew?"

"Yes."

"Well, your right hand is what we call your dominant hand. Your left hand will show me the characteristics you were born with, and the right hand will tell me how those characteristics have changed over your lifetime." She studied his hands. "Though, in your case, the two hands are rather surprising – in fact I can't see any difference between them. I don't think I've ever seen anything like this before."

"Can it predict my future?"

"Sometimes. Not always."

She ran her fingers first over the ball of his thumb and then over the lines on his palm. "I don't think you're a very social person, Andrew. You tend to keep your true nature hidden from those around you. You didn't have a very happy childhood, did you? I don't think you felt you fitted in with the other children at school. I think you were alone much of the time."

Gilbert flinched.

"You're sensitive. You think a great deal – perhaps too much. And you're searching for something."

That bit was obvious, thought Gilbert. If he wasn't searching for something, then he would hardly have asked for a palm reading. The woman was just making things up as she went along.

"There's a break in your life-line, just here – do you see?"

He sat up straighter. "Does that mean I'm going to die young or die suddenly?"

"No, it could just indicate a major change will happen in your life, or a major decision. The predominant feeling I'm getting about your past is one of sadness. Is that right?"

"Yes – it is."

"But that's not the feeling I'm getting about you now. It's turned into something else. Anger, I think – perhaps that's the major change that your palm is showing me."

"What about ... what can you tell me about love?"

"You're married, I think."

Gilbert nodded.

"But not very happily, I can tell. Yet you yearn for love. Also, there is a slight difference between your hands, just here – see? I hadn't noticed it before. It indicates a trauma of some kind. Something violent." She gripped his hand and looked up, into Gilbert's eyes. "Does someone with the initial 'D' mean something to you? A woman, I'm fairly sure."

"D?" he said. "I don't think so. You wouldn't have mistaken it for 'B'?"

He expected Serenity to immediately agree with him – that's what these so-called psychics did, wasn't it? Just picked up on what their customers said or how they acted.

"No, it's definitely an 'D'."

He felt deflated.

"This 'D' – she has some kind of power over you."

"No, I don't know any one with that initial."

"Then perhaps it's in the future? But you will take away that power: you will come to dominate the relationship." She relinquished his hands and sat back in the chair. She looked exhausted. "That's all I can read, my love. Do come again if you would like to have a tarot reading."

*

Harry insisted on giving Barbara a lift back from the art show, an offer she was a bit dubious about, as he seemed to have consumed most of a bottle of wine. But she had little choice in the matter as Andrew had not turned up. The back seat of the car was entirely taken up by a stack of stretched and primed canvases and she had to arrange her feet around a cardboard box of oil paints that was in the passenger seat-well.

"All the more reason why learning to drive is a good idea," said Harry. "When do you take your test? Don't forget you'll need to tell them you are taking the test in the 2CV, otherwise an ordinary gearstick is going to confuse you completely."

"I don't think I'll be allowed to do that. I can have a few practices in Ian's car to get used to the gears. Anyway, haven't booked it yet. I've got to swot up on the Highway Code a bit more."

"You'll be fine. Then once you've passed, you can get Andrew to buy you a nice little car of your own."

"And pigs may fly!"

As they reached the Straight Mile at Ampfield, he began to sing 'No Particular Place To Go' but when he got to the part about 'cruising and playing the radio' he waltzed the car to the other side of the road.

"Harry, for goodness sake!" shouted Barbara.

"The road's empty – it's fine!"

"You're drunk, Harry!"

"Drunk? I've hardly even begun, dear girl. Just enjoying myself."

"Well, enjoy yourself a little more modestly, please."

He pulled up outside Barbara's house and kept the engine running.

"Sure you don't want me to come in?"

"Quite sure. Thank you for the lift." She leaned over and kissed him on the cheek.

When she let herself into the house, the lights were on in the hall and sitting room, but there was no sign of Andrew. He was probably in his workshop, she thought, and walked through to the back of the house to look out of the kitchen window, but the workshop was in darkness. Until now, she had felt aggrieved that he hadn't come to the show: now she began to feel worried. She checked her watch: 10pm. She couldn't believe he'd miss News at Ten: his life totally revolved around routine. She took off her coat, kicked off her shoes and walked upstairs to put her handbag away in the wardrobe. As she clicked the bedroom light on, she saw a shape under the continental quilt.

"Andrew! Are you OK?"

He grunted but did not stir. He was lying on his side.

She walked round the bed so she could see his face but he immediately turned over so that his back was to her.

"Are you not well? I was worried when you didn't show up tonight." She was conscious that this was not entirely true. "The show went really well – I wish you could have seen it."

"I'm perfectly well," he said, his voice muffled by the pillow. "I didn't come to the show because I didn't want to come. And now I want to go to sleep."

Barbara addressed the back of his head. "Couldn't you have told me earlier that you didn't want to come? Didn't it occur to you that I might have had difficulty getting home afterwards?"

"I'm sure one of your new-found friends was only too pleased to run you home."

"That's hardly the point."

"It is, indeed, precisely the point. Now, perhaps you'd be kind enough to go and sleep in the guest bedroom tonight so that you don't wake me up again, clattering about?"

She stood for a moment, fighting back tears. She was damned if she was going to let Andrew know how upset she was. As she left the room, Snob slinked in through the closing gap in the door and jumped up on the bed, pummeling the quilt and looking smugly over at Barbara.

*

Gilbert stepped out from the hedge in the darkness and swung the spade wildly in a kind of arc as soon as Ian got into the driver's seat of his car. The spade was heavier than he expected, its metal handle and shaft cold against his hands and slippery from where his palms had been sweating. He wished he had thought to wear gloves. He had mis-timed the strike, the sharp edge of the blade glancing off the rim of the door and smashing into the side window which cracked with a loud report. The jolt of the impact ran from his hands right up to his shoulders.

Moving back slightly, he raised the spade again, crouching in order to find a better angle. Ian, still sitting in the driver's seat, reached out to try and pull the door closed but was too slow. This time Gilbert's aim was better and the spade came down neatly on Ian's arm, halfway between elbow and wrist. He let out a gutteral howl and fell out of the car sideways onto the gravel driveway.

Holding the spade horizontally across his body, Gilbert looked down at the figure illuminated by the light from the car. A 'courtesy light', they called it, and the incongruity of it made him give a bark of laughter. Ian looked up at the sound, cradling his broken arm as if it was a precious new-born baby or some valuable antique artefact. 'Please please please,' saying it over and over again. He raised the spade once more, this time two-handed, and brought the flat of it with a satisfying swoosh down onto the back of Ian's head. As he began to raise it again, this time aiming for the head, Ian let go of his injured arm and grabbed the other end of the metal shaft with a surprisingly strong grip. They wrestled for a moment, both tugging at the spade for possession, until Ian suddenly shoved the spade towards him, the handle catching Gilbert a direct blow on the nose. He staggered back, astonished at the pain and at the amount of blood pouring from his face.

Ian was kneeling now, throwing the spade away from him like a javelin into the rose-beds and then lunging at Gilbert, grabbing his ankle so that he toppled over backwards, his head hitting the tiled border that marked the edge of the lawn. The arm of his coat had caught on one of the shrubs and he tugged at it to free it, unable to see properly in the darkness and bemused by the pain in his head, but somehow taken with the thought that he shouldn't tear the fabric.

When he looked up again, the clouds had moved away and the moon was visible, just a slender slice of moon almost resting on the roof tiles of the house. The engine of the car started, the gears made a graunching sound and the gravel spurted up as the car reversed, the driver's door still wide open, its edge just grazing his chest as it went by. The car swerved crazily in the drive, glancing off the brick gatepost before reaching the road. Gilbert rolled over and watched as the door swung to, half-fastened, and the car roared away in first gear.

*

The coach was almost full when Myra and Sandra boarded, and they had to find a seat near the back. Myra fretted that they were going to be sitting over the wheel arch, always the most uncomfortable spot, but Sandra told her not to fret. Myra glanced around.

"Everyone seems much older than us, Sandra."

"We'll soon get them going! Well at least," said, casting a sidelong glance at Myra, "I'll soon get them going."

The journey seemed interminable and there was a long queue on the Exeter by-pass, but by then the coach had stopped for a couple of 'comfort breaks' and Myra and Sandra had got talking to some of the other passengers. By the time they cleared Exeter, Sandra was leading the coach in some rousing community singing. She seemed to know endless risqué verses to 'She'll Be Coming Round the Mountain'. Myra tried to doze, conscious that they had a long evening ahead of them with dinner followed by 'live cabaret entertainment', as the brochure put it. She didn't want to bring on one of her 'turns' – she was determined to make the most of this weekend. Gilbert had been very subdued when he dropped them off at the coach station. He had seemed distracted and had had to be prevented from loading their luggage onto the wrong coach. He was probably wondering how he would manage to fend for himself for a whole weekend, thought Myra.

The Grand was a Victorian hotel on the seafront and their room provided a sweeping panorama of Torbay, even if the vista was somewhat bleak and windswept on this winter afternoon. The palm trees were looking a bit bedraggled.

"They are a lot more healthy looking than the ones in Los Angeles, though," said Sandra, always keen to show off about the far-flung places she had visited. "All you get there is about forty feet of skinny trunk with a couple of fronds right at the top where you can barely see them without binoculars. I told Gerald that they never looked like that in the pictures, but he said they bring some potted ones in especially and just set them up in front of the cameras. It's all smoke and mirrors, he says."

Myra was wondering whether she'd be warm enough without her cardigan when Sandra announced it was time to go and find the bar.

"You're not going down to dinner like that, are you, Myra love? Haven't you got something a little more glamorous to wear?"

"I'm not really the glamorous sort, Sandra."

"Nonsense. Come over here – let me put some of this lipstick on you. I got it at Edwin Jones last week."

"It's a bit too red for me. I like something a bit more subtle."

"It will make you look terrific – just wait and see." She patted the dressing-table stool and Myra obediently sat down. Sandra applied a generous coating of red to Myra's thin lips. "Here!" she said, taking a blue silk scarf out of her bag and draping it around Myra's neck. She then fluffed up Myra's hair with her fingers. "Look at yourself now!" She spun her round to face the mirror.

Myra couldn't believe how something so simple could have wrought such a transformation. She didn't look like herself at all, but like a younger, carefree person; someone who whom all possibilities were still open.

*

Twice on the way home, Gilbert had to pull the car over as the rising feeling of nausea overcame him. The second time, he opened the driver's door and threw up in the gutter. Despite the cold, his hands were sweating on the steering wheel. Blood was still pouring from his nose and now his mouth tasted foul, his teeth furred. As he pulled into Forest Close, his head was beginning to throb and for the first time in his life, he craved alcohol – a large glass of brandy, to be precise. He wondered whether Myra still had some in the sideboard left over from last Christmas. He eased the car gently onto the drive and opened the door quietly, not wanting to attract the attention of the neighbours. He decided to come back for the spade, which he'd placed in the boot, so – holding a handkerchief to his nose – he crept up the drive and into the porch. He waited for a moment, but all was quiet, the house itself, of course, in darkness because Myra had gone off that morning with Sandra on her 'turkey and tinsel' trip to Torquay: he had dropped them at 7am at the coach station in Bedford Place and then come back to disable the PIR light over the front door. As he walked into the hall, the telephone started ringing. He ignored it, shrugged off his mud-caked anorak and went to run a bath, all without turning on any lights. The phone rang for a long time.

He wasn't sure how much brandy to pour, but he took it like medicine, gulping the whole glass down in one go. Initially it was like being hit over the head, but then its warmth spread throughout his body in what seemed a miraculous way and he was filled with a sense of power and triumph. He had achieved his goal: although his intention had been to kill Ian, he felt he must have inflicted sufficient damage on him that he would never bother Barbara again – she would be safe at last. And she'd be grateful to him, he knew, once he explained. She would realise what an unselfish act it had been. He must call her in the morning and ask to see her. He staggered back upstairs into the bedroom and fell on the bed.

It was four hours before he awoke suddenly from a dreamless sleep and remembered that the spade was still in the car. His nose wasn't hurting so badly now, but it was swollen and a dark bruise was starting to appear. His glasses wouldn't fit properly over the swelling. Still in his clothes that he'd worn the night before, he went out to the car, hurriedly retrieved the spade and took it into the back garden to wash it under the outside tap. The paint had been scraped off the spade in a number of places, the blade was dented on the side, and a surprising amount of blood ran down the drain as he washed it. He then wrapped it in his muddy anorak, put it in a corner of the shed and went upstairs to pack an overnight bag. It was still dark outside, though he could hear Roy next door, thumping about, presumably getting ready for work. He worked shifts, doing something called coil-winding for the railway. Gilbert had no idea what that meant.

By 5.30am, Gilbert was getting back into the car with his overnight bag. He looked quickly through the AA road-maps in the glove compartment, selected the one marked 'south west' and set off.

*

By the following night, Myra was feeling more relaxed. She had not been away anywhere with Sandra before and initially it was a bit of a strain because of Sandra's relentless enthusiasm for everything – and her insistence that they share a twin-bedded room so that they could have 'girly' talks late into the night.

Myra tried to overlook the fact that it was only just November, and tucked into her full Christmas dinner: the hotel had even erected a Christmas tree, and carols were drifting from the loud-speakers. The tape must have been on a loop, because Myra could swear, by the time they got to the mince pies, that she had heard 'White Christmas' three times. She was glad that Gilbert wasn't with them, but slightly niggled that on both occasions when she had phoned him, there had been no reply. He was probably sitting there right next to the phone, determined to punish her by not answering.

The cabaret began with a comedian who was a bit 'blue' for Myra's taste, but Sandra laughed heartily and he picked her out for special attention. Myra stared fixedly at her coffee cup, terrified that he might pick on her next. After that, came a snake-charmer, a young girl of about seventeen, wearing a sequined bikini bottom and with silk tassles covering her nipples. All the husbands woke up at this point, stopped telling dreary stories to each other about other holidays they had been on which were much better than this one, and started to pay attention. The snake seemed somewhat superfluous to the act. Myra wondered how the girl stuck the tassles to her nipples and whether it hurt to take them off again.

By the time the band appeared on stage, Myra had drunk two rum-and-Cokes and was feeling quite relaxed. She thought she might broach the topic of the mysterious Barbara later, if Sandra was in the mood for confidences. Quite how long they would remain confidences once Sandra knew them, however, was another matter, but Myra needed to talk to someone and Sandra was the only option. She watched the couples dancing: the floor was now packed. The band had just finished playing 'SuperTrouper' and were starting on 'Take That Look Off Your Face' when a tall dark-haired man in his 40s approached Myra's table and asked if she'd like to dance. She hesitated, but the rum-and-Cokes had weakened her usual resistance and she followed him onto the dancefloor, trying to avoid Sandra's over-curious gaze. He danced well and didn't, to Myra's relief, hold her too tightly or make inane conversation. As they turned around the floor, Myra caught glimpses of the bar, the girl singer, the big sign over the stage that read 'It's like Christmas every day', and the doors out to the corridor that led to reception. Someone was standing in the doorway, silhouetted against the light, but despite the fact she could only see his outline, she knew instantly who it was.

"I'm sorry," she said to her dance partner. "I have to go."

He relinquished his hold and looked at her, puzzled.

"Have I done something to offend you?"

"No, not at all – it's just ... I'm sorry," she said, and pushed her way through the dancing couples towards the door. When she got there, the figure had disappeared.

*

"Barbara? It's Cass. I'm calling from the hospital."

"Is the baby going to be early? Is Ian with you?"

"No – it's not the baby. Not for a couple more weeks, hopefully. I'm afraid Ian has been badly hurt – that's why I'm calling. They found his car in a ditch late last night. He's in intensive care." Her voice, usually so calm and controlled, was quavering.

Barbara mentally replayed the previous evening when Ian had come round to drop off the flyers for their antique fair at Eastleigh and had stayed for a glass of wine. She'd waved him off at the front door – it had been a beautiful clear night and the stars were out – then she'd gone straight back inside because the phone was ringing, so she hadn't seen him drive off. But surely one glass of wine wouldn't have been enough to make him lose control of the car? Perhaps he'd swerved to avoid an animal in the road? A rabbit or a pheasant?

"Wait a minute," said Barbara. "You said 'late last night' but he left Ampfield about 8.30 – did he go out again after he'd been home?"

"He never made it home. It must have happened shortly after he left you, but it was a couple of hours before anyone found him and by that time he'd lost a lot of blood. The thing is, Barbara, it wasn't just an accident."

"What do you mean?"

"Sorry – I've got to go. The doctor wants a word with me. Can you let Harry know what's happened?"

"Yes of course. But what do you mean about it not being an accident?"

But Cass had hung up.

*

As soon as he saw Myra, he knew it had been a terrible mistake to drive to Torquay. He remembered little of the journey and thought later that he must have still been suffering from shock. Traffic had been light because he had started out so early and he had arrived well before lunchtime. The resort was cold and windswept and there had been a hail shower just as he'd got out of the car to put money in the pay-and-display machine on the seafront car park. The Grand Hotel was an imposing Victorian sprawl. He had hung about for a while watching the entrance and though many guests came and went, he hadn't seen Myra. His tiredness and the enormity of what he needed to tell Myra was beginning to overwhelm him: she had no idea about the loss of his job, who Barbara really was, and what he had just done to protect her. To clear his head, he had gone in search of a café and had found one with a steamed-up window in a side street: it had formica-topped tables, but it was warm and cosy. He had sat there over a mug of strong tea while he tried to organise his thoughts. He rubbed a small circle of steam off the window, so he could see out, but passers-by could still not see in.

Presumably, the police would have been called by now, either by Ian Avery if he had survived, or by someone else if they had found his body. He wasn't sure whether, by coming to Torquay, he had been trying to establish an alibi, or just running away from a frightening situation. Should he just hand himself in to the local police station? He could explain that he had done what he did for perfectly honorable reasons. They would they understand that, surely? Or should he phone Barbara? He was glad that he had waited until she had shut the front door before making his move on Ian so that she hadn't seen anything distressing. He checked the change in his pockets: he had enough for a trunk call.

He used the call box at the end of the street to phone – he knew the number by heart now – but there was no reply.

He went back to his car and sat in the driver's seat for a while. What if the police didn't understand? What if he were to be punished just like some ordinary criminal? He began to shake, whether from cold or from fear, he wasn't sure. His nose was throbbing and he took off his glasses that were pinching the bridge. By now, it was dark. He took a deep breath, got out of the car and went through the main hotel doors into Reception. At the desk, he asked for Myra Smart.

"I'll try her room for you. One moment," said the young blonde receptionist. She tapped her long painted nails on the top of the desk as she waited for the phone to be answered. "No, no-one is picking up, but I think you'll find that they are all in the ballroom at the moment because it's the big

Christmas Dinner Dance tonight." She indicated the corridor that led to the ballroom.

"Thank you," said Gilbert. She had been staring at his nose, he felt sure. He touched it self-consciously and nearly yelped with pain.

He could hear the music from a hundred feet away. An Abba song was blasting out and as he looked carefully in through the open doors, anxious not to be spotted, the dancefloor was full.

"Don't be a wallflower!" cried a female voice. "Come and dance!"

An elderly lady with too much make-up was beckoning him hideously with a scrawny finger. Gilbert smiled faintly and shook his head. He couldn't see Myra anywhere, then remembered that he hadn't got his glasses on. The room swam into focus and he was astonished to see Myra in the arms of a good-looking tall man, being whisked around the dancefloor. At least, it looked like Myra, though there was something different about her that he couldn't quite identify. She looked younger and her face had taken on an expression that it rarely wore these days – a look of happiness.

At the split second that he realised that coming to Torquay had been totally the wrong thing to do, their eyes met. Her partner turned her immediately afterwards, but Gilbert was one hundred percent sure that she had spotted him. He fled back down the corridor, heart thumping, and straight out of the hotel. Throwing his bag onto the back seat of the car, he started the engine. In his panic, his foot slipped on the brake and he reversed straight into the low wall that bordered the car park. He thrust the gear lever into first and accelerated away. As he reached the esplanade road, he saw Myra coming through the revolving doors of the hotel onto the steps outside. He didn't look back.

*

When the coach pulled in to Bedford Place, Gilbert was ready and waiting, jangling his car keys nervously. Myra handed him her suitcase and gave him an intense look but resisted the temptation to ask him what on earth he had been doing in Torquay. She had not told Sandra about seeing him, partly because Sandra would ask a lot of questions which Myra didn't think she would be able to answer, and partly because she half-believed that she must have been seeing things. Why would he come all the way to Torquay and then run away without talking to her? It would be ridiculous, but then Gilbert *was* rather ridiculous. If he wanted to tell her, she was sure that he would do so in his own good time.

Sandra, of course, was not so circumspect.

"My God, Gilbert – what have you done to your nose? Someone given you a punch in the face? A jealous husband, perhaps?" She laughed uproariously. "It looks like a strawberry!"

"I bumped into a door," said Gilbert, "in the dark. I was trying to change a fuse."

"Yes, I'd stick to that story," said Sandra. "The old excuses are the best ones."

Myra tutted and moved off to towards the car, hoping that Sandra would drop the subject. Did Gilbert acquire this injury before he'd come to Torquay, or afterwards? She tried to imagine someone thumping him on the nose. Gilbert was so absent from himself much of the time that the punch might have met with thin air. A non-person, that's what he was. Things happened to Gilbert, but he never actually made anything happen himself.

As Gilbert lifted up the boot lid, she noticed the dent in the back bumper.

"I suppose the car ran into a door as well," she said.

"I accidentally reversed into a wall in the car park at work. The garage are mending it on Tuesday – it's all covered by insurance."

"Just as well," said Myra, "after what we spent on this weekend jolly."

"Did you have a good time?" he asked, rather stiffly.

"Yes thank you."

"We had a snake-charmer!" said Sandra, excitedly. "She wore nipple-tassles! And Myra 'pulled'. Didn't you, Myra?"

"For goodness sake, Sandra! It was just a dance."

*

Gilbert was upstairs when he saw the police car arrive. He stood to one side of the bedroom window so he couldn't be seen from the street. Two men got out; one was rather tubby and tugged at the jacket of his uniform where it had rucked up from sitting in the patrol car. They both put on their peaked caps. As soon as the bell rang, Myra's feet could be heard tapping down the hall. Gilbert moved quietly to the head of the stairs.

"Is this the residence of Mr Gilbert Arthur Smart?" said the slimmer of the two.

"Yes, it is," said Myra, sounding almost eager. "He's upstairs – I'll fetch him." She hesitated. "It's not bad news, is it?"

"No need to fetch me," said Gilbert, descending the staircase. "I know what they're here for."

"Gilbert Arthur Smart, we are arresting you on suspicion of the attempted murder of Colin Ian Avery."

Colin, thought Gilbert as the policeman read him his rights. Ian was his middle name. Colin sounded like a wholly different person – solid, dependable.

"Do you wish to take a coat or anything with you, Mr Smart?"

Myra silently handed him his beige anorak from the hall-stand. On impulse, he picked up the copy of *The White Company,* an Arthur Conan Doyle novel, from the bookshelf in the hall. The policeman gripped his arm.

"If you'd like to come with us, sir."

"Aren't you going to handcuff me?"

"I don't there's any need for that, sir, if you behave in a sensible manner."

"Goodbye, Myra," said Gilbert, but Myra had already started walking back down the hall towards the kitchen.

As they stepped onto the path, the PIR light came on over the front door and Gilbert was irritated to see that his Austin was looking dusty and could do with a good clean. He'd have to do it on Sunday. As they drew level with the curb, he glanced back, and saw Roy and Anne framed in their doorway, looking avidly at the scene unfolding before them as if it was something on the telly. The tubby policeman opened the rear passenger door of the patrol car. Gilbert felt as if he was in an episode of *Softly Softly* – it used to be one of Myra's favourite programmes. He hoped the policeman was not going to do that stupid thing of pushing Gilbert's head down as he guided him into the back seat. He did. The car drew away. The front door of Gilmyr was still wide open with the hall light on, but Myra was nowhere to be seen. Gilbert clutched the book to his chest and stared straight ahead as the car swung out of Forest Close onto the main Sholing road and headed for the city centre. It was only then that he noticed he was still wearing his maroon slippers.

*

Myra stood in the kitchen completely still for a good ten minutes after the police car had driven away. She couldn't exactly say what was going through her mind – her thoughts seemed to have ground to a complete halt. She hadn't wanted Gilbert to think she was shocked by what had happened and, indeed, she couldn't suppress a tiny glimmer of pleasure that he had got his come-uppance – but come-uppance for what, exactly?

Attempted murder, the young copper had said. The name had meant nothing to her – Colin something or other. Who the hell was that? She couldn't recall anyone at Gilbert's office called Colin. Anyway, it had to be a mistake – at the thought of someone as wimpish and repressed as Gilbert trying to commit murder made her laugh out loud. He had certainly been behaving oddly in the last few days, but then he was always odd, so she had not paid any extra attention to it. He'd cried out in his sleep the previous night, something that sounded like 'sword straight, blade true', and she'd stomped off to the spare room for a bit of peace and quiet. But then again, he was already having nightmares, thrashing about and sweating.

A shout from the hall roused her. Four or five tough-looking policemen were clustered in the doorway, one of them lifting up the seat of the hall-stand and rooting about inside it. This time there were no courtesies.

"We have a warrant to search these premises," said the stocky one with a blond buzz-cut. He was brandishing a piece of paper in Myra's face. "So, if you'll allow us to go about our business ..."

They swarmed in as if they were on some army exercise, fanning out across the small semi-detached house. One went straight out through the back door to the shed.

"Guv?" shouted one from the top of the stairs.

Blondy went up the stairs two at a time, while Myra shrank back against the wall of the hall.

Blondy thundered down again.

"Mrs Smart – can you explain why all your husband's belongings seem to be boxed up? Was he about to do a runner? He sneered at her.

"I threw him out, that's why they're in boxes. Only ... well, I took him back and we hadn't had chance to unpack them."

Blondy raised his eyebrows but any sarcastic remark he might have been planning to make was cut short by the tall thin policeman coming through the kitchen from the back door.

"What?" said Blondy, rudely.

"Better calls the SOCOs – I've found something."

Blondy followed the thin one out to the garden shed. They returned, looking important and speaking into their walkie-talkies.

"Stay right where you are, Mrs Smart. Or better still, maybe you could make us all a nice cup of tea."

Myra huffed, but went to the kitchen. Suddenly feeling faint, she leant over the sink and stared at the plughole. When she noticed it was stained and needed a good scrubbing, she deemed she must be feeling better and straightened up. The policeman never did ask what had happened to the tea.

Later, a man in a suit went out the front door carrying a spade wrapped in a big plastic bag. Myra didn't recall that they ever owned a spade.

After they had gone, she sat on the sofa. It wasn't until the clock struck midnight that she accepted that Gil was not coming home.

*

"You've brought this entirely on yourself. I warned you and warned you, but you were in no mood to listen." Andrew flung the *Daily Telegraph* down onto the coffee table and stood up. Snob, alarmed by the shouting, jumped off Barbara's lap and headed for the door, looking back reproachfully as he slid through the gap.

"How can this possibly be my fault? I've not done anything – you're just being irrational," said Barbara.

"I think I'm entitled to be irrational at the moment," Andrew retorted. "I've stood by as you took up with Ian Avery and I've watched him turning your head with all these new ideas. I no longer recognise you. You're not the person I married. You're never here – you're always running around doing antique fairs, or playing at being an artist, or drinking in pubs with that disreputable Harry character. As for Gilbert

Smart, you encouraged him too. What did you think was going to happen? Did you not see this coming?"

"What on earth are you talking about? How could I possibly have known that he'd attack Ian?"

"Fighting over women – that's what men do, isn't it?"

"That's a ridiculous thing to say. They weren't fighting over me. I'm in business with Ian and that's all. As for Gil, I felt sorry for him."

"Yes, and look what it led to. He was obsessed with you."

"Only in a puppy-dog way..." She trailed off. "Or, that's how it seemed at the start."

"Well you were wrong, weren't you? And now you've got your just desserts."

"That's a terrible thing to say. What about Ian? He's the one who was nearly killed – or had you forgotten that? Do you think he got his 'just desserts' too?"

"I don't really care about Ian. What I care about is that I am being punished for something that's nothing whatsoever to do with me. Police crawling all the over the place, reporters camped outside, people slowing down in their cars to take a look at our house."

"And what do you think it's been like for me? You're hardly ever here – at least you can escape to London. I have to be here every day. It's me who has to face the stares in the Post Office or the bakery; the whispers every time I appear. They are too cowardly to say anything, but they clearly think I've brought this scandal down upon the village."

Andrew sat down on the arm of the sofa and plucked absently at the corner of the cushion. "Well it's true – if you hadn't been messing around with Ian, none of this would have happened. He told me, you know, months ago."

"Ian told you what, exactly?"

"Not Ian – Gilbert."

With shock, Barbara remembered the confrontation she'd had with Gil when she accused him of spreading lies.

"When did he talk to you?"

"When he came to my office."

"Let me get this straight – Gil came to your office? In London? And you never told me?"

"After what he said, I certainly wasn't going to tell you about it, no."

"But how on earth did he even find out where you worked? I've never said." She thought for a moment, remembering catching sight of someone who looked like Gil one lunchtime in the car-park of the Royal Oak. It was only a split-second and the man had turned his back to them almost immediately. Had he been following them? Had he followed Ian to London?

"How he found out where I worked is not really relevant, is it?"

"I have a feeling it might well be," said Barbara, "when it comes to the trial." She felt sick even at the word 'trial'.

"Aren't you going to ask me what he said?"

"I think I already know," said Barbara. "The point is, you could have prevented all this – you had the opportunity there and then to put him right, but you didn't. You chose to believe his lies. So if anyone is to blame, it's actually you."

Andrew sighed, got to his feet and went out of the sitting room, closing the door carefully and quietly behind him – an act that had more of a sense of finality about it than if he'd slammed it.

*

Barbara had never been to the Magistrates' Court before and was glad to have Harry, who was maintaining his customary air of insouciance, with her. She was surprised how shabby the waiting area was: notices were peeling off the wall, the coffee machine had an 'out of order' sign on it and a variety of rather unsavoury-looking young men were leaning on the walls of the corridor, awaiting (so Harry told her) their duty solicitor to spend two minutes with them apprising themselves of the case in order to defend them. All the young men turned to stare openly at Barbara and one rolled his tongue lasciviously around his lips. She moved closer to Harry.

Three courts were sitting that day, and Harry learned from the clerk at the door that Gilbert's case would be in Court Two, where a district judge was presiding. Barbara went in, following Harry, and they both nodded to the magistrate, as they'd been told to do, before sitting in the seats allocated to the public, at the back of the courtroom. To sit down, they had to ask the skinhead seated at the end of the row to remove his huge boots from where he was resting them on the panel in front of the seats. He slid them down the panel, making sure they made a loud scraping noise, then deposited a wad of chewing gum on the arm of the seat. A case was in progress as Harry and Barbara sat down: a young woman with dyed blonde ratty hair was slouched in the dock and a solicitor in a dusty-looking suit that had seen better days was telling the court that the only reason his client had called the policeman a 'filthy pig' was that she was in drink at the time. She was deeply remorseful and had already made changes in her life regarding alcohol. The magistrate gave her a suspended prison sentence: as she left, grinning, the skinhead turned to Barbara, murmured 'result!', shuffled to his feet and followed the girl out. During the procession of cases that followed (habitual stealer of aerosols, car thief, wife-beater, drink-driver, vandal) Barbara listened with a horrible fascination. It was the politeness of the whole process that amazed her. Dyed-in-the-wool villains were addressed as 'Mr', solicitors, ushers and clerks bobbed up and down constantly, standing up every time they spoke, in deference to the magistrate. Even the defendants were asked to be seated if there was a long delay. She looked at the panel in front of where the skinhead had been sitting. Names had been scratched and etched all over it and the perspex sheet protecting its end had been picked off by patient fingernails.

"Who is that?" Barbara whispered to Harry, pointing at a young man at the side of the court, who was scribbling in a notebook.

"Reporter – from the Romsey Advertiser, I imagine," said Harry. "It'll be a big story for them."

Barbara was horrified: it never occurred to her that the paper would print anything else other than the report of the attack: that was quite bad enough, the photographs of the scene clearly identifying it as being her house.

"So, in crown court, if I'm called as a witness, they'll write it up?"

Before Harry could reply, the clerk called Gil's case. Like the wife-beater before him, Gil was brought up from the cells in handcuffs by a custody officer. Barbara could not see his face because the public gallery was at the back of the courtroom, behind the dock. He wore his suit jacket, but no tie; it was the first time she had ever seen him without a tie. He faced straight ahead. The case was over in less than two minutes. Gil said his name and address; the charges were read; and the magistrate asked him how he pleaded. "Not guilty, your honour," said Gil, barely audible. He was then ignored while court officers conferred and phone calls were made, before finally being given a date for his trial at Crown Court. The date was set three months' hence: there was no appeal for bail, so Gil was remanded in custody. He turned to follow the custody officer back down to the cells and, as he did so, he glanced over at the public gallery. Barbara looked away quickly, not meeting his eye, but she saw him give a tight smile as he was led away.

"Why such a long delay?" she asked Harry.

"Probably so they can compile psychological reports. Let's go," he whispered. "A large brandy in the White Horse is called for, I think."

*

Gilbert had often driven past Winchester Prison, a suitably forbidding Victorian edifice next door to the hospital on the road into Winchester from Romsey. But the prison van in which he was transferred afforded no view of the street: it had only one barred window at the rear and the lurching of the van soon made Gilbert feel queasy. He was sharing the ride with two other prisoners, who were being remanded in custody until their trial, both young men with skinhead haircuts. One wore tartan trousers and a leather jacket that had been deliberately slashed to reveal his T-shirt underneath. Gilbert felt very old and staid in his suit and tie. The two lads didn't speak a word to him, or to each other, on the journey.

Going to prison had been a surprise to him. He'd never really considered what being 'remanded' meant and when he told his solicitor that he did not want to ask for bail, he somehow assumed that he would continue to be held in the custody suite at the court. His solicitor had not enlightened him. The custody officer explained that is was because Crown Court cases took a long time to come to trial, but not to worry because he would be housed in a special wing of the prison, away from the convicted criminals.

"And if you're found guilty," he said cheerfully, "the time you've spent on remand will count against your sentence."

He would be allowed visitors and his barrister would be coming for regular briefings. He was also to have a psychological assessment, whatever that was.

Used to routine and a circumscribed existence, Gilbert found that life in prison was relatively bearable. The governor had quickly identified that he was a white-collar worker, and asked him to help out in the library, where he spent most of his time checking out books on True Crime for inmates and helping them to fill in forms or write letters. Most were barely literate. Having always been an underdog at work, it was strangely pleasurable to have these men look up to him.

When Gilbert was told he had a visitor, his heart always leapt, only to be disappointed to find that it was not Barbara but his barrister, a florid-faced man called Stevenson who wore a chalk-stripe suit and looked as if he should be selling dodgy TVs that had fallen off the back of a lorry. He came once a week to talk about the case – his main concern seemed to be who they might get on the bench that day and who would be prosecuting.

Gilbert wrote letters every day, but received none in return. Many of the letters that he wrote to Barbara he never even posted, and it was a week before he wrote one that he felt confident enough to send. He wondered whether the prison staff read all the letters and censored them. Writing to Myra proved even more difficult. After 'Dear Myra' he felt unable to continue. He remembered some of the messages on postcards sent by serving soldiers during the war – he'd seen them when he was collecting cards. In beautiful copperplate handwriting they would say something like 'Dear Edith, I hope this finds you well. I am fine. Thank you for the scarf you sent. Your loving husband, Tom'. They revealed absolutely nothing of the hell that soldier must have been going through.

Gilbert was sitting on his bed when the guard put his head through the open door of the cell.

"You've got a visitor."

"But it's Wednesday – my barrister doesn't come until Friday."

"It's a woman. Bit of a looker, too. Better comb your hair and look presentable."

A woman? At last, thought Gilbert – she's come. I knew she would. He remembered that first time he had seen her, just a fleeting glimpse as she had passed him in the corridor at Wendell Court. She had smiled at him, her eyes kind. She had a distinctive way of walking, of holding her handbag with one hand and swinging the other arm. He checked his face in the small shaving mirror above the sink before following the guard.

As he entered the Visiting Hall, he looked around anxiously for her. Most of the tables were already occupied – prisoner on one side, visitor on the other – both seated on orange plastic chairs. It never failed to astonish him the way the girlfriends or wives of the prisoners managed to wrap their legs around their men under the table. Snogging took the place of conversation most of the time.

"Over here," said the guard, pointing to a table where a woman sat alone. She was unknown to Gilbert. She was young and petite, with a mass of curly shoulder-length black hair, dark eyes and an olive-skinned complexion – almost Italian looking, or perhaps Greek, he thought. Not a pretty woman, but there was something striking about her.

Gilbert sat down, puzzled. The woman smiled.

"Hello, Mr Smart. My name is Lola. I'm from the prison visitors' service. I'm a volunteer, attached to Winchester Prison. I heard that you've not had any visits from your family, so I thought I'd come and introduce myself and see if you wanted a chat. You can talk to me about anything and I can call in once a week if you would like. Anything you tell me is completely confidential."

Gilbert didn't reply immediately, but looked at her well-manicured hands, which she had placed on the table. He was still numb from the realisation that it hadn't been Barbara in the visitors' room. The sense of loss was physical – an ache in the solar plexus like someone had kicked him. He thought that this was what grief must feel like. He tried to collect himself.

"Lola, did you say?"

"Yes, that's right. It's a Spanish name – my mother was Spanish."

She had no trace of an accent. He looked up, curious about her. She wore a silver cross on a chain round her neck and it glinted against her dark skin.

"Why would you want to be a prison visitor? Here, with all these men?"

"Perhaps I'll tell you later, when we know each other a bit better. But first, tell me about you. I know you're on remand – how are you coping?"

He started stiffly and hesitantly, but she was a good listener, smiling and nodding as if there was no-one else she would rather talk to. As his only visitors had been his barrister and the psychiatrist – and he had had to be guarded about what he revealed to them – it was a relief to be able to talk to someone who was entirely neutral. He wanted to talk about the case, but each time she carefully steered him away from the topic, encouraging him instead to tell her about what the prison food was like, or what he'd seen on TV yesterday, or to recall something from his childhood. She revealed little of her own background, but just enough to make him feel that they might have things in common. At the end of visiting time, he plucked up courage to ask her whether she would be able to post a letter for him. He suspected that his letter to Barbara had been blocked by the prison governor and that's why he had not received a reply. Lola explained firmly but pleasantly that she couldn't do that because she was not allowed to take anything out of the prison, or bring anything in. Despite this, he found that when she asked if he would like her to visit again the following week, he said 'yes' straight away.

Next time they met, two cups of coffee were on the table and the atmosphere was less formal. She didn't object when he started to tell her about Barbara, and by their third meeting, he felt able to express his fears about what was going to happen to him at the trial. Every time he had tried to think about it, it was as if a grey blind had been pulled down in his brain, preventing him from even imagining it.

"Will you be there?" he asked Lola, anxiously.

"No, I'm afraid not. My commitment to you is to be your friend all the time you are here in prison. But I will find out what happens, of course."

"I don't think there will be anyone there for me, except Barbara of course."

"She will be called as a witness, I imagine, so she'll be there. What about your wife?"

"I hadn't really thought. I suppose so." He pictured all the cardboard boxes with his belongings in them, stacked in the spare room. "Are you married?" He glanced at her hand, but there was no wedding ring.

"No, I'm not. I'm still waiting for the right man," she said, laughing. "My mother keeps introducing me to potential husbands, all of them completely unsuitable. Being Spanish, she feels that if her daughters are not married off by the time they are 25, then they will be on the shelf forever and a disgrace to the family. All my sisters are older than me and they are all married with kids."

"I always wondered what it would be like to have a brother or sister."

"It's like being in hell and heaven at the same time. I've just got sisters now, but I had a brother, once. You asked me why I became a prison visitor. Well, he's the reason. He got into bad company when he was in his teens and eventually he went to a juvenile detention centre and then to prison." She looked away and her voice shook. "He hanged himself in his cell."

Gilbert didn't know how to react to this, so he took off his glasses and polished them carefully.

"I'm so sorry," he said, avoiding her eye to allow her time to compose herself. He imagined himself hanging from the doorway of his cell, strangled perhaps by a belt smuggled into the prison, his feet dangling a few inches above the floor.

"I probably shouldn't have told you that," said Lola. "I've not told a prisoner that before, so forgive me."

"What was his name?"

"Alejandro."

"Do you miss him very much?"

"Every day. So, because of Alejandro, I will be here for you right up to the date of your trial – you can count on me."

*

Barbara was restless. She put down her book, got up from the sofa, made some minute adjustments to the ornaments on the mantlepiece and caught sight of her reflection in the gilt-framed overmantle. She looked ugly, she thought and pulled a face to exaggerate her perceived ugliness. There was dust on the mantlepiece and she drew her finger across it in a lazy arc. She took her coffee cup out to the kitchen and put it down on the oak worktop. She gazed absently out of the window to the back garden as she waited for the kettle to boil. The wind was lashing the bare branches of the whitebeam tree. A grey squirrel hopped across the lawn, stopping every few feet to dig in the grass and then to move on. Barbara tapped the glass and the squirrel froze in mid-dig, regarding her with one intelligent eye before soaring effortlessly up the fir tree and away ... into next door's garden.

When the kettle boiled, Barbara decided she didn't want another cup of coffee after all. She wandered out into the conservatory, feeling irritated to see the paint peeling from the window frames where they met the sill. She suddenly wished she lived in a flat, somewhere new and unsullied; somewhere without all these layers of history. They had seemed to add character – that's why she had been drawn to the place – but now they seemed overbearing. They stopped her thinking. All she could do was go round and round the same thoughts, over and over again. She crossed the garden on the flagstoned path and went into Andrew's workshop. This was his sacred space: she never normally intruded, but he was in London, so what did it matter? And where was her sacred space, she wondered? Did she even have one anymore? There didn't seem anywhere where she could escape her thoughts. She picked up one of Andrew's white balsa-wood models, turned it round in her hands, then without considering what she was doing, threw it to the floor and stamped on it. She lifted up her shoe: the model had split into a dozen pieces. Leaving them there, she walked back into the house and picked up the telephone. Her palms were sweating despite the coolness of the hall.

"Harry? It's Barbara – I really need to see you."

*

Barbara got off the bus at the end of the lane and walked up the track. Some of the puddles were still iced over and the grassy area down the centre of the track gleamed with frost. She wished she had worn more suitable shoes. She checked the note she'd scribbled down when she was speaking to Harry on the phone: after a hundred yards, the track would divide and she should turn right and go through the farm gate. She found it with no problem and unlatched the heavy gate on her second attempt – the barn was straight ahead. Harry's 2CV was parked outside at a crazy angle, and alongside it was a black motorbike with a crash helmet balanced on the seat. The door to the barn was slightly ajar, so Barbara put her head inside and shouted 'hello'. A young man of about 20 appeared. He was tall and slim with dark hair and was totally naked.

"Hi!" he called out. "Come in – you must be Barbara." He seemed completely unconcerned that she had seen him without any clothes. Feeling very middle-class and conservative, she endeavoured to keep her eyes fixed on his face as he spoke.

"Harry's just gone into the next field to pick some sorrel – I'm cooking lunch today. He'll be back in a minute. Coffee?"

"Yes please," she said, wondering if it was quite such a good idea to be alone with this naked stranger in a barn in the middle of nowhere and beginning to replay in her mind all the horror films she'd seen. As he busied himself at a rudimentary kitchen unit in the corner of the barn, Barbara took a quick look around. The barn was heated by an old iron stove in the middle of the floor, with a long stovepipe leading up to the ceiling. Next to it was a raised platform with a straight-backed chair on it, and facing it was Harry's easel, which was surrounded by a mess of paint-tubes, palette knives, and old brushes soaking in a jam jar. In the corner of the barn was a rumpled camp-bed. Her gaze strayed back to the young man – he moved with slim-hipped grace and his hair curled pleasingly on the back of his neck.

"Take a good look if you want!" he called, still with his back to her.

She jumped with guilt.

"It's only the second sitting, so it's a long way from finished."

Barbara almost laughed with relief. She walked over to the easel. Harry had been painting the young man in profile, standing behind the chair and leaning towards it, with his hands placed on the rail of its back.

"Here – I hope you can manage without milk."

"That's fine. Thank you," she said, taking the cup. "I like the painting."

"Well, Harry's a certified genius, isn't he? At least, that's what they think in Germany. But then no man is a prophet in his own country."

Barbara revised her view of the young man as being a lad from the village who probably worked as a barman in the evenings to coming from a rather more educated background. Perhaps he was an art student.

"Have you been modelling for him for long?"

"A couple of years now. I expect he'll get fed up with me soon and trade me in for a younger model."

The barn door banged open and Harry entered, his clothes covered in paint splashes. He was wearing a fur hat with ear-flaps.

"What's this about a younger model?" he shouted. "And, for goodness sake, Ashley, put some bloody clothes on. Barbara is from Ampfield – they don't run around stark naked there, you know. They are rather more civilised. And throw another log on the stove, or your bits will shrivel up with cold."

"Sorry," said Ashley to Barbara, grabbing a bathrobe from the end of the camp-bed. "I didn't think."

"The frost got the last of the sorrel, even the ones in the cold-frame. So we'll have to do without. You're staying for lunch, aren't you Barbara? It's rabbit casserole, the rabbit kindly donated by the farmer. Might still have a few pellets in it, of course, but we can pick our way around those. And before that, I will give you your first painting lesson."

Barbara was seized with anxiety. She had assumed she would be alone with Harry, so that she could unburden herself about everything that had happened. Now she was supposed to concentrate on a painting lesson, be polite over lunch, and make conversation with this Ashley chap.

As if he'd heard her thoughts, Ashley began to pull on denim jeans and a thick sweater. "I won't do any more today, Harry, if that's alright," he said, picking up a leather jacket from the back of a chair and stepping into motorcycling boots. "I'll see you same time tomorrow." He flung a casual arm around Harry's neck and kissed him briefly on the mouth. He waved vaguely at Barbara and strode out of the barn door. After a moment, she heard the motorbike roar into life.

"Charming boy," said Harry. "He's just started training for the priesthood."

Barbara laughed, despite herself.

"No, really – he is. His father is a rector over Micheldever way, but Ashley wants to be a city vicar." He took Barbara's hand and looked seriously into her eyes. "I know you need to talk and we'll do that over lunch. But you're clearly in a very agitated state, so I suggest we do some painting for an hour first – that will help relax you and give you time to arrange your thoughts. So finish your coffee, and let's get started."

"It's ghastly – the coffee."

"I know. Ashley has no idea how to make a decent cup. I'll pour it down the sink."

Harry was right: after an hour of carefully mixing colours, and concentrating on what he was telling her about the 'colour wheel', Barbara felt her tensions ebbing away, though he had to remind her twice not to hold the brush with quite such a fierce grip.

"It's not a weapon, you know – you look like you're about to bayonet someone with it."

"Perhaps I am," said Barbara.

Over the rabbit casserole, which Harry served with fresh noodles, Barbara talked – and talked. She felt as though she were emptying herself: every emotion, every conflict came pouring out. Initially she had cried, but Harry had just sat there patiently until she had gathered herself again, and towards the end, she felt strangely calm and detached.

"The most important thing, Barbara, is that none of this is your fault," he said. "None of it. I'm sure that Andrew knows this in his heart, but right now he's just lashing out and you happen to be the target. That will pass. And Ian *didn't* die, which must be some kind of miracle, and he *will* get better. As for Gilbert Smart, you weren't to know, so stop torturing yourself about it. He'll go to prison and you'll never have to worry about him again."

"Harry, you're such a comfort. I really don't know what I'd do without you."

"Well, you'd certainly not to have to encounter naked men in barns, or drive cars that appear to have an umbrella for a gear-stick. Which reminds me – we need to fit in some more driving lessons soon if you're to be ready for your test."

"I can't really concentrate on that right now. Once Ian's well again, perhaps I will. Or perhaps not, if Andrew continues to make a fuss about it. And then there's the trial to worry about; they'll call me to give evidence. Will they cross-question me? What if there are things I can't remember? Or what if I get it all wrong and Gil gets off? ..." She was aware that she was babbling again, so she picked up her coat and bag and told Harry that she was now off to visit Ian in hospital.

"Wait – I've got something for him," said Harry. "You could take it for me. It's only small."

"What is it?" she asked as he handed over a tiny package wrapped in velvet.

"You'll have to wait and see." He put on his fur hat again and headed for the door. "Come on – I'll drive you into the village, so you can get the direct bus."

*

Myra cautiously drew back the edge of the net curtain in the lounge. The two cars were still outside and their two drivers were leaning on the bonnet of the larger car, smoking cigarettes. One had his camera around his neck – one of those huge cameras that looked more suitable for taking pictures of rare birds several hundred yards away than for dashing off a snap or two of Myra putting the bins out. The other one was a reporter: she knew that because he had rung the doorbell every day, trying to wear down her resistance and get her to tell 'her side of the story.' He had an over-loud, rather uncouth voice and kept calling her 'love'. He wasn't from a newspaper at all, but from an agency and he said this was because he wrote for all the papers. He had been adept at wedging his foot in the gap between the door and its frame, but after she'd closed the door fairly briskly on it a couple of times, he'd retreated to the car. For some reason, they were both kitted out in clothes that made them look like Israeli resistance fighters, with those khaki-coloured waistcoats with lots of pockets and olive-green baggy trousers that had a buttoned pocket halfway down the leg.

They hadn't given up and she had got used to their presence now, even nodding a good morning to them when she couldn't avoid going out. One day she even took out tea and biscuits on a tray. They had asked her if she had a photograph of Gilbert, but she said she didn't. She really only had their wedding pictures, and she wasn't going to give them one of those.

They had tried knocking on the neighbours' doors as well, but Elsie and Tom across the road had given them short shrift. Myra suspected that Anne and Roy next door would probably welcome them in with open arms and tell them all kinds of stories about Gilbert, even though they barely knew him other than to say 'good morning' to, but because they were both out at work all day, thankfully they hadn't seen the reporter. Myra was careful not to invite Sandra to the house: the thought of Sandra spilling her guts to the press and repeating things that Myra had told her about Gilbert was too awful to contemplate.

The vicar came round once, much to Myra's astonishment. She only knew he was the vicar because he was wearing his dog-collar. She'd certainly never been through the doors of his church and never intended to, especially as it was one of those 'smells and bells' churches with Catholic leanings. But he was a nice enough young chap – it was apparently his first parish – and he asked Myra if she would like one of his 'counselling team' to come and see her. The thought was horrifying: some busy-body do-gooder pretending to console her while really burning up with curiosity to hear all the dirty details. She knew what these churchy people were like. Myra was also not quite sure what she needed consoling for. For having married Gilbert in the first place? For the fact that Gilbert was probably going to prison for a long time? She didn't want to offend the vicar, so she said she would think about it.

*

Barbara sat by the hospital bed, tears pricking her eyes. Ian reached out his good hand and she gripped it.

"Come on Babs, it's not the Death of Little Nell you know. As Oscar Wilde once said, you'd need a heart of stone not to laugh at the death of Little Nell."

She smiled. "I'm sorry, Ian – I just can't stand to see you like this."

"You mean in this rather unflattering hospital robe? I'm not surprised. Don't they make them in leather?"

"You know what I mean. You're so – bouncy – normally."

"Yes," he said, "I know. But at least I'm conscious now, even if I do have a rather avant garde hairstyle. I might join the Sex Pistols once I'm better."

He reached up and touched the side of his head where his hair had been shaved away. "And I'm eating, too."

"Glad to hear it. Thin does not suit you."

"And how are you, my little Barbarian?"

"Me? It's not about me."

"I rather think it is," said Ian. Seeing Barbara's face fall, he added hastily: "What I meant was, you're looking a bit peaky. Oh God, I didn't mean you should be feeling guilty about what happened."

"But I do, Ian – I do. Andrew thinks this is all my fault."

"He's said that?"

"Very directly. And very forcefully. Apparently you were attacked because I have too many interests or something. It's hard to follow his logic, but he's very vehement about it. And he said something else – something I found very disturbing."

"Go on."

"He said that Gil had come to his London office – months ago now – and told him that you and I were having an affair."

Ian reached behind him and tugged the pillows into a more comfortable position.

"And he never mentioned this to you at the time?"

"No. And he chose to believe Gil instead of bouncing him off the idea, which he could easily have done. Then none of this would have happened. So how it could be my fault, I really don't know." Barbara looked down, twisting her wedding ring round and round on her finger. It spun easily – she had lost weight. Why was it, she thought, that the first parts of your body to lose weight were always your fingers and your feet? "Of course, it all makes sense now – the sabotaging of the Brighton fair,the tyre-slashing. There we were, looking askance at every disgruntled stallholder when the answer was staring us in the face. I just never thought ..."

"Never thought he'd do something like this?"

"No – he seemed so pathetic really. I felt sorry for him. He was like a little dog, following me around. A waif and stray, begging for crumbs."

"Well he certainly seemed more like a Rottweiler when he clouted me with the spade. Not that I could see him clearly – it was dark and mostly I was in the car and he was standing by the door. It could have been anyone, to be honest."

"So, what if it wasn't him?"

"Don't be ridiculous – of course it was him. He'd been building up to this, hadn't he, over weeks and weeks? It just never occurred to me that he'd do something physical. Poison-pen letters would have been more his style, I think."

"Do you remember the attack?"

"Every day, every night, over and over – yes."

Barbara squeezed Ian's hand.

"I was frightened you might die. Or worse ... because it was so long before anyone found you. And your head injury ..."

"But I didn't die. And I still have the same pitiful number of brain cells I had before he tried to kill me. I'm on the mend now – I'll probably still be here when Cass has the baby, though. Just a few more tests to do on my conk."

"Poor Cass."

"Poor Cass? What about me, you dreadful woman?"

Barbara laughed. She reached into her handbag. "I almost forgot to give you this," she said, taking out a small, flat object wrapped in velvet.

"You'll have to unwrap it for me – I've only got one working arm at the moment."

She unfolded the cloth to reveal the miniature painting inside.

"It's Cass!" he said. "Cass as a mediaeval maiden – how fantastic!"

"Harry painted it and I framed it."

"It's beautiful," said Ian. "Though if Harry painted it, I guess we have to be grateful that Cass is actually depicted as having two eyes and a nose in the right place."

*

"Fiona? It's Barbara." There was a clinking noise in the background. "Hello?"

"Sorry, Barbara – just putting my wine glass down. Some perfectly divine Châteauneuf-du-Pape that Nigel brought round last night. He can be such a dear."

"You're still seeing Nigel then?" said Barbara, recalling Fiona's trauma over him only a few months ago.

"Yes – everything's fine now. He's going to leave his wife and come and live with me. It's such a relief."

"Really?" said Barbara, the surprise evident in her voice.

"Yes, he's just waiting for the right moment to tell her."

"Aah – I see."

"And we're working on this wonderful project at an old castle outside Dundee. Bespoke order for dozens of yards of custom-made fabric with the family's heraldic crest woven into it. Nigel says without me, they'd never have clinched the deal."

"Sounds wonderful," said Barbara. She picked up the framed picture of her and Fiona that stood on the hall table. They had both been in their teens and they were pictured standing in their parents' back garden in front of the rose bushes. Barbara had her arm around Fiona's shoulders and they were both laughing at something. Six months after the picture was taken, Fiona had left home, in the wake of yet another dreadful argument with their father. Barbara could hardly reconcile the carefree girl in the picture with the needy, neurotic, self-obsessed woman that her sister had become.

She waited patiently for Fiona to ask how she was, but had to endure another ten minutes of Fiona's real or imagined woes before – about to bring the call to an end – Fiona said: "Everything OK with you, I assume? Your life running on its usual smooth tracks?"

"Actually – no," said Barbara.

"Don't tell me – your cleaning woman has run off with the family silver? Or you've leaving Andrew and moving in with the vicar?" Fiona laughed, but her laughter tailed off when she realised Barbara wasn't responding. "What, then?"

"Do you remember Ian Avery from when you were staying with us?"

"The hunky chap with the leather jacket – very fanciable. Yes, of course I remember." There was another clinking sound, presumably Fiona trying a little more of Nigel's 'perfectly divine' wine.

"Well, he's not looking very fanciable at the moment. He's been attacked: someone tried to kill him. He's in Southampton General. He's been in a pretty bad way."

"The General?" said Fiona, immediately latching onto the trivia of the story. I would have done with him on my ward, when I was in there. He'd certainly have aided my recovery."

"Fiona," said Barbara sharply, "he nearly died."

"Sorry – I didn't mean to sound flippant. Poor Ian. Do you remember when we were six and we both had the whooping cough?"

Barbara sighed, but Fiona rattled on, oblivious. "Frightened Ma and Pa horribly. They said there was that awful pause before the whoop when they thought we'd stopped breathing altogether." There was a slurping noise as Fiona took another swig of wine. "Did you say 'attacked'? Who by? Some spurned female?"

"A man – no-one you know – but the thing is, I'm to blame. Or that's what everyone thinks. To tell the truth, Fiona, I don't know what to do – I've been beside myself." Her voice broke and she gripped the handset of the phone more tightly to try and fight back the tears. She was damned if she was going to cry in front of Fiona.

"Dear girl! Don't take on so. Do you want me to come down to Ampfield?"

"No, no," blurted Barbara, horrified at the prospect.

"Or you could come up here and stay with me for a bit," she said, "or nearby," she added slyly.

"I have to stay here – for Ian. And for the court case."

"You must tell me all about what's happened. I'll have to call you back, though – that's Nigel at the door. I'll call you in half an hour. Or make that an hour."

"OK." Barbara put down the phone and sank onto the hall chair.

Fiona never did call back.

*

Myra got the train to Winchester but hadn't realised what a long walk it would be from the station. She felt chilled to the bone by the time she reached the prison gates. She checked her watch: five minutes early. She asked the uniformed man at the gatehouse about where visitors should go; he didn't reply but pointed with his biro at the straggly queue of people forming along the pavement.

As Myra walked to the end of the queue, everyone stared at her in what she felt was an intimidating way, so she fussed with her gloves to avoid meeting their eye. They were all women, all very young, and several had enormous hoop earrings. None of them were dressed for the weather – they looked more as if they were about to go out to a nightclub. One turned her head to look at Myra, blowing an enormous bubble-gum balloon in her direction.

The noise was what struck Myra most when they finally went inside: everything seemed to be made of metal. Gates clanged, trolleys squeaked, clipboards banged, keys rattled and chairs made loud scraping noises when moved. In the echoing, high-ceilinged visitors' hall, they waited for the prisoners to be let in. Myra wondered what prison clothes were like: she didn't imagine that they wore stripes any more, but the only recent films she'd seen that featured prisons were American, where they all seemed to be clad in orange jumpsuits and have chains on their ankles. Would Gilbert be chained? Surely not. When he appeared, she was surprised to see he looked better than he had done for a long time: his face was thinner, and he was wearing denim jeans – an item of clothing he always said he'd never be seen dead in – and an open-necked blue shirt. He looked surprised and a bit flustered to see her. He didn't smile.

"I was expecting someone else," he said, sitting down in the plastic chair opposite her.

"Why? Who else would visit you here?"

"No-one. I mean, just the person from the prison visitors' service. She's been a number of times."

"I've heard about women like that – they think it's romantic, getting off with a prisoner. They write dirty letters to convicts on death row and offer to marry them."

"Don't be ridiculous."

"Anyway, I'm here now."

"Yes."

They lapsed into silence. Myra was now too hot in her coat. She glanced sideways at the next table where a young man with spiky hair was sitting opposite his girlfriend. He had kicked off his shoes and had placed one of his feet on the chair opposite, up the skirt of the girl, who was gazing at him and licking her lips. Myra looked away, shocked.

"I'm here for a reason."

He did not respond.

"There's no money in our joint account. I've had this letter from the mortgage people." She opened her handbag and extracted an envelope, pushing it across the table to him. He picked it up, opened the letter and smoothed it with his hand on the table, but didn't look at it. "There wasn't enough money to pay the mortgage this month and now they're making all kinds of threats. And when I wrote a cheque for the butcher, it bounced. What's going on? What have you done with all the money? Given it to that Barbara woman?"

"Of course not. It's just that ..." He hesitated. "... there hasn't been any money coming into the account."

"What about your wages?"

"I've not been earning any wages. They fired me."

"When? When you were arrested?"

"No. They fired me three months ago. I meant to tell you, but I didn't know how."

Myra couldn't take this in. She replayed in her mind the scene that had been repeated every morning when Gilbert went off to work in the car, carrying his briefcase and sandwiches. Every evening he had returned at his usual time and made some anodyne comment about what kind of a day he had had. She had never once suspected.

"Where on earth had you been going every day?"

"The library mostly. And the park."

Myra thought for a while, imagining Gilbert wandering aimlessly around Southampton, checking his watch every few minutes to see if it was time to go home yet.

"Why did you get the sack?"

Gilbert was obviously reluctant to say. He took the mortgage letter, folded it up and carefully put it back in its envelope.

"Why?" she persisted.

"I'd been spending too much time out of the office."

Myra suddenly remembered phoning the office and being told he wasn't there because he was having a day's leave. In fact, she distinctly recalled him coming back that evening, exactly as usual, even having a moan about Mr Harding, the boss. He had probably been out seeing that Barbara, though she certainly wasn't going to give him the satisfaction of telling her now. She also remembered noticing that he was putting petrol in the car much more often: with a husband like Gilbert, you could rely on an absolutely invariable routine. Every Saturday morning, he went to the garage to fill up, but she'd seen some petrol receipts in the hall drawer, where they tended to empty their coat pockets, for midweek dates as well.

She was quiet for a couple of minutes; long enough, she felt, to make him feel uncomfortable.

"So what am I supposed to do – about money?"

"I don't know. You'll need to talk to the bank and explain the situation."

"Tell them that my husband's in prison for attempted murder? Oh, thanks very much. I'll be a laughing stock."

"What about your parents? Could they lend us some money?"

"I haven't told them about you. Whenever I speak to them on the phone, I pretend you've gone out or that you're in the shed or the garage."

The tannoy sprang into life. "Five minutes until the end of visiting time."

"I've torn up your list, by the way," said Myra.

"List?"

"Of jobs around the house. Not much point in keeping it now. I managed to fix the shed door myself and Roy has offered to put those shelves up in the kitchen." That was not all that Roy had offered, but Myra didn't see the point in telling Gilbert that.

Gilbert gave a shout of laughter. What was funny? Myra never could understand his sense of humour. You'd tell him jokes and there would be no reaction whatsoever, yet you'd tell him something serious and he'd laugh.

"I'm not coming to your trial. I just wanted to tell you that. So don't look for me."

Gilbert didn't say anything.

"It was you, wasn't it – in Torquay?" For some reason, it felt more important to Myra to establish this than it did to find out whether he really had tried to murder this Colin Avery person.

"Yes."

"Why? Why did you come all that way? And then why did you run away?"

"I don't know, really," he said.

He was silent again.

"I've booked another holiday with Sandra, by the way. We're going to Benidorm. Straight after your trial. Thankfully, we'd already paid the full amount."

"So you won't be there when I come home?"

"When you come home? You won't be coming home, Gilbert Smart. You're staying right here – don't you realise that?"

*

"I'm pleased to say that I'm the proud father of a beautiful baby girl. Six pounds, five ounces."

"That's wonderful, Ian," said Barbara." How's Cass?"

"She's doing fine. I wasn't able to be at the birth, obviously, though if I could have hung out the window of the ward by my ankles, I might have just glimpsed the maternity unit down the road. I'm hoping that they'll let me go and see her and the baby tomorrow. The baby's going to be in intensive care for a while."

Barbara didn't quite know what to say. "Oh?"

"A heart problem to be sorted out. Should be fine."

She found herself choking up and coughed to clear her throat. "What are you going to call her?"

"Annabel Rose."

"That's lovely."

"She's – a special baby."

"Yes of course – she's your first."

"It's not just that, Babs – the thing is, she's got Down's Syndrome."

"You mean she's a mongol?" blurted Barbara, who was then instantly ashamed of what she had said. "Did you know – I mean, before?"

"Yes, but it wasn't going to change our minds. This baby means everything to us – and especially now, because I might not even have survived long enough to see her. She might never have known her daddy." Ian, always so cheery and upbeat, let his mask slip just a little and Barbara was almost grateful – that he trusted her enough to tell her these things and to show his own vulnerability.

"I can't wait to see her," said Barbara, finding that she really meant it. "Will you be looking after Annabel yourselves?"

"What do you mean?"

"It's just that – a lot of people feel these children are better off in institutions."

Ian went quiet and when he spoke, there was an iciness in his voice. "And that's what you think, is it Barbara – that she belongs in an institution? Over my dead body!"

He realised what he'd said and laughed, though it was strained.

"You know I didn't mean that, Ian. It's another world now – not like it used to be. When I was young, that's just what happened. We thought it was normal. Fiona and I thought it was normal."

"What are you saying – you and Fiona?"

"We had a younger sister, Sarah. But we never really knew her. Our parents couldn't cope, or maybe they didn't want to cope. Anyway, the outcome was the same: she was sent to Knowle Hospital. She was only seven. I hardly remember her, to be honest. Father said it would be cruel to visit her, so we didn't. She died there and it was months before our father told us. She'd drowned in a pond in the grounds."

"Oh, Babs," said Ian.

"I thought you might wonder why Andrew and I had never had children. Well that's why, really. I felt I might repeat the kind of mistakes my own parents made. But I'm so glad for you and Cass – you'll be such wonderful parents."

"Thank you, Babs." Ian's voice had choked up.

"I'd better not tire you any more or I'll be in trouble with Matron. I'll come and visit tomorrow."

"How are bookings for the Midhurst fair coming along?"

"Ian?"

"Yes?"

"Shut up."

*

"I've never felt less Christmassy in my life," said Barbara as they loaded the car.

"And I've never felt less like spending it with your parents," said Andrew.

Even writing the Christmas cards had seemed like a chore this year; it was a task that Barbara usually enjoyed, taking care to add a personal message to each, to counter all those cards they received where people just signed their names, often not even bothering with 'to Andrew and Barbara', so that they could presumably just sign a pile of cards and them put them randomly into envelopes. Barbara had refused a number of social invitations in the build-up to Christmas, and everyone had been very understanding, but because she had not yet told her parents about the attack on Ian and the impending court case, they had felt obliged to agree to spend Christmas Day with them.

"We can leave after lunch on Boxing Day – it's really only 48 hours to get through," said Barbara. "Can you just try and be nice to me for that period? And to them, of course."

"I'm always nice to your parents."

"I know. Sometimes I think you'd have been better off marrying my mother."

"Don't be ridiculous."

"At least Fiona won't be there too."

"Thank God – that really would have been beyond the pale." He shut the boot of the car. "Let's go."

Barbara's parents had moved ten years ago from their well-proportioned Edwardian villa in Fareham, where Barbara and Fiona had grown up, to a boxy modern house on the outskirts of Ledbury in Herefordshire, a town they had chosen because it was where they had spent their honeymoon. The town itself was attractive, with its quaint shops and black-and-white timbered buildings, surrounded by rolling countryside. But it always felt strange to Barbara, visiting them in a house that had not been her home, and being accommodated in the rather characterless 'spare room', but perhaps on the positive side it did take away the unhappy childhood associations – being sent to her room by her father for talking during dinner; Fiona being punished for escaping out of the bedroom window to meet her rather unsavoury boyfriend, the one with the long hair and the black motorbike. There had been happy memories of their childhood home too: sitting on the bed exchanging secrets with Fiona in whispers; having a midnight feast of biscuits and ginger beer raided from the pantry; their mother standing on a stepladder glueing glow-in-the-dark stars to their bedroom ceiling.

"You know I said I wanted to tell them in person what's been happening," said Barbara as they drove into Cirencester, where they planned to stop for coffee. "Well, I really don't see how I can. Not on this trip, anyway."

"Why ever not?"

"Well, if I tell them tonight, it will spoil their Christmas."

"Then tell them on Boxing Day morning, before we leave. You should have told them weeks ago, to be honest."

Barbara mulled this over while Andrew circled the car park, looking for a free space.

"Aha! That red car is just pulling out – we can nab their space," he said, swooping the Audi into the slot a split second before another motorist tried to do the same thing. He switched off the engine and turned to Barbara. "I know why you don't want to tell them – you're still frightened of your father, aren't you?"

Before Barbara could reply, there was a sharp tap on the driver's side-window and the angry face of a middle-aged man appeared. Andrew did not wind down the window, so his protestations went unheard. Andrew smiled sweetly at him without saying anything and eventually the frustrated man walked back to his car.

"I feel I should be past being frightened of him. I'm an adult, I'm married, I have my own life. But I'm not. Anyway, he'd only cause a row, and that would upset my mother too, so let's just leave it and try to enjoy Christmas with them."

*

Christmas in the prison felt very strange to Gilbert. In a way, it was something of a relief to be there, without the stresses and strains of having to buy presents, send cards, attend carol concerts, trail around the supermarket, visit Myra's parents, or even – he admitted to himself – see Myra. She had not returned after her visit to talk about money: presumably she had managed to borrow some from her father. He wondered if she was at home for Christmas, picturing her pulling both ends of the cracker, and sitting alone at the dining table in her paper hat. But she'd probably gone round to Sandra's for the day, or perhaps they'd gone to a hotel for a slap-up meal and hadn't thought about him at all. He did miss watching the Queen's Speech, though, and settling down for a game of Monopoly with Myra afterwards – she always won, but that was because she cheated. She thought he hadn't noticed that she always acted as the banker so she could sneak the occasional hotel onto one of her properties instead of a house, or filch the odd £100 from the bank.

The prison did its best to introduce a festive air. There was a big Christmas tree on the Visiting Hall and some singers came in on Christmas Eve to sing carols. They were an earnest-looking group from a local evangelical church. Gilbert was careful not to get into conversation with them after the concert.

He only received one Christmas card, and that was from Lola. It said 'Feliz Navidad' inside it, so she must have bought it on one of her trips back to Spain to see her family. He put it on the bookshelf in his cell. There was no card from Myra and none from Barbara. Perhaps she had been forbidden to communicate with him? Perhaps by Andrew, now that Gilbert's task was accomplished?

The prison Christmas dinner consisted of pre-sliced processed turkey roll, not real turkey, and was very like the office Christmas dinners that he had attended, joyless affairs that had to be booked six months in advance and at which Old Harding would give a sentimental speech after a couple of glasses of port. Being teetotal, Gilbert had always found these dinners to be interminably boring.

At least it would be his first and last Christmas in prison, he told himself.

*

The visit had gone well: Barbara's mother was as gracious and charming as she always was, although anyone, thought Barbara, can seem gracious if they continually defer to whatever their husband says or wants to do. She had always seen her mother's behaviour as being the oil in the mechanism, that helped it run smoothly, but now she began to see the continual denial of her own needs and her own opinions as a sign of weakness. She felt guilty for seeing her mother that way, but once the thought had occurred to her, everything her mother did was seen through his new lens. A lens of clarity or of distortion? She couldn't decide.

She even felt a twinge of scepticism when her mother exclaimed delightedly at the present the Barbara and Andrew had given her – a pair of bronze book-ends in the shape of owls, a bird that her mother had always admired. Barbara heard a horrible echo of all the times that people had given *her* unsuitable presents and she had pretended that they were exactly what she had wanted.

If her parents detected any sense of strain between Barbara and Andrew, they did not comment on it. It wasn't until Christmas night, when they were sitting around the fire – one of those fake electric log fires with a 'glow bulb' that Andrew always said were kitsch – having just finished watching the Morecambe and Wise Show, that the visit slid into catastrophe. Her mother had been telling Barbara about one of her niece's children who had just had a baby.

"Oh, I forgot to tell you," said Barbara. "Ian – you know, my business partner in the antiques business – has just become a father for the first time. His wife Cass has had a little baby girl."

"How lovely," said her mother. "Aren't they rather old for having a first child? I thought you said he was about 40."

"Yes, he is. I think Cass is slightly older than me but I don't know exactly. She wanted to have a proper career before she became a mother – she's an art teacher and a sculptor. Very talented."

Barbara's mother made a face to express her disapproval of women who put careers before motherhood.

"They are naming the baby Annabel Rose. She won't be out of hospital for a while, because they have to fix a heart problem first." Suddenly decided, she took at large sip of her brandy and replaced the empty glass on the coffee table. "The baby has Down's Syndrome."

There was a silence.

"How distressing for them," said Barbara's mother.

"They love her to bits."

"Yes, of course. But it will be hard for them, won't it?"

"Did you love Sarah to bits?"

Her father thumped his glass down onto the table. "What kind of question is that?" he said, glaring at Barbara.

"I think it's a perfectly reasonable question because it's one I just don't know the answer to. And one I've never asked before."

"Of course we loved her," said her mother.

"So why did you send her away? Why could we never visit her? Why did she die there, all alone, if you loved her?"

Andrew put a restraining hand on Barbara's arm. She could feel her face getting flushed and the adrenalin surging through her.

"That's enough, Barbara," said her father. "You're upsetting your mother."

But it was too late for Barbara to stop now.

"No, it's not enough. All my life I've thought about this. All my life you've never spoken about it. It's as if Sarah never existed."

"It would have been wrong to take you and Fiona to the hospital to see her," said her mother soothingly, glancing across at her father as she spoke. He nodded for her to continue. "You were just little children – you wouldn't have understood. And it might have been disturbing for you."

"Disturbing to see all those 'mad' people? Yes, it probably would have been. But Sarah wasn't mad, was she? She was just a poor kid who needed more love and attention than most. Tell me," she said, looking directly at her mother. "Did you and dad visit her?"

Her mother would not meet Barbara's eye and her father jumped in to answer the question.

"She had a regular routine there," he said. "A routine she was comfortable with. We didn't want to interrupt that and risk upsetting her. She thought of the nurses as her family, I expect."

Barbara sat back on the sofa. She had always suspected this but it was still a shock to hear her father say it. Tears sprang into her eyes, but they were tears of rage rather than sorrow.

"Do you know why I've never had children?"

"No ... your father and I always hoped that you would."

"Can you not guess?"

"Barbara ..." said Andrew, warningly.

"Well I'll tell you. I was frightened to have a baby. I was frightened that I might not love it, that I might feel able to send it away like you did with Sarah. That's why."

Barbara's mother began to cry and her father leapt to his feet, knocking over a glass.

"Now look what you've done, girl!" he shouted. "Have you taken leave of your senses?"

Barbara stormed out of the room and they heard her thumping up the stairs. Andrew stood up and placed his hand on her father's shoulder. "I'm sorry," he said. "She been under a bit of stress recently – she's not been herself. I'm sure she didn't mean to upset you both. We'll leave first thing in the morning."

*

The week before the trial was Lola's last visit. Gilbert was seated in the Visiting Hall before she arrived and he thought how different she looked from all the other visitors streaming through the door. It was partly her exotic looks but also something about the way she carried herself: although her clothes were casual, they were clearly of good quality and she wore them well. She waved and smiled as soon as she saw him.

They talked mostly about the trial and as their conversation neared its end, Gilbert kept glancing nervously over at the clock, willing time to slow down a little before he had to go back to his cell. He told Lola about Myra's visit and mentioned that she had booked a holiday in Benidorm.

"Do you know it?" he asked.

"I've never been – my mother's family are from Cordoba, so that's where I tend to go when I visit. I don't think Myra will experience the 'real Spain' in Benidorm," said Lola.

"I'm not sure that the 'real Spain' is what she's looking for. It's more about sun and sangria, I think. She's not invited me, not that I'm the 'sun and sangria' type really. She's going with a friend instead. A perfectly dreadful woman called Sandra."

If Lola had noticed that Gilbert was assuming that he would be released after his trial, she did not give any indication. He was pleased about this. Perhaps now she knew him a little better, she realised that he was an honourable man and that it should have been Ian Avery in prison, not him.

"I hadn't come across anyone called Myra before," said Lola.

"Myra Hindley, perhaps?" suggested Gilbert, smiling.

Lola laughed to cover her embarrassment.

"Actually, I hadn't come across anyone called Gilbert either."

"Well, it's rather an old-fashioned name these days," said Gilbert. My father was an admirer of an architect called George Gilbert Scott. He designed workhouses, I believe, though I'm not sure that he got around to designing prisons. What about your name? Is Lola a popular Spanish name?"

"Yes – it's mainly used when babies are born on Good Friday, as I was. It's a diminutive of Dolores, which means 'sorrows'. It refers to the Virgin Mary being Our Lady of Sorrows."

"I hope that sorrow does not visit you again in your life," he said, rather stiffly.

"That's a very nice thing to say, Gilbert. Thank you."

"May I write to you after the trial? Just to say thank you for visiting me? It's meant a lot to me."

"Yes of course – I can't be your pen-pal, but just a thank you note would be very much appreciated. You can address it to me care of the prison."

*

Myra didn't go to the trial. After all, what was the point? Sitting looking at all those stuffy old farts in their wigs and gowns, pontificating about evidence and obscure points of the law. Gilbert probably not saying a single word throughout the whole process. Anyway, the verdict was obvious to anyone with an ounce of commonsense. Come to think of it, perhaps she would go to court on the day of the verdict. That would be interesting, watching as the judge delivered the sentence. Watching Gilbert's face. Watching as he was taken down into the cells. Would he turn and look for her in the public gallery? That's what they did in these courtroom dramas on the telly. She thought not.

She fingered the air tickets that were on top of the bureau: she'd put them as bookmarks into the page of the travel brochure that described Benidorm and the five-star hotel she and Sandra would be staying in. Live entertainment every night – probably flamenco dancers or something, she thought. And that wonderful phrase 'all inclusive' – that meant as many G&Ts as could pour down your throat: Sandra had liked the idea of that. And handsome dark-eyed Spanish waiters, maybe, for a little harmless flirting. There was a day excursion midweek to see the orange and lemon groves in the hills behind the town. Myra had never seen an orange growing on a tree: it sounded so exotic and she imagined herself picking one, putting the fragrant skin close to her nose to smell it. She suddenly had a thought, and opened the bureau, removing Gilbert's expired passport. She trotted upstairs to the spare bedroom, where neatly stacked cardboard boxes filled the entire floor-space, each box sealed with sellotape and labelled 'Charity'. She added the passport to a box marked 'Throw Away' and went downstairs again to read the *Echo*. Only one more hour and she'd be going round to Roy and Anne's. Roy was going to teach her something called the West Texas Waltz, though judging by the looks he'd been giving her recently, he had something else in mind entirely.

*

Although Andrew refused to come to the trial with Barbara, there had been some kind of climb-down in his attitude and, oddly enough, his mother had been the cause of it. Barbara had never liked her; the way she cosseted and protected Andrew might have been excusable when he was a young and impoverished architectural student, but her attitude to him had not changed at all over the years, despite the fact that he was now married and a partner in a successful London practice. Barbara always felt under suspicion when she spoke to Andrew's mother – as if she would let slip something that would cause her mother-in-law to say 'see – I told you so. Barbara never was good enough for our boy.' The fact that

Andrew had consulted his mother on something so trivial as Barbara attending the course at Wendell Court just summed up the mother-and-son relationship. She dreaded to think what Andrew had been confiding lately, or what advice his mother might have given him.

Although she had hidden the broken architectural model in the kitchen bin, she knew he would notice it was missing and felt she had to say something.

"I'm afraid I broke one of your models yesterday," she said.

He took off his headphones and she repeated what she'd said.

"It was while I was dusting."

"What were you doing the dusting for?"

"Well, if you remember, we don't have Mrs H any more."

"Oh no, so we don't. I'm surprised it broke – perhaps the glue hadn't set properly. Not to worry. I'm sure I can resurrect it."

"Actually ..." She took a deep breath. "... I stamped on it. I broke it deliberately. I smashed it to smithereens."

But it was too late: he had replaced his headphones and was listening to Mahler again.

At dinner, she had tried to raise the subject of how hurt she had felt that he had not come to the art show as he had promised. He clearly didn't want to talk about it, but could see no way of getting out of it.

"Well, I concede that I may have slightly over-reacted," he said, grudgingly, fiddling with his knife on the dinner plate.

"I thought you'd be proud of me, not jealous."

"Jealous? I wasn't jealous. Why would you think that?"

"I think you were, Andrew. You've made it clear you don't want me to have any kind of independent life, any friends who are not your friends, any interests that are not yours." She heard her voice starting to shake and was annoyed not to be able to sound calm and rational. Andrew was always contemptuous of women who broke down in tears to 'get their own way', as he put it. Like Fiona.

"Having these things has got you into a lot of trouble, though, hasn't it? Let's face it."

Barbara was silent.

"I liked you better when you weren't running around with Ian Avery and that artist chap, and inviting psychopaths into our house."

"You probably liked me better when I wasn't clearing up blood off the drive, or being interviewed by policemen, or giving evidence in a Crown Court. Which, incidentally, I'm having to do alone, without your help or support. Have you any idea what I've been going through? Or is it all about you and how it affects you?"

"No, of course not. I'm sorry. I've talked this over with my mother ..."

Barbara froze.

"... and she says you've got a point about Gilbert Smart – that I could have stopped it and I didn't. I'm sorry I didn't. I'm sorry about a lot of things. She did suggest something that might cheer you up, though."

"What's that?" asked Barbara, wondering what horrors were in store – a joint holiday with his parents, perhaps.

"I told her about your driving lessons and she thought they were a good idea."

A good idea? Andrew's mother must have had a few drinks when they had this conversation, thought Barbara.

"So, with your test coming up, she said I ought to buy you a car. So I did. It's being delivered on Tuesday."

"What?"

"A car – your own car. It's a Ford Fiesta. Just the basic model."

Barbara didn't know which was the more astonishing: Andrew's climb-down, the fact that she would now be truly independent, or his mother's role in all this. The only unsurprising aspect was that Andrew had assumed that he, and he alone, would choose the car and Barbara would not be consulted on the matter at all.

"What colour is it?"

"Blue. I'd rather have had white to be honest, because it would have looked better when parked in the drive, from an aesthetic point of view, but I thought you'd probably prefer blue."

Barbara reached across the table to embrace Andrew, knocking over a wine glass in the process.

"Steady on!"

"Thank you, Andrew. Thank you."

*

"The court calls Desmond Robert Harding."

Barbara watched as a short, rotund man took the witness stand. He was about 50 with slightly bulging eyes and thick lips. He was wearing a grey suit and blue striped tie. He grasped the stand tightly with hairy fingers wrapped around the wooden rail. Though this might have suggested he was nervous, everything else about him exuded confidence. It appeared he was Gil's employer and he rattled off the details of Gil's job with ease, supplying details of Gil's increasing absences from work. Barbara thought back to the time when he'd visited her, claiming a business appointment in Romsey. Maybe that had not exactly been the truth, she realised. And the day Ian had spottted his car up on the hill above the house – that had been a working day too, surely?

"And what can you tell the court about Gilbert Smart's character?" asked the barrister for the defence.

Desmond Harding seemed disconcerted. He ran his tongue across his lips and then looked down at the stand.

"What kind of man is he?" encouraged the barrister.

Harding kneaded his hands on the rail.

"I'm sorry, your honour, but I really couldn't say."

"Can't – or won't?" interjected the judge.

"Can't," said Harding hastily. "What I mean is – it's hard to say. I don't know how to describe it."

"Please try," said the judge, drily.

"I'm sorry – it's just that he was always a blank slate. No personality whatsoever that I could discern. I can't tell you about his character because I don't believe he has one."

"Thank you, Mr Harding. You may step down."

*

"I don't think I can do this," said Barbara to Ian, as they stood in the hallway of the courts after the first day of the trial. "I don't actually know for certain that he stole the house-keys; I don't know for certain how his tie-pin got upstairs; I've only got your word for his spying on us. I didn't see the attack. There's very little I can tell them."

"I thought you were here to support me?" said Ian fiercely, gripping her firmly by the arm.

"I am – of course I am."

"Then you need to back me up. Don't lose your nerve. Without your testimony, how are they going to convict him? They'll think I'm just making up all that other stuff and that it was just a fight between two blokes over a woman and that it might just as well have been me wielding the spade. Who on earth tries to kill someone with a spade, anyway? He'll get off on account of his 'balance of mind being disturbed' or something. Or a crime of passion – do they still have that?"

"Please stop holding my arm so tightly, Ian."

"Sorry." He let go of her arm and led her over to a long wooden bench against the wall of the hallway, where they sat down. "I know why you don't want to say any of that. You feel sorry for him, don't you? He tried to kill me, yet you feel sorry for him."

"No, that's not true. Or perhaps it is – I just don't know any more."

"He's not a harmless little man, not a puppy dog or however it was that you first described him. He's dangerous, he's a potential killer and I hope they lock him up for a long time."

"But he was deluded, Ian. He thought he was doing the right thing. He was doing it for me."

Ian slammed his hand loudly against the wall, and the court ushers turned around to look at him.

"It's you who's deluded, Babs. It's time you took a good long look at yourself."

She started to cry.

"I'm sorry."

He hugged her. "I'm sorry too. I didn't mean that. It's just that the world is a wicked place – you need to stop assuming that everyone you meet is a good person just because you're a good person."

"I know. But what a horrible, cynical world it would be if I did that. To trust no-one – that would be a wretched thing. A lonely thing. Who would want to live in a world like that? What about you, Ian?"

"What about me?"

"Do you still trust people?"

"I trust you, Babs. I trust you to support me at this trial, but now I'm frightened because you've wavering."

"I think I need to go home now."

"Can I give you a lift?"

"No, I've got my car."

"You never told me."

"I passed my test last week. Andrew bought me a car at the weekend."

"Well, well, Barbara Blaize. You are amazing. I'm going home too – I've got a beautiful daughter who's just waiting for me to come and give her a big cuddle."

*

Gilbert found the Crown Court trial all rather bewildering. He was bothered by the fluorescent lights, the constant opening and shutting of the courtroom door as people came and went, the bobbing up and down of clerks, ushers and lawyers, the vast ring-binders and bundles of papers that the judge was constantly sifting through. Most of all, he found it difficult to hear through the glass screen that surrounded the dock, even though he stood as close to the small slot in the glass as he could and listened intently. It was like being underwater, or in a tank, and consequently everything seemed unreal. He couldn't see the public gallery without turning round, and he never seemed to be able to bring into sharp focus the individual faces of the jury, who were seated to one side. He felt strangely distanced from it all – as if the whole proceedings were not about him at all, as if he were peripheral to it. Witnesses came and went in a blur. He was surprised at one point to see Old Harding in the witness box, and wondered what on earth he was doing there. Was it about how much time off Gilbert had taken? Surely that wasn't relevant now? Old Harding was followed by Barbara's house-cleaner Mrs H, who Gilbert learned for the first time was actually called Mrs Hart. Then came Barbara, but Gilbert found he had to shut his eyes and hum quietly because he could not bear to hear what she might say. Next came Ian Avery and for a moment Gilbert wanted to tap the glass to attract his barrister's attention because there was hardly a mark on Avery, so how could it possibly be a charge of attempted murder? Then he remembered that three months had gone by: Avery had recovered. His wounds had healed. A bitter, black bile came into Gilbert's mouth at the thought.

Strange objects were handed around the court, sealed in clear plastic bags. A large spade, the binoculars from his car, the gold tie-pin in the shape of a pair of spectacles. They were passed among the jury like ceremonial objects from some newly discovered tribal society. The psychiatrist who had interviewed him in the prison spent a long time giving evidence, but to Gilbert it all sounded like mumbo-jumbo. He didn't recognise any aspect of himself in the psychiatrist's description.

Gilbert felt inexpressibly tired. He had not had a full night's sleep since his arrest three months earlier. When the trial started he had been moved from Winchester prison to the cells underneath the courtroom: they were white-walled, utilitarian, built of breeze-block, and the lights never went out. They'd taken his spectacles away so everything had been a blur. When he was due to be brought up to the courtroom he was handcuffed to the guard and they ascended the steps together awkwardly as there was not room for two people to walk side by side. The steps led straight into the dock. Gilbert thought of those theatre organs that rose up out of the ground, the organist on his stool, playing as the organ rose. He'd always felt there was something creepy about them.

He was not called upon to speak at his trial, though he'd asked his barrister if he could do so. So that people would understand that his intentions were honorable, that he was only protecting Barbara. That he'd actually been asked to protect her by her own husband. That she would have been in danger if he'd not put a stop to Avery. That it was Avery who should have been in the dock, not him. The barrister said he thought it best if Gilbert did not speak.

Once the jury retired to consider their verdict, Gilbert had the best night's sleep for as long as he could remember. No bad dreams came to haunt him, the noise from the other cells did not wake him, and he slept peacefully under the thin blanket until the guard shook him awake at 9am.

'They're coming back,' he said.

*

On the day that the verdict was anticipated, Myra went to court. They searched her handbag at the entrance, as if she might have a knife or a gun in it and suddenly run amok in an attempt to free Gilbert. The court usher told her where the public benches were and she was surprised to see how many people filed in once the door to Court Four was unlocked.

She squeezed onto the end of a row, close to the dock, and next to a chap who looked as if he was some kind of tramp. Perhaps he'd come in to warm up a bit, thought Myra – it was a cold and blowy day. Although she'd not been to the trial, she had followed the reports each night in the *Echo*. They seemed to be making a bit of a meal of it, but at least the paper was no longer using a photograph of Gilmyr every time they reported on it. She'd had a procession of sightseers, ghouls really, coming down Forest Close with their cameras around their necks. Sandra seemed to think it was all a bit glamorous and kept talking about what a 'dark horse' Gilbert was.

"He's more like an onion," Myra had said.

"What do you mean?"

"You keep thinking he must have hidden depths, but as you peel away the layers, each one underneath is exactly the same. There's no 'core' to reach."

Myra had thought of all those 'pass the parcel' games she had had to endure as a child at birthday parties, and how she had cried in frustration as the parcel got smaller and smaller and still had not revealed its secret.

There was a stirring in the court – the jury was about to return.

"All rise," said the clerk and various chaps in wigs and gowns took their seats under a rather ostentatious royal crest on the wall. Myra realised that on the other side of the tramp was the man she knew from press photos to be the victim, Colin Avery – the same man who had called at the house that day and said Gilbert was to leave him alone. He looked like he'd survived pretty well, though there was a walking stick propped up against the bench in front of him and something was wrong with the side of his head – a scar visible where the hair had not grown back properly.

She craned her neck further round as they all took their seats again. Colin was sitting next to an attractive, slim woman with long red hair. This must be Barbara – Myra recognised her from the pictures snatched by the paper of her leaving the court. Myra had been asked by the police about Barbara but she'd denied all knowledge of her, never mentioning the letter she had found and pieced together.

Gilbert was brought up from the cells and Myra was shocked to see that he was handcuffed to a uniformed guard. He seemed to have shrunk – such a small, slight man – it was as if she were seeing him for the first time. He looked very calm in the dock, impassive even. He did not turn his head to look at the public gallery.

*

Barbara nudged Ian.

"That must be Myra," she whispered. "And about time too."

"Yes, that's her all right."

"You've seen her before?"

"Yes – I went to their house. Gil wasn't in so I gave him a warning via Myra."

"What – you threatened him?"

"Just said he should leave us alone, that's all."

"You never told me. You never told the court either."

"Didn't want to worry you – anyway, I though it would do the trick, but I was wrong."

"What did she say to you?"

"Nothing at all. She just looked stunned. I'm not sure she even knew who I was."

As the jury filed back, Barbara looked at their faces, trying to discern what the verdict might be. One of them, a young obese woman with her hair scraped back in what the *Daily Mail* called a 'council house facelift' appeared to be doing a word-search puzzle as she waited for proceedings to resume.

Barbara chanced another glance at Myra – she was short and slight, like Gil, with her hair unfashionably 'set'. Her face wore a tight expression as if she had spent her whole life disapproving of what she saw. Myra turned her head and their eyes met. Barbara looked quickly away, embarrassed.

The foreman of the jury stood up and the rustling of papers and general fidgeting ceased. The court seemed to hold its breath.

*

Barbara was beginning to get used to driving the Fiesta, but still felt nervous as she turned onto the narrow lane that led to Knowle Hospital. It had twists and turns and she was worried that she'd meet a tractor coming the other way and there wouldn't be room to pull over. She hadn't yet gauged the width of the car and often left far too much room when passing parked cars. The gates of the hospital appeared sooner than she expected and she turned in, following the signs to the visitors' car park. She had phoned ahead, so they were expecting her.

As she got out of the car, holding the bouquet of flowers, a young, neatly dressed woman with long dark hair approached her.

"Hello. It's my birthday today," she said, peering into the car through the rear passenger window.

"Hello. Happy birthday."

"Are those flowers for me?"

Barbara had been about to address the young woman as a member of staff, but at this point realised she must be a patient. "No, I'm sorry they're not. Perhaps someone else will bring you flowers for your birthday."

She started to edge away, but the girl followed her.

"Are you going to see Matron? I can show you the way."

"Thank you," said Barbara, heading briskly for the door marked 'Reception'.

"I know all about this hospital and everyone in it. I've been here for years and years."

"How old are you?"

"I'm not sure. I might be 23. I'll ask Matron."

Once inside the office, the uniformed woman behind the desk efficiently separated Barbara from the young woman, encouraging her to go over to the kitchen garden to see if she could help with picking the brussel sprouts.

She then summoned someone called Brian, who whose job it would be to escort Barbara. A middle-aged man with grey hair and a considerable paunch, he sighed as if it was the hardest task on earth that he'd been given.

"Number 231 – well, I'll do my best," he said in a distinct Meon Valley accent. "Walk this way. We'll take the short cut through the main building."

He led Barbara down a hallway that smelt of polish. The tiled floor gleamed and their footsteps echoed. Brian nodded at an open door.

"That's what they call the show-ward."

She looked in as they walked past. It was achingly clean; beds were lined up in a regimented fashion and nurses bustled around, smiling and talking to their patients who were sitting in chairs next to each bed. They looked calm and well cared-for.

"Why is it called the show-ward?"

"Because if you're about to commit a relative, it reassures you that it's a good hospital. We don't put the noisy patients in there, or the ones with filthy habits, or the ones who are drugged to the eyeballs. Just the acceptable ones. The real wards are down there," he said, nodding towards another wing.

Barbara clutched the bunch of flowers more tightly.

Brian pushed open some double doors and they emerged into daylight. The cemetery lay immediately in front of them. He consulted a rolled-up plan that he was carrying.

"Plot 231 – well, that's fine in theory. It should be over here." He pointed off to the right. "But finding it will be another matter."

"How many people are buried here?"

"About 5,000 in all."

Hardly any of the graves had markers. A few had headstones, but most just had plain little rusting iron crosses. Many of them had come adrift from the graves that they had originally marked and lay in a tangle alongside the path.

Brian strode on.

"I'd say it's here. You've got a choice of two or three, because they did tend to cram them all together, especially if they died in the same week as each other, but if you want my opinion, then here is about right."

He nudged the grass with his foot to indicate the spot.

"I'll leave you now. When you're ready to leave, just follow this path around to the right – keep walking and eventually you'll come out at the front of the building".

"Thank you, Brian," said Barbara. She wondered whether he was expecting a tip, but he walked off.

A watery sunshine had broken through the clouds and the air was still. There were banks of snowdrops in flower around the big oak tree and Barbara caught sight of a rabbit standing absolutely still over by the fence. She made a slight movement and it leapt away, white tail bobbing. Hardly any of the graves had flowers on them and she realised that she didn't know whether her parents had ever visited Sarah's grave; if they hadn't visited while she was alive, then they were hardly like to have do so after she died. So many of these seemed to be forgotten people. She laid the flowers on what might, or might not, be Sarah's plot. There was nowhere to sit down, so she took off her wool scarf, laid it on the grass and then knelt on it.

She had expected a headstone with Sarah's name and dates on it – even a loving epitaph: instead, it was just a bit of grass that was indistinguishable from any other. She struggled to find the right words to say, perhaps because it was hard to feel anything at all. Then she remembered Ian's baby and how different a life that baby would have from the brief one that Sarah had lived.

"I'm sorry," she said to the grass. "I'm so sorry. I was just a child – I accepted what our parents told us. That the hospital was the best place for you. That you were happy here. That it would be cruel to visit you. I hope you did find some happiness here, however unlikely it seems. I can't make it up to you, but I promise to be a good friend to Ian's daughter. I can at least promise you that."

Barbara got up off her knees, walked to the path and picked up one of the iron crosses that were lying there. She tried to push it into the turf on Sarah's plot, but the ground was too hard. In the end, she took off one of her shoes and used it as a hammer. The cross finally stood, slightly lopsided, at the head of the plot. Barbara bowed her head and recited the Lord's Prayer, propped the flowers up against the cross, and then walked back to her car. On the way back, she could hear shouting and screaming coming from one of the buildings, but she encountered no-one.

*

The opportunity to start being a 'good friend' to Ian and Cass' daughter came sooner than she had anticipated. When the phone rang, she knew it would be Ian wanting to talk about the next fair, but what he also asked surprised her. He sounded diffident about it, as if anticipating a refusal.

"The thing is, Babs, I'm not what you'd call a Christian, and I haven't really been to church since Sunday School, but I do want Annabel to be brought up in the right way and we want to have her baptised. I don't suppose you'd possibly consider, well, being her godmother, would you?"

Barbara could not believe how quickly her prayer at Knowle had been answered.

"I'd be honoured, Ian. Nothing would please me more."

*

Myra put the front door on the latch and went out to the car, carrying a Sainsbury's plastic bag. The man from the car dealer's was coming this morning so she needed to clear everything out of it. Roy had done the negotiations for her and got a good price from someone he said was trustworthy, though looking at the wreck that was his own car, Myra wasn't too sure that his judgement could be relied on. He said there was no point in keeping Gilbert's car outside in all weathers, unused, for three years – and besides, Myra needed the money.

She stacked up the AA maps, emptied the glovebox of a torch and a set of screwdrivers and cleared up the sweet-wrappers and bits of rubbish. In the boot, there was just a folded picnic blanket in blue check, though she didn't recall them ever going on a picnic. In her experience, they were uncomfortable occasions: sitting on the ground was awkward and she always ended up being the one to prepare and dole out the food, which never tasted quite the same out of Tupperware containers. As she grabbed the blanket and tucked it under her arm, something fell out onto the road. It was a small bag. She picked it up and examined it curiously. A very pretty clutch-bag made of silk in a subtle shade of jade green, the front of it covered in a swirling pattern of tiny beads. She ran her finger over them. It looked like the kind of bag a flapper would have carried in the 1920s. It would be just the thing to take on holiday.

*

"To Annabel Rose!" said Ian, raising his glass.

"To Annabel Rose!" everyone echoed.

The centre of attention herself was unaware of the toast, having become distracted by a pink ribbon attached to the wrapping of one of her Christening presents. She strained out of Cass' arms, trying to reach for it.

"Nice to see you having a real drink at last, Ian," said Harry, who had dressed for the occasion in a crumpled cream linen suit and was looking quite debonair.

"Yes, it's my first alcohol since The Awful Incident. Half a glass of champagne will be enough, though, or so the doctor tells me. After all, I don't want to be accused of being drunk in charge of my number one daughter." He smiled fondly at Annabel and tweaked her tiny foot with his fingers. She switched her gaze from the ribbon to her father and laughed delightedly.

"And how does it feel to be a godmother?" asked Ian, turning to Barbara.

"It feels wonderful! Annabel was beautifully behaved in church, wasn't she? At least, until she had the holy water poured over her head, but that's understandable. It was probably freezing cold."

"I thought the vicar was going to drop her at one point, when her Christening robe got caught up on his sleeve. I saw you make a lunge towards them, just in case."

"Well, I'm taking my role very seriously!"

"More champagne, anyone?" asked Andrew as he approaching carrying a bottle in each hand.

Harry held out his empty glass but was beaten to it by Ashley.

"When I'm a vicar, I shall drink champagne every day, courtesy of my parishioners," he said.

Harry laughed and punched Ashley in the arm. "Not unless you're going to be vicar of Mayfair. I think all vicars get offered are endless cups of tea by little old ladies in cardigans."

"In that case, I'll have to make a swift rise to bishop, or archbishop. And you can be my 'artist in residence', Harry."

After the cutting of the Christening cake, Ian walked over to Barbara and drew her into a quiet corner, away from the boisterous chatter, much of it centring around Dylan, who had made a re-appearance on the art scene, to everyone's surprise and not-very-well concealed amusement. He had made no reference to his absence, or the reasons for it, and if he thought everyone knew about his well-publicised stint as a fake hospital doctor, he showed no sign of it and was his usual charming, insouciant self.

"Are we OK, you and me?" asked Andrew, looking seriously into Barbara's eyes.

"Yes, of course."

"You were very brave, Babs, at the trial."

"You forced me to be, you great brute."

"I'm sorry about that. I thought it was necessary."

"You were right – it was."

"And it was the right result, wasn't it?"

Barbara sighed. "Yes, I suppose so. I can't help thinking of him, though, and how he'll cope with being in a place like that. Three years is a long time."

"It would have much longer if they'd found him guilty of 'attempted murder' instead of 'grievous bodily harm'."

"I know." She ran her finger round the top of her glass. "But he'll find it hard. He gets so depressed – he told me about his dreams once, when I first met him at Wendell Court. Horrible dreams about life being like an conveyor belt that is moving so fast that you can't get off."

"Well he nearly tipped me off that belt, so I'm afraid I can't feel any sympathy for him."

"Will they treat him, do you think? I don't really know what 'secure mental facility' really means."

"Lots of sedation and high barbed-wire fences."

Barbara recoiled in horror.

"Only kidding, Babs. Well, not about the fences perhaps. Anyway, tell me – how are you and Andrew?"

She looked over at her husband who was talking animatedly to Cass and was waving his hands about as if he was conducting. Annabel was watching his hands, entranced.

"I think we'll be OK. I think he's grudgingly coming around to the idea that it wasn't all my fault."

"And to the idea that you have a life of your own to lead?"

"That's still some way off, I fear."

"Perhaps you should have burned your bra back in the sixties."

Barbara laughed. "Is it too late now?"

Andrew turned at the sound of their hoots of laughter.

"Really!" he said to Cass. "I don't know what's got into my wife these days!"

Epilogue

Three years later:

The traffic queue at the Hockley lights was interminable and Gilbert fretted that he wouldn't arrive in time. At 5pm he finally reached the city centre and swung off past King Alfred's statue, around the one-way system and towards Hyde. On a 'dry run', he had rehearsed the route, including the right turn into the small side-street and the best spot to park, about fifty yards away from the house. But because he was running late, the parking space he wanted had already been taken, and he was forced to pull in nearer the house than he would have liked. He turned off the engine, grabbed the bouquet of flowers off the back seat and hurried across the road. Opening the garden gate, he walked up the short quarry-tiled path to the open porch and propped the bouquet against the front door. He checked his watch again before retracing his steps to the car, hesitating before he got into the driver's seat and glancing anxiously down the road. All was quiet. He settled down to wait, his eyes trained on the rear-view mirror. He drummed his fingers on the steering wheel impatiently.

Just five minutes later, she appeared at the end of the street, a briefcase in one hand and a supermarket carrier bag in the other. His heart leapt. She was wearing a black leather jacket over a smart skirt and blouse. Her hair was a little shorter than he remembered it, but she did not look a day older than when he had last seen her, three years ago. As she passed him on the pavement, he leaned forward, pretending to get something out of the glove-box so that she wouldn't see his face.

She pushed open the gate with her hip and put down her bags to get her front door key out of her handbag. Then she spotted the flowers. She picked up the bouquet, turning it round to see if there was a card attached, but found nothing. Leaving her bags in the porch, she walked back to the pavement and looked up and down the road. Gilbert slumped down in his seat so he wouldn't be visible. She then disappeared into the house and he saw a light come on in what must be the sitting room.

It hadn't been hard to find out where she lived, but it had taken considerable patience. He had saved up his weekly phone calls so that he could make enquiries about her. Other than that, when he was released it was simply a case of putting together the small pieces of information that she had told him during her visits: her brother's death in custody, and his unusual first name – Alejandro – had made it easy to trace the newspaper reports of the case. From that, he had found out her surname and although her home phone number was ex-directory, he remembered her saying that she worked part-time at the teacher training college. By posing as a member of the Prison Visitors Association, he was able to call the college on the pretext of having to get in touch with her urgently to rearrange her rota at the prison. If she'd been there at the time, he would have had to hang up, but fortunately she wasn't, and equally fortunately he was put through to a chatty colleague who spent ten minutes telling him that she couldn't really give him Lola's home number or address before saying that she was happy to make an exception for Gilbert, as he did such valuable volunteer work.

He had worried that perhaps Lola had now married, but a quick check of the Electoral Roll revealed that she lived alone. An attractive woman like that, particularly one in contact with prisoners, might be prey to all kinds of unwanted attention. But he could protect her from that. It was the least he could do. In fact it was nothing less than his duty.